HOW DEEP IS THE BODY?

HOW DEEP IS THE BODY?

A JAKE AND MALLORY THRILLER

IVANKA FEAR

First published by Level Best Books 2025

Copyright © 2025 by Ivanka Fear

Author Photo Credit: Amanda Belec

First edition

ISBN: 979-8-89820-063-3

Cover art by Level Best Designs

This book was professionally typeset on Reedsy.
Find out more at reedsy.com

To my husband, Brian, who helps me weather the storms.
And to our family
With all my love.

Praise for How Deep is the Body?

"In Ivanka Fear's third novel, *How Deep is the Body?*, the author skillfully blends crime thriller elements with profound personal stakes for the returning protagonists, Mallory and Jake. This is a domestic thriller at its finest, where home becomes both sanctuary and crime scene, and the past refuses to stay buried."—Gayle Brown, author of *A Deadly Game*

"Fear weaves suspenseful tales driven by amazing characters and the intriguing dilemmas they find themselves in, perfect for fans of B.A. Paris or Alice Feeney. If you're looking for a puzzling murder mystery or an enthralling domestic suspense, this book is perfect for you."—Michelle Godard-Richer, multi-award winning author of The Fatal series

"Jake and Mallory think country life will be more peaceful than the city, but this third installment of the series proves that it's anything but. With unexpected adversaries appearing from every shadow, and Mallory expecting their first child, the strength of their bond will be tested more than ever. You will be as addicted to Jake and Mallory as they are to each other."—E. R. Hann, author of *Heart-Shaped Karaoke Box*

"Fear masterfully blends domestic drama with criminal intrigue, set against the stark, unforgiving Canadian winter. The landscape itself becomes a character—cold, isolating, and filled with secrets. As truths begin to surface, it becomes clear: no one is exactly who they seem. *How Deep is the Body?* is a chilling, suspenseful ride that fans of the genre will devour. Ivanka Fear has once again proven her skill at crafting thrilling, emotionally layered stories. I can't wait to find out what lies ahead for Jake and Mallory."—Joseph Souza, bestselling author

Prologue

Two Months Ago

Ryan surveys the property that would have been his had things gone differently and thinks how easily he crossed the line from cop to criminal. The lure of easy money and the excitement of slipping out of 'good guy' mode have been the ruin of many solid police officers.

A cold wind blows across the vast expanse of open fields, the first skiff of snow covering the ground. The weathered red barn to his left has seen better days, but he understands why it serves its current purpose.

Obviously unused and abandoned, stalls devoid of livestock, hay bales left to rot, farm machinery rusting, it's clear no one has been there for some time. The unlocked doors indicate it holds nothing of value to the owners. Or perhaps, its isolated location provides them with a sense of security. No one would think of coming here to rob the place.

It's ideal. The perfect spot to store a cache of stolen jewelry until the heat dies down. A stash house.

When rumors began circulating that the small town of Idlewood was a haven for jewel thieves, Ryan wanted in on the action. Its proximity to Brampton Heights, lack of police presence, and trusting citizens had attracted the attention of a major crime ring.

But Ryan has a more personal reason for asking to be recruited for this mission.

When he ran a title check on the several-hundred-acre farm nestled in the woods, he could hardly believe his luck. The property matched the photos he had discovered boxed-up in the basement of his family home.

This place must be worth millions on today's market. So this is the home Great-grand-dad built? All this could have been mine.

Ryan turns to the stately old farmhouse and imagines what life was like back then. Simpler times. Things have changed. He considers the present occupants and wonders.

Will this put them in danger?

Chapter One

There's the shovel.

Blade shoved so deep only the top of the shaft is visible. The wind buffets a small Canadian flag, knotted onto the handle, the red making it easier to spot in a landscape of white. Not that it will do any good at this point. Dusty white grains swirl across the front lawn, gathering in waves, culminating in a hummock at the walkway, a foot from the base of our wooden porch. Gusts of wind drive flakes from the crest onto my bay window, threatening to obstruct what little view it provides through the driving snowfall.

Things will only get worse, according to the weather report on my app. The winter storm of the decade is underway. Tonight will be a nightmare. Severe blizzard conditions. Snowfall amounts up to twenty inches within the next forty-eight hours. Expected wind gusts of 60 mph. Travel will be impacted. Probable power outages. Possible damage to property from falling tree limbs. Danger from downed utility poles and wires.

Jake will downplay the weather conditions, laughing it off and telling me, as usual, that it's not as bad as they make it sound.

It's fine, Mal. They always blow it way out of proportion. Those reports come from the city, where they declare an emergency over five inches of snow and haul in the army to handle it.

It's easy for him to remain calm; he's not the one carrying our precious bundle of joy. I pray to God he doesn't decide to make an early entry into the world. An emergency trip in an ambulance through a snowstorm during labor isn't something I can deal with. Especially without Jake by my side.

Thanks to our neighbor, Paul Winston, and his new enclosed riding snow blower, the laneway isn't totally blocked. He cleared it early this morning, and Jake took several more swipes with the push snow thrower after lunch, before leaving for his 3 to 11 shift. But you'd never know it now as darkness advances to blanket the milky canvas. And with twilight, unease sets in.

Across the road, dark, lifeless branches mix with evergreens in the woods. A long expanse of lawn separates me from whatever lurks beyond the trees bordering the gravel shoulder. Little traffic travels down our street, situated on the outskirts of a small town. Fields of white on either side of us and to the back allow for lots of privacy.

I won't venture outside and put myself and the baby at risk. The possibility of slipping on the steps keeps me indoors where it's safe. Jake can shovel aside the drifts when he gets home.

The next seven hours will test my patience, not to mention my sanity. Waiting for Jake to arrive home from his evening shift frays my nerves in good weather. It's going to be a long, stressful wait till 11:30, possibly till midnight if the plows don't clear the roads shortly before he sets out.

A soft meow distracts me from the weather, if only momentarily. Nellie, our long-haired black and white cat, and Lucky, our short-haired black kitty, sit on the sill and stare out into the gray and white world. Without their calming presence, I'd be talking to myself, rambling around our large two-story red brick farmhouse, trying to convince myself that I'm safe, Jake is safe, and more importantly, the baby is safe.

I'll leave the drapes open. Switch on the outdoor lights. Keep an eye out for the storm. Keep an eye out for Jake. Try to occupy myself with a book, maybe a movie. Stretching my legs out on the sofa, I open my iPad to the novel I'm currently reading. My eyes flit from the print to the window. I should know better than to read a murder mystery about a group of strangers trapped in a resort during a snowstorm while a storm brews outside my cozy home. Although it feeds my anxiety, I can't resist.

You should stop reading those scary books, Mal. They scare the shit out of you. Shouldn't you be singing lullabies to the baby instead? What if he picks up on the bad vibes and ends up being a serial killer like one of those characters in your stories?

Whenever Jake sees me reading something that isn't romance or women's fiction, he eases the book from my hand, as though fictional evil might somehow seep into the baby's blood, scarring him for life.

The rumbling in my stomach prompts me to set aside the book. Outside the window, darkness has overtaken the white, and I strain to see whether the storm has intensified. Although the snow is steady, it seems the call for a blizzard may have been exaggerated. Jake's probably right. The media like to cause panic. As I walk down the hall to the kitchen, the cats trail alongside, eager for their own supper. Once I scoop expensive chicken pâté (the only canned cat food deemed acceptable by former homeless strays) into the cat bowls, I check the back door off the mudroom, then the side patio doors off the dining area in our new addition. All locked up tight. Curtains drawn.

Jake and I love our home which has been in his family for generations. We've made it our own with renovations over the last three and a half years, the upstairs nursery and the basement office being the most recent changes. But sometimes—more often than not—it creeps me out.

From the refrigerator, I grab the containers of roast beef and potatoes and prepare a plate to microwave while I chop cucumber, tomato, and feta cheese. I add a whole wheat roll and a glass of orange juice to my tray, then make myself comfortable on the sofa in the adjoining family room.

"Here you go, guys." Like every night, Nellie and Lucky share my supper after they have eaten their own. Tidbits of beef hit the floor, and they wolf them down as though they haven't eaten in days.

When I flip on the television to catch the six o'clock local news and weather, the words 'No signal' flash across the black screen. Snow must be covering the satellite dish. I could go out to the deck and sweep it off with the snowbrush Jake fashioned out of two broom handles, but climbing the ladder would be foolish in my condition. I'll wait for Jake to take care of it when he gets home.

Settling in for a wintry evening, the four of us (baby Jakey still in my womb) search for an online movie instead. Something romantic. Heartwarming.

Something to drown out the howling outside. Not the first, and certainly not the last, evening of my married life spent alone. Working opposite shifts keeps the spark in our marriage, but makes for a long and lonely week.

My mind flits to my job as an early childhood educator. Although I'm looking forward to seeing the kindergarten kids again, the two-week Christmas vacation doesn't seem long enough. Only a little over a week left to relax. In a few days, we'll be ringing in the new year. Hopefully, a better year than this past one.

Best not to think about that. Some things are better left forgotten.

I switch the television to our streaming service and click on the all-Christmas selection. A movie looks promising, set in a small town where Christmas is a community project. It reminds me to switch on the lights strung on the Christmas tree in the corner. On screen, the young couple, former high school sweethearts, bump into each other fifteen years after graduating. The guaranteed happy ending of these types of movies draws me to them on nights like this. Happy, like me and Jake. Ever after.

Despite the fact that he's never around when I need him. Why can't he work normal hours, like everyone else?

I'm selfish, wishing he were with me every hour of the day. He has a secure job at The Auto Supply Warehouse as supervisor in the humongous facility. I'm proud of him. And plenty of other spouses sit at home alone in the evening while their better half works to pay the mortgage, including my best friend, Vicky. Her husband, Craig, works with Jake at the warehouse, making a lot less than she does as a lawyer. And I don't hear her complaining.

Would you rather I quit my job and work at the casino? Dom says his offer's open anytime I decide I need a change.

Jake reminds me more often than necessary that he's not thrilled I made him turn down the new job prospect. But with his past record of gambling away our money, there is no way I'm going to allow him to work in a casino.

My phone pings partway through the movie.

Hey how you doing?

Today's second text from Jake. The first was letting me know he got to work. I never relax until I'm sure Jake is safe. The events of the past summer have heightened my anxiety. It's only the baby that stops me from regressing to a dependence on prescriptions.

I respond, telling him I'm okay, but worried about his drive home.

Chill. I'll be fine. Don't stay up worrying.

Of course, I *will* stay up worrying. He could end up in a ditch. Or worse. Smash into a pole. A head-on collision. Freeze to death in the middle of nowhere. It wouldn't be the first time he's nearly made a widow out of me.

Ok drive safe. Love you.

Stay calm, think of the baby. The doctor said I need to keep my blood pressure down.

Love you more. See you soon.

Another five hours of waiting.

Easing myself off the sofa without disturbing the cats, I tidy up the remnants of my supper. The roar of an engine, then another, startles me as I open the dishwasher. Peering through the family room blinds into the back yard, I glimpse a flash in the distance.

Snowmobiles. Jake says we should charge a fee. Just because we own a huge tract of land doesn't mean it's free for everyone to use for their own pleasure.

Like a chainsaw slicing through logs, the revving ramps up as the lights grow brighter, the sleds zipping toward the house. Three sets of headlights bear down in my direction. I rush to the back door and flip on the exterior lights to discourage them from coming closer. The police won't respond to a report of trespassing on our farmland. I know that, and so do the snowmobilers. But knowing their presence has been noted often deters them.

Leaving on, as well, the interior lights at the back of the house, with the blinds open to allow the glow to filter outside, I call Nellie and Lucky to follow me, then pull the hall doorway closed and head to the living room to continue my TV viewing, hoping the front of the house is quieter. With only the glow of the screen, I watch through the window as snow flows from the sky, on an angle now, swept to the right underneath the glow of the streetlight. The timer has switched on the Christmas lights adorning the evergreens lining the driveway. Their colors bleed onto the white canvas, red, green, yellow, and blue, muted by snow blanketing the trees.

A craving hits. Hot chocolate with whipped cream, a perfect treat for a night like this. Back in the kitchen, the whirring continues. Headlights circle in the field. Kids out for a joyride. Heating milk in the microwave, I watch and listen. Once the wind picks up, they'll tire of their games and head home, so I can have some peace and quiet. With the hallway door closed behind me, I retreat back to the living room with my steaming mug and set it on the coffee table.

Closing the drapes shut tightly against the storm and snuggling under the throw, I curl up and immerse myself in the rest of the movie, the cats settled next to my feet. About four hours to kill till Jake bursts through the door. Sips of the soothing hot liquid and the Christmas decorations in the movie's fictional town temper my thoughts of Jake driving on snow-covered roads.

My eyelids grow heavy, the television sending me off to slumberland. No point in shutting it off and heading to bed. The minute my head hits the pillow, I'll be wide awake. With the volume turned down, cat snores and wind gusts intrude upon the actors' conversations. I close my eyes and imagine Jake gazing into the bassinet, so proud of his son. He hadn't been sure he was ready to start a family, but I know he'll be a great dad.

Baby Jakey kicks, reminding me he's strong and healthy. Nellie and Lucky's contented rumbling assures me everything is right with the world. The happy couple in Christmasland smile. Jake and I are due for some of that bliss. I drift off to sleep with thoughts of our happy little family next Christmas, opening presents by the tree, Jakey gleeful as he rips open packages. Maybe I'll be pregnant again by then.

The house shakes me back to reality with a crack that splits my ears.

Then again. A roar through the very foundation of our home, threatening to rip it in half.

Chapter Two

"It's really starting to come down out there." Craig swings open the door to my office, plops his lunch pail on my desk, his butt following suit onto the utilitarian chair in front of it.

If it were anyone else, I'd demand they turn around and try again with a polite knock on the door before barging in and making themselves at home. But Craig and I go way back. We've shared this god-awful job for ten years, coveted each other's wives (although that's all in the past), lied to the police for each other, and kept secrets from each other. If that's not the definition of a best friend, then I don't know what is.

"Jay's saying it's only going to get worse. They're likely to close roads before long. Maybe you should think about shutting down early, send everyone home before we're all stuck here for the night," Craig continues, opening his container of microwaved lasagna, the steam wafting upwards.

Jay's our evening radio host on The Edge. What does he know about the weather? Nothing. About as much as he knows about music, playing that modern rock stuff, but The Edge is the station of choice in the greater Brampton Heights area.

You call that rock? Back in the day, they played the hard stuff. None of this namby-pamby garbage.

I'd like to smack Dad's voice clear out of my head, but it's rooted so deep into my psyche it'll snap back like an elastic band.

My mouth waters as my best bud digs into layers of cheese, meat, and sauce, prepared by *his* wife using *my* wife's recipe. When I pry open the lid of my own plastic lunch box, I'm pleasantly surprised to find Mal packed a heaping helping of pot roast and potatoes instead of the usual sandwich. In place of the cookies or granola bar, there's a slice of apple pie. She must have taken pity, watching me freeze my ass off earlier, pushing the snow thrower to clear the lane.

As I head toward the door to heat my meal in the staff cafeteria, I wave my hand in the air to dismiss Craig's concerns. "Any moron who can't drive through a bit of snow shouldn't have a license in the first place."

The metal steps clank as I descend from the mezzanine to the warehouse floor, where the rank and file receive, sort, shelve, and ship auto supply parts. I used to be one of the worker bees before I stepped up to management a few years back. From drone to queen bee by the age of twenty-five. Not bad. But I've got bigger plans. Thirty years ancient and a kid on the way. I never expected to get this old.

Time to grow up, Jake. Take care of that lovely family of yours.

I shake my head to dislodge my old man's voice. Since he's come back into my life, he's always there, like some demon trying to possess me.

Snagging an available microwave, I survey the staff while I wait two minutes for the ding. Mostly guys of various ages, with a few chicks and older women mixed in. We're an equal opportunity employer. If you can hoist it, forklift it, or shove it, welcome to The Auto Supply Warehouse, where our parts make it whole again. Your dream job, complete with benefits and a retirement package.

Several sets of eyes meet mine, and heads nod, acknowledging my presence. Here, I'm their superior. In the bar, after hours, we're all equals. You've got to mix with the employees, show you're one of them, just another cog in the wheel, working for the boss man.

"Hey, Jake!" One of my drinking buds waves me over to his table. "Any chance of getting off early tonight?"

Conversation dies down as the crowd awaits my answer. My brain sifts through the pros and cons. An early start to the weekend. Relieved spouses. Happy employees. Scoring points with my drinking buddies. Beating possible road closures. Safer driving conditions. No sleepover at the warehouse.

Company policy: The warehouse remains open except for emergency situations.

"Not likely." My roast beef dinner and I exit the lunchroom to a chorus of boos. I'm not the bad guy here. They know that. I answer to my boss, who answers to his boss, and I'm not sure who she answers to, but in the end, Company policy rules us all.

And speaking of bosses, I need to check in with Mal. Back in my office, I fire off a text before grabbing my fork. Wife first, stomach second. If I've learned anything in three and a half years of marriage, it's this: If you value your life, look after your wife. Especially if she's a tad on the nervous side and overreacts. Ready to pop. Like an overwound clock or a covered boiling pot or…a sizzling frying pan.

But, God, I love that woman. Anxiety and baggage included.

Craig's still in the honeymoon phase, married a few months. He's tapping away on the phone with one hand, shoveling lasagna with the other. "Vicky says I'd better get home safely, or you'll have to answer to her," he says, looking up from his phone, his expression a mix of lovestruck puppy dog and whipped husband.

The fact that Vicky makes a shitload of money compared to Craig defines their roles, even though Vick doesn't lord it over him. She can't help it if she's one of those fancy lawyers at a big firm. Craig pretends it doesn't matter. But I know better. Why else would he seriously consider tagging along with me and my offer of employment with a more prestigious company? A position with plenty of perks, along with a nice salary. Dom is giving me free rein to hire support staff, and I've told my best buddy he'll be nicely compensated for joining me at the casino. If I take the job.

The half-hour passes a lot faster than the rest of the shift. Craig packs up and springs from his chair. "I'll talk to you later."

Through the glass panes, I observe as the drones below get back to their appointed duties, moving car parts along conveyor belts, carrying them up ladders, shifting them to shelves with forklifts, while others do the same job in reverse, preparing products for shipping. In and out. Out and in again. A finely oiled machine.

After checking my computer for the status of incoming and outgoing orders and accepting new orders into the system, I sneak a peek at the weather forecast for the rest of the night.

Mal is going to freak out. She'll take the forecast literally, the fear-mongering, and exaggerated conditions. I can picture her pacing from one door to the other, peering through each window, waiting for the worst, imagining me dead in a drift. And it's hours till quitting time. By eleven o'clock, she'll have bitten her fingernails down till the skin around them bleeds and twirled her hair till clumps come out like fur balls. She does it without fail every single time. The least bit of a problem, and she flies off the handle.

And every time, I eventually come home as expected. Except for the few times I went missing this past year. A fourth time might just send her over the edge.

Down on the floor, I make my rounds, checking in with my staff to see how it's going. "Oh, it's going," everyone assures me. Rows of blue industrial shelving border wide aisles, a hive of activity reflected as work boots clip and clop on the shiny epoxy flooring. I spy Craig lifting a box over his head, the toned muscles in his arms a result of hard labor. A flash of jealousy hits me as I think of those arms around Mallory.

"There's nothing between Craig and me. We're just friends." Mallory assured me there was no way he could be the father of our baby. And I believe her. Because I love her. "Nothing happened. He cares about me because I'm his best friend's wife, that's all."

At the loading dock doors, product rolls down the line and is packed into trailers, boxes stacked on skids. A circle of truckers stands off to the side, their conversation piquing my interest. I know them, but I'll be damned if I can recall their names. They come and go, like the product.

"She's blowin' in good," says a burly guy, about my age.

"Won't be surprised if they shut down traffic overnight. Maybe best not to head out," an older dude says, scratching his head.

No, no, no. Not good. Those goods need to get out to the stores and garages. We can't have a delay.

"Hey, is there a problem?" Best to nip this in the bud. "My guys will have the trucks loaded and ready to roll soon. In plenty of time to beat the storm."

"Have you looked out there lately?" Tall mustached guy raises his brows. "She ain't pretty."

Echoing his sentiment over the loudspeakers is Jay, The Edge's doom and gloom host, interrupting namby-pamby repetitive lyrics. "Highway Six North is now closed. Police are cautioning people not to travel unless absolutely necessary. We're in for a wild ride tonight, folks. Stay tuned to The Edge for updated closures as this storm system closes in."

The truckers shake their heads. Looks like our product is going nowhere tonight. I wave them off, releasing them from their duty. Maybe I should consider doing the same with my staff. I don't need accidents on my conscience. If the hard-as-nails truckers aren't driving, it can't be good. I've only made this call a few times in the last five years. Taking it upon myself to shut down isn't in my job description, but my boss won't shoulder the responsibility. He tells me to make an educated decision based on the conditions in the countryside where the warehouse is located. Then he adds, "In inclement weather, all employees are expected to be at work during regular hours, provided they can travel safely."

What the hell does that mean? Sounds like something out of the employee handbook.

The side emergency exit door resists the pressure I apply. Asking the truckers for assistance is no longer an option, as they took off the second I suggested it might be okay to do so. I shove the door again, but it shoves back. I pull out my phone and send a text.

Hey, get over to the west emergency door. ASAP.

Minutes later, a forklift rumbles down the back aisle, past the loading docks, toward the west wing, beeping to clear a path. Craig hops off. "What's up?"

"Door's stuck." I jerk my thumb toward the metal escape hatch.

Craig's muscles strain as he pushes. "Maybe give me a hand?"

We force the door open only to have it fly out of our grip and slam against the side of the building. Craig and I brace ourselves along the interior wall as the roar threatens to swallow us whole.

"Was there a reason you wanted the door open?" Craig shouts as snow invades the warehouse, swirling in a ghostly formation. "It's freezing out there."

"I wanted to see how bad the storm is."

"Did you get your answer?"

A couple of guys show up from around the corner, looking for the source of the sudden blast of frigid air and howling. With the effort of four men, the emergency door locks back into position, leaving us covered in white dust and shivering like newborn babes.

"I'm calling it a night. Time to shut down and head home." My words follow the two men as they jog down the aisle, calling it quits before I make the official announcement.

Overriding Jay and The Edge, I get on the horn and tell everyone to clear out before it gets any worse and to drive safe. I don't need to say it twice. Within minutes, Craig and I are wandering through the warehouse, checking the aisles, and finding ourselves alone.

"Well, I guess that's it. You go ahead, and I'll do one more shoutout over the system before locking up." I head up the stairs to my office, but my best bud follows and sticks with me until I'm convinced everyone is out.

Craig checks his phone for the latest on road conditions. "You're out of luck, man. They just closed ten north of here. You'll have to stay over at our place. We better get out of here before they shut down the rest of the highway."

Highway ten leads to the city of Brampton Heights and Craig and Vicky's new home in the suburbs, twelve minutes to the south. Ten north leads to Mallory and our farmhouse, eighteen minutes away in good weather.

"You know I can't leave Mallory alone in this. Not in her condition. I'll take the back roads. There won't be any traffic. And I'll take it slow. I've got those new snow tires."

"You won't do Mallory any good if you wind up in the ditch. I'm sure your neighbors, Paul and Linda, will be there for her if she needs help. You can head home in the morning, once they clear up this mess."

"I appreciate the offer, but Mallory needs me."

The employee door resists as we push, then falls forward into the driving snow. We shove the door closed behind us, and I yank at it, checking that it's locked. Despite the black night, the lights on the building and in the parking lot would normally illuminate the exterior of The Auto Supply Warehouse. But not tonight.

Whiteness has obliterated the night and the light like a fog. A sheet slips down all sides of the lot, a blanket between us and the rest of the world.

Pressing in. Entombing us. Claustrophobic. Smothering. Crushing.

Mallory will be freaking out.

"I need to get to Mallory." Pressing the remote start on my key fob, I venture out in what I hope is the direction of my new Honda. I feel Craig's hand on my arm, then it slips away, and I turn to shout, "I'll call you when I get home."

I'm not sure he hears. I keep trudging.

Toward the car. Toward home. To Mallory.

Chapter Three

For weeks, he's been watching the property, although he was told to stay away and mind his own business. But this *is* his business. Not the store heists, not the stashing of stolen goods, and not the possibility of a dirty cop. The operation itself doesn't concern him. But the consequences of a failed mission do.

That this particular barn has been chosen as a cache for the jewelry is a stroke of luck. He has a personal investment in what lies hidden within the wooden red structure. Hours spent gazing at the treasures, at the risk of being caught by one party or another, affirm his decision to infiltrate the family.

The question is how to do so without exposing the criminal activity on their land and jeopardizing the entire operation.

He waits for the opportune moment and is rewarded by Mother Nature.

Chapter Four

Shock shoots through to my core, like an arrow through the heart. In that instant, I'm certain I'm going to die. Anxiety leaves no room for reason. Sitting ramrod straight, I survey my surroundings, willing the breaths to come, slow and steady. In and out. Breathe and listen.

Wind. Snow. That's all it is. This old brick house is sturdy enough to withstand it. The generator will automatically kick in if the power goes out. Jake made sure it's fueled for the winter, with an extra can of gas ready. No danger of being alone in the dark and cold. I need to stay calm. My hands instinctively cover my swollen belly as a loud crack assaults the house again.

Thunder? In winter?

Nellie and Lucky's ears twitch as the rumble shakes the house. Easing myself off the sofa, I shuffle to the window and move the curtain aside a couple of inches. The woods across the road, the road along the woods, the lawn between the road and the house—have vanished. The walkway off the porch is barely visible in the exterior lights, a drift separating the house from the rest of civilization.

The jingle startles me as much as the sounds of stormy weather. Grabbing my phone off the table, I notice it's 9:46. I don't know whether to be relieved or concerned that Jake is calling.

"Is everything okay?" My heart pounds, expecting the worst.

"I'm fine, hon. Just shutting down early. Heading home now. I wanted to let you know not to worry if it takes a while. They've closed the highway, so I'm taking the back roads."

My mind works to process what he's saying, but all I can think is that I want him home with me. "Okay. Jake?"

"Yes, hon?"

"Drive carefully."

"Love you, hon. See you soon."

Once he ends the call, my brain starts to clue in. Jake could die. And the last thing I said to him was that he should drive carefully. As if he planned on driving recklessly. I should have told him to stay at work till the storm settled, or at least wait till daylight. Not that he would listen. Jake has driven through the worst storms, on closed roads, on unplowed roads, on roads with vehicles lining the ditch on both sides. And he's always made it home somehow. He's been lucky.

But his luck could run out.

"It's okay, Jakey. Daddy is going to be fine. He'll be home soon." I draw circles on my belly, reassuring the baby that nothing bad is going to happen, when another boom makes me jump out of my skin.

The cats turn their heads in all directions, searching for the source of the turbulence intruding upon our home. Their eyes meet mine, questioning whether I have the answer.

"It's just the storm. It's okay." If I can convince the cats, maybe I'll believe it, too.

Keep busy, Mal.

Jake says that's the best thing to do when I'm waiting for him, and he's later than expected.

Before you know it, I'll be there.

Jake figures if you just wait long enough, problems will fix themselves.

But I know better.

Opening my iPad, I check the weather forecast again. More snow, wind, and cold temperatures overnight and through tomorrow. The latest news report is still labeling it the first real blizzard of this winter, shaping up to be the storm of the decade. Another rumble rocks the house, sending me on an internet search for the possible cause of the noise. Thundersnow? Frost quakes?

Watching storm videos keeps me occupied for a while. But Jake is wrong.

Keeping busy only feeds my anxiety. I close the iPad and head back to the window, opening the curtains fully to stare into the void, waiting for Jake's headlights to pierce through the whiteouts. A sudden flash of lightning illuminates the sky.

Right middle finger in my mouth, teeth clicking against my nail, ready to chomp, I come to my senses.

Stop it. Jake will be fine, like always.

Focusing on the seconds as they tick and staring at the deluge of snow won't make Jake come home any faster. Removing my finger from my mouth, I close the drapes, turn off the television, and retreat upstairs to our bedroom, iPad and phone in hand, cats racing past me to claim premium bed space.

Once settled under the covers, I close my eyes and listen to an audiobook, choosing a romance this time to avoid scaring myself to death. Jake said it would be a while, not to worry. If he comes home to find me strung out, it won't do our relationship any good. I hate being the meek, frightened, submissive little wife, and Jake knows it. He didn't always.

The volume turned up on my iPad, in an attempt to drown out the howling and roaring, my concentration wavers between the romance novel and my own romance with Jake, the man who saved me from a deep and dark depression after my parents died in a fire. I've been told that time heals. How much time? Weeks, months, a year? It's been five years, and I'm nowhere near healing. But Jake gives me a reason to live. And now he's given me baby Jakey. Since the moment I gazed into Jake's blue-green eyes more than four years ago, I knew he was the one.

Not that he's perfect.

Far from it. His fear of becoming like his abusive father nearly drove him to follow in his footsteps. Raised by a father whose drinking reached a point where he lashed out at his wife and two sons as though they were the reason for his stupor of a life. But Jake has always managed to restrain himself from actually striking me, even when his fury builds to a crescendo. The abusive face of Jake rarely comes to the surface, eclipsed by his sense of humor and easy-going nature. I calmly explain to him, as though he were one of my kindergarten charges, that his derogatory comments sting as much as a slap and his controlling behavior is NOT acceptable. And he whimpers, like the little boy beaten by his father, begging me not to leave him. Accepting that he has a problem, while understanding that he is not destined to become his father, is difficult for Jake. But he's learning.

Just as he's learning to deal with his gambling addiction, having finally agreed to counseling and group therapy. I didn't sign up for this when I married Jake. But then, he didn't sign up for me either. We're still getting to know each other and the burdens we carry, three and a half years after signing the marriage certificate that sealed our fate.

My heavy lids close, the iPad slipping from my hands as my mind transports me back to the day we said "I do". So much promise in those words. For better or worse. Jake's smile and the twinkle in his eyes, pledging there would be better things yet to come.

If only life were that simple. Jake and I love each other more than we love ourselves. That's never been the problem. It's life that's the problem.

Another boom intrudes upon my thoughts as they morph into dreams, shaking me from near-slumber. I rise from our bed and pull the curtains to the side, startled to see only white splayed across the black canvas, the color of our outdoor Christmas lights having been obliterated from the painter's palette. Does the rest of the world even exist beyond the dots and splotches of snow on my window and the spraying of nature's pure white paint upon the blacked-out landscape that belongs to Jake and me?

Letting the curtains fall as a flash illuminates the sky, I check the time on the clock radio next to our bed. 11:06. Shouldn't Jake be home by now?

The ringing that follows my question prompts more questions. Why didn't I hear his car? Why doesn't he use his key? I ease my way down the lit stairs to the front entry, flip on the hallway light, not thinking twice about whether or not to turn the knob. The outer door pushes against me, barring access to the wintry world. Shoving my weight against it, I feel a sudden pull on the handle, a hand trying to pry open the storm door, like the lid on a vacuum-sealed plastic food container. With a whoosh, the door springs open, snow blowing into the hallway.

No one is there. As I wrestle to close the storm door, another flash brightens the sky, momentarily shedding light on the driveway. With snow drifts nearly as tall as the garage, it's not surprising Jake's Honda hasn't made it up the lane. I can barely see the shape of my Toyota under the blanket of white.

A banging startles me. I hurry to the mudroom. Why is Jake using the *back* door?

The white shape outside, barely discernible from its background of snow, even with the house lit up inside and out, resembles a snowman ousted from his spot on some child's lawn and dropped onto my doorstep.

Thank goodness he's made it home. "Jake! You must be half-frozen to death!"

Jake stumbles into the mudroom, collapsing on the floor, sending flakes of icy snow in all directions.

Door slammed, I turn the lock. Safe and secure in our home. Jake, me, and baby Jakey.

But as the snow melts, the beginnings of a small puddle form, bringing forth an image of Frosty the Snowman. Only this isn't a cartoon, and the shape transforming by my feet isn't Frosty.

Nor is it Jake.

Chapter Five

I battle the biting snow, pressing forward with my arm shielding my face. With each step that sinks into the fluff, I thank Mallory for having the good sense to insist I drive to work in the pricey winter boots she bought me for Christmas. I raise my head between the gusts and spy the headlights of my Honda, the engine a faint purr. Grabbing my gloves and the snowbrush from the back seat, I clear the several inches of snow from my windshield, windows, taillights, and headlights. After a few swipes along the hood, I turn the brush on myself, sweeping snow from my black jeans and the front of my jacket. If I had been smart enough to put on the Christmas red plaid trapper hat Mal bought, I wouldn't be freezing my ears off right now. And I sure as hell wouldn't be concerned about how ridiculous it looked. But there's no point in bothering now.

Snow brush tossed in the rear, I sink into the driver's seat and press the heated seat button, flip the front and back wipers on full blast, crank up the heat, and shut off the radio. I psych myself up for the trek home, my eyes closed for a few moments. I've driven through my share of blizzards, but this is the first of the season. And I've got a kid in my wife's belly who's going to need his father to make it home safe.

As I maneuver the car through the lot, tracks from previous vehicles guide me to the exit. Red taillights prompt me to stop and put the car in park. My phone rings.

"Hey, you sure you want to drive home?" Craig asks.

"I'm good, thanks anyway."

"If you change your mind, let me know. Call me either way. Drive safe."

"I will. You too."

Craig pulls out onto the road leading to Highway 10. I follow, but once I reach the main thoroughfare, I hesitate and consider whether to risk a fine and demerit points on the closed highway. I stick with my initial thought and take a chance on the backroads.

Slow and steady. A brand new all-wheel drive vehicle and the best snow tires money can buy. Except, I can't see shit.

Hands at ten and two on the steering wheel, and my eyes glued ahead as the wind bombards my windshield with flakes, I creep along with just enough speed to plow through. I focus on where I need my vehicle to head—down the road, which, mercifully, is free of twists and turns, unlike many of the roads in the area. At the first side road, I turn northwards, the sense of isolation increasing as I remember there are no towns along this route. The high beams only make it worse, illuminating the sheer force of the blizzard, but I flip them on and off to get my bearings. Now and then, I glimpse the sides of the two-lane road, narrowed to one lane by drifts. Fortunately, there's no oncoming traffic, and the road runs along a straight course angled toward home. The banks lining my way, and the grit and slush beneath my tires indicate the county plow has been through at some point tonight. Trees border the road, their branches heavy with snow.

A glimpse of the dashboard tells me it's 10:22. Up ahead, to the right, a faint glow beckons. I slow down, pull into the driveway of a farm equipment dealership, keep the engine running, and slump down in my seat. Time for a breather. And a text to my wife, who is no doubt pacing the floors, wondering if I'm dead.

All good. Stopping for a bit. It's slow going. Be a while. Love you.

Five minutes later, I'm ready to face the storm again. Inching toward home, I focus straight ahead as time drags like molasses in winter. I could swear this trip is stretching into an overnight journey.

And then I spot a landmark—the feed mill. I'm so close to home, I can almost smell Mal's hair, taste her lips, touch her round belly. I'll be home before 11:00. She'll be so relieved to see me, I'm guaranteed some lovin' tonight. I pick up the pace, anticipating my welcome home. Another five minutes and I'll be home free.

Is that the lights of the town I see up ahead? Our turnoff will be coming up any…

There it is. I slow down to make the turn onto our back street, our paradise off the beaten track.

Where the hell is the road?

I make out the road sign on the corner, buried under a mound, whiteout having smeared the lettering. A six-foot drift obstructs the way to paradise. Which means I will have to circle around town and come in from the other side, extending my trip by a good ten to fifteen minutes.

Resigning myself to the fact that it's going to take longer to get home than I figured, I drive into town, pull over to text Mal again, and realize my phone's dead.

Shit!

All I can do is keep moving. Through town, left onto the next county road, and left again down the side road bordering our property. Fields of snow all around, it's hard to see what's road and what's not. A sense of pride strikes me, knowing I own most of the surrounding land. Mal and I own it, that is. Thanks to Mom's generosity, my grandparents' homestead is ours. Someday, all this will be baby Jakey's.

I'm blindsided by the glare of headlights barreling toward me. I move as far to the right as possible, allowing the oncoming vehicle space. A pickup with a blade in front whizzes by, honking, barely missing me.

A flurry of snow and slush slaps my Honda, throwing me for a loop as my wipers whack away the obstruction. But I keep moving, eyes piercing through the explosion of white in the beams, hands steady on the wheel, foot letting up on the gas, swearing up a storm to rival the one blazing outside.

You drive a fuckin' pickup, you think you own the fuckin' road.

Once I realize the guy has done me a favor by clearing a path, I calm down. Some vigilante young hotshot is taking matters into his own hands, making the roads passable and checking for stranded motorists. Foolhardy, but well-meaning. A lucky break for me. It's easier going now.

Several sets of eyes glow beside the road ahead. My reaction is swift. Brakes slammed on, the Honda skids, and I overcorrect, going into a spin. The snowbank races toward me.

Chapter Six

So, who is it? The shape takes form, lying semi-prone on the floor, the puddle seeping closer toward me. He moans. Yes, it's clearly a man, his outerwear, not Jake's. Why is this man here?

"Are you o…kay?" Backing away, I wait for a response.

He rolls onto his side and curls up. "C…c…cold."

A shudder rolls through me, my arms instinctively folded and rubbing the prickles under my flannel sleeves. A black balaclava encrusted with snow covers his head, only the eyes and mouth visible.

There's a stranger in my house.

"Who are you? Why are you here?" I back away further, keeping my eyes on him.

"Truck. Stuck." He pulls off his balaclava and rolls onto his back, staring at the ceiling, his chest rising and falling.

"I'll get you a blanket. Be right back."

I tilt my head to the side to catch any movement from him as I tread down the hall. I ease one foot onto the step before realizing that's a mistake. If he follows, I'll be trapped upstairs. But my phone is on my nightstand, and I feel exposed in my nightgown. I turn to call down the hall before continuing the climb. "Stay there. Don't move. My husband and kids are sleeping."

In our bedroom, I grab my cell and call Jake. It goes to voicemail, so I text. **There's a man here stranded in the storm.**

Before I can click send, I realize there's nothing Jake can do. He won't get here any faster knowing that. It might even worry him enough to rush and get into an accident. I dial another number instead.

On the fifth ring, a man's groggy voice asks, "Mallory? Everything okay there?"

"Yes. No. A man is here. His truck is stuck in the snow. Jake isn't home yet."

"I'll be right over."

The line goes dead. I pull my robe over my flannel nightie, pop my phone into a pocket, and grab Jake's baseball bat from our closet. In the hall, I stop to pull a thick towel and a blanket from the linen cupboard before returning downstairs.

"My husband will be down in a while. And he called our neighbor. Maybe they can help get your truck unstuck. I'll get you a hot cup of coffee. Here." I toss the towel and blanket onto the tiles next to him, where he now sits, leaning against the wall with his legs spread out. I back away toward the kitchen, baseball bat tucked behind me. If he sees it, he doesn't let on.

"Thanks. Appreciate it." He pushes himself off the floor and removes his parka. After hanging his drenched coat on the door handle, he dries himself off and wipes the tiles with the towel, leaving his gloves and balaclava on top of it.

I get a glimpse of a beer-belly body that matches his lightly lined face and the touches of gray in his short hair.

"You can go into the living room and sit down." I motion down the hall.

In the kitchen/family room, I unlock the patio doors, have second thoughts, and lock them again. It might provide an easier escape for me, if needed, and allow Paul another way in if I can't get to the front door. But what if this man brought others with him and they're waiting outside to see if I'm alone?

As I prepare the coffee, Nellie and Lucky appear from wherever they were hiding and circle my legs, rubbing against me, meowing. Tossing some cat treats on the floor, I commend them for their guarding skills. "Good kitties, you'll take care of Mommy."

They disappear after scarfing down the treats. I call Vicky, hoping that will make me feel safer.

"Mallory? Is everything okay?" Vicky's voice sounds strained, not her usual perky tone.

"Yes, I think so," I whisper. "But Jake's not home yet, and there's a strange man here; he says his truck got stuck in the snow. I told him Jake's upstairs, so he wouldn't think I'm alone. Paul's on his way over, but I'm a bit creeped out."

"Ohh…that is creepy. Out there in the middle of nowhere."

That doesn't reassure me. "Do you mind staying on the phone with me till Paul comes?"

"Of course. Maybe you'll feel better if you put me on speaker so the three of us can chat till Jake or Paul get there."

Cup of coffee in one hand and the phone and bat in the other, I tiptoe down the hall and peer into the living room. The leather club chair holds an average-sized male, save for the beer belly. Nothing about him is threatening. In fact, he looks as uncomfortable as I feel, ankles crossed, his hands rubbing his knees.

Blinking as he glances up at me, his eyes widen. "What's the bat for?"

I look down at the metal bat hanging from my hand. Setting the cup on the coffee table, I sit on the sofa facing him. "Oh, this? My husband left it in the kitchen."

He nods, accepting that as a reasonable answer.

"So, you got stuck in the snow?"

The man's eyes dart around, looking for the source of the voice that isn't mine. "Uh, yeah."

"That's too bad," Vicky continues, and he zeroes in on my phone. "Hopefully, Jake and Paul can get you out. What happened? How'd you get stuck?"

"Going too fast, I guess. Tires slipped off the road, slammed into the snowbank. Rocked it back and forth. Couldn't get out. Just down the road, so I got out and walked, hoping there'd be a farmhouse nearby. Got lucky. This nice lady answered her door." For the first time, his lips turn up in a smile. He leans forward, his hand inching out to reach the coffee cup.

This is the most I've heard him speak.

"What's your name? Where are you from? What were you doing traveling out there in the boondocks in this weather?" Vicky fires off questions as though he were a client accused of cheating on his wife.

"Um…Dave. I was just heading home to Brampton Heights after visiting a friend in Orangetown. The highway's closed, so I took the backroads."

"Bet you're wishing you'd stayed over at your friend's place."

"Figured I'd be good with the monster tires on the truck. Should have watched my speed." He shrugs, sips his coffee, and relaxes back into the chair.

The doorbell rings, startling us both. I shuffle toward the door, bat tagging along. "That must be my neighbor."

The wind howls into the hallway as I unlock and pull the door. Paul stands on my covered porch, a dusting of white on his puffy jacket, a bulge protruding in the middle that puts the stranger's beer belly to shame. He forces the storm door open, bracing himself to stop it from slamming shut.

"Everything okay, Mallory?" A furrowed brow and gentle eyes show his concern. Paul Winston, proud grandfather of two little ones, has taken on a fatherly role since learning Jake and I are expecting our first child, going so far as to offer his wife, Linda, for free babysitting services.

I step out into the frigid air, arms crossed. "I think so," I whisper, half closing the door behind me, "but Jake's not home yet, and I'm not comfortable being alone with a stranger, especially with the baby to think of. I told the man that Jake's upstairs, but I'm sure he's wondering why he doesn't come down."

Paul ushers me out of the cold. "It's okay. I'm here now. And I brought Russ for protection."

Standing in the hallway, Paul unzips his jacket and greets the stranger. "So, I hear you got stuck."

The man, who *claims* his name is Dave, takes in Paul and the Jack Russell terrier pup who leaps from Paul's chest and bounds toward the club chair. He jumps and yips around the stranger's legs. Dave's eyes flit from Paul, to my bat, to my phone, and to Russ. "Yeah, my truck's stuck in a couple of feet of snowbank. Just down the road, past the corner."

"I could try to blow you out. Once the wind settles down and we've got some visibility."

Dave stares at Paul.

"I've got one heavy-duty snow blower. Got me here, no problem, but I'm not sure I want to venture much further down the road. Don't want it to end up in the snowbank like your truck. If you don't mind waiting till morning or till the storm quits..." Paul rubs his scruffy chin, appraising the stranger. His eyes narrow, and his voice changes from friendly to authoritative. He pulls his phone from his pocket. "Or we could call emergency services—my cousin, Ralph, he's a cop, lives in town—could probably authorize a plow truck to get out here ASAP. If you're hurt or need immediate assistance."

"No, no need for that. I can wait it out." Dave's mug shakes as he brings it to his mouth. Russ sits on his haunches, eyes glued to the stranger.

Paul pries the bat from me and taps it in his hand. "Why don't you go into the family room and lie down. I'll wait here with..." He motions to the man.

"Dave."

"Dave and I will keep each other company till Jake gets his lazy ass down here." Paul winks at me. "You go on and rest."

I switch places with Paul. He sits on the sofa facing Dave, firmly gripping Jake's bat, while I stand in the hallway. "Okay. Let me know if you need anything."

Leaving the kitchen door open, I lie on the family room sofa. Although I feel more secure now, I won't sleep. Not until Jake gets home.

"Mallory?" I jump at Vicky's voice, having assumed she ended the call when Paul arrived.

"It's okay. Paul's watching him. I just wish Jake would get here."

Silence for a moment, then Vicky speaks, her voice quivering. "I know how you feel. Craig hasn't come home yet either."

It's nearly midnight. Where are our husbands?

Chapter Seven

reat. Just great. So frickin' close to home.

Shifting into reverse gear gets me nowhere. The tires spin, pulling me in deeper. Rocking back and forth doesn't work; it drives me further into the bank. I step out of the Honda, grab a flashlight from the glove box, and survey the damage. Front end embedded in the snowbank, inches from a utility pole.

Could be worse. At least I'm not wrapped around the pole.

Can't call Mal. Phone's dead.

Shit! She'll be thinking I'm *dead.*

I flip the hatch and pull out the shovel and have a go at the snowbank. Three or four shovelfuls later, I decide that's not the issue. I need to back the car out, not move it forward into the snowbank. Out come the traction mats, positioned at the back tires. I rev the engine in an attempt to jolt the car backward. Then I use a gentler approach. Still slipping. When I get out to reposition the mats, a flicker of light in the distance catches my attention.

Eyes shielded, I stand and gaze to the left, waiting for another lull in the gusts that threaten to pull my feet out from under me. Could that be our house? What else could it be? Our property is the only one out here. The town's behind me. I must be near the intersection. So close.

Ears burning, I sit my ass down on the leather seats and let the car unfreeze me. A few more tries to rock the car out of the snow and…The snowshoes! I saw them in the back when I grabbed the shovel. Still there from when a buddy at work returned them after borrowing the shoes for a weekend at the cabin.

Time to bundle up. It's going to be a long walk. But with Mallory at the end of it, I can do it. She'll have the home fires burning, so grateful when I fling myself through that door. I grab my snowpants, parka, and plaid hat from the backseat, slip on the snowshoes, guzzle what's left in the metal water bottle from my lunch pail, and I'm ready to hike across the field. The winter emergency and first-aid kit Mallory put together and forced me to carry in the car catches my eye in the cargo area. I unzip the huge canvas bag and root through, wondering how that's going to save me in the middle of nowhere in a blizzard.

Jesus, Mal, everything in here but the kitchen sink. Silly girl. A scented candle? Might have been a good idea to pack a phone charger instead. A change purse with coins and a couple of twenties? That'll come in handy out here. And what the hell am I supposed to do with this? Referee a game?

Always be prepared in winter. Especially in rural Ontario. I wrap the whistle cord around my neck and grab a pouch of trail mix in case I get the munchies. Then I spy something I really *can* use and pull another lanyard over my head. A compass—just need to head southwest. A country and western song about a cowboy riding into the sunset rolls through my head. The heavy-duty flashlight, along with the compass, is a must-take so I don't get lost. And maybe the bright orange thermal blanket in case I *do* get lost. God, I love my woman.

I keep in mind the image of Mallory and what she'll do to warm me up once we're tucked into bed as I trudge past the Honda, feeling for the fence. It's got to be here somewhere. The wooden rails enclose our property, and I'm fairly confident this *is* our property. Or it could be the woods behind it. And who knows what or who lies in there. Those sets of eyes that sent me into the ditch came from there. Most likely, just raccoons.

I wave the flashlight to my left. No trees. Nothing but white and more white coming down, whipping my face. There's the glimmer of light again, on a diagonal from where I tramp along parallel to the road. One hand reaching out, sweeping through drifts as I meander along searching for the rail, the other hand holding my flashlight to guide the way, my eyes flit between the powdery path ahead and the roadway, both barely visible. The last thing I need is to get lost in the cornfield. I need a reference point.

Something solid brushes against my glove. I stop and bend for a closer look.

Hallelujah! Thank you, God!

I've never been a regular churchgoer, and Mal gave up on church after her parents died in that horrific fire. But Mal insists we attend for the baby's sake.

"You need a church to christen a child," she says.

So we show up at 10 a.m. at the local church on the occasional Sunday when we're not too worn out. Because we're both believers, whether we want to be or not.

The fence is my assurance that I'm on my own property, and the light at the end of this long tunnel of white is home. And home is Mallory. And the baby.

I hoist myself over the fence. If I can move in a straight diagonal and not a circle, I'll be fine. Need to watch for the light. One foot (or snowshoe) after the other, I plod along, trying to keep my balance, arms braced against the wind, hood pulled and fastened as far as it goes, sheltering my bare face. I can handle the cold. Thoughts of Mallory on the beach in her bikini during our honeymoon burn me up. Or, it could be I'm sweating like a pig from the exertion of lumbering through a snow-covered field in the middle of the night in the worst blizzard I've ever had the misfortune to hike through.

Things are going along smoothly, considering I could die out here, and they wouldn't find my body till spring. My legs are giving out; fatigue is wearing me down. If I could just stop for a minute and rest…

Keep moving, Jake. Mallory's waiting. The baby needs you. You're almost there.

But, the truth is, I have no idea whether I'm almost there. I can't see the light. I continue my monologue, out loud, hoping the pep talk will give me strength. Then I stumble. And trip. Down, onto the snow. Down, onto something hard.

Bracing myself against the object that sent me flying, my mind tries to make sense of it. A rock? No. A stump? A fallen tree?

Out in the middle of the field? How lost am I? GET UP JAKE!

I scan the area with my flashlight. I'm not lost at all. To the left, the old barn is a faint silhouette. I could make it there, rest, then continue straight down to the house. Five minutes, ten?

The knowledge that I'm nearly home encourages me to push myself up, using the hard object as leverage. But it's not a rock. Not a tree.

An old farm implement on the lane? Under the tarp?

I haven't been back here in years. Guess grandpa didn't have a chance to clean up before he kicked the bucket. My glove wipes the snow off its surface, the occasional lull in the howling wind allowing me to get a better idea of what lies buried in the snow. Before I do, I notice something next to it.

A snowmobile? Grandpa didn't sled. Who the hell left that *here? And why?*

On my feet, considering which way to turn—to the barn for a breather or straight home—the decision is made for me. Something latches onto my lower leg, pulling me down into the snow. I flop onto the powder, like a fish being tossed onto a boat deck, struggling to catch my breath as the wind snatches the scream exiting my throat.

Next to me on frigid ground, a face pokes through the drift.

Chapter Eight

"I'm starting to worry," Vicky says. "Craig called a couple of hours ago and said he was helping someone who slid off the road into the ditch. I haven't heard from him since, and he's not picking up his phone."

Knowing Craig hasn't made it home soothes me. Craig has a shorter and easier drive than Jake. Some nasty, jealous part of me is glad that Vicky, too, is worrying. Why should I be the only one tearing my hair out? Now that she's married, maybe Vicky will have a better understanding of my anxiety. Loving someone too much isn't all hearts and roses. Sometimes it's so painful your heart can't bear it.

Curled up on the sofa, I'm ever mindful of the fact that a stranger sits in our home, and Jake still isn't here. At least Vicky knows what Craig is doing. It's just like him to help others. "He's probably still busy trying to get them back on the road. And maybe his phone's in his car," I assure her.

"What about Jake? Have you heard anything?"

"Same as you. Not since 10:30. He said it was rough out there, and he was stopping for a bit. But he should have been here by now, and he's not picking up his phone either."

Vicky hesitates before answering. "I'm sure he's fine. Maybe he fell asleep waiting for the storm to blow over. What about you? Are you okay with that man in your house?"

"Yes, I think he's genuinely stuck and came here to get out of the cold. Paul and Russ have things under control. And we have Jake's baseball bat in case there's a problem." My words make me sound braver than I feel.

"Okay, text me when Jake gets home, and I'll let you know about Craig."

Ending the call, I slip into the hall and listen to the voices coming from the living room. I sensed Paul was apprehensive about the stranger. Why else would he mention his cop cousin, Ralph, who doesn't exist? He and I know there is no police presence in Idlewood. In this weather, it would take a while to get help from our closest station.

"Can't get through that mountain of snow at the corner of our place," Paul says. "And it's a long way around the block."

It sounds like Dave's truck is on the road leading to the main highway. Which, according to Paul, is inaccessible at the moment. So how is Jake going to get through?

"So there's no way out of here?" Dave says.

"We'll figure something out. I'm curious, though, why you didn't come to my house. It's closer to the road." Is there suspicion in Paul's tone?

"I could barely see a thing. Looked like lights from a town in the distance, but then I noticed a glow off to the left, so I took my chances. Trudged through the field in knee-deep snow to get here. I'm just thankful this nice lady opened the door for me, or I'd be freezing to death out there."

"I guess we were already hunkered down for the night. Lucky for you, Mallory had the lights on. If I were you, I'd let your wife know it'll be a while."

"Uh, yeah. I'll text her."

There are likely more than a few wives waiting to hear from their husbands tonight. How many *husbands* are pacing the floor, wondering where their wives are? Do men panic when their wives don't arrive home on time in a snowstorm? Or maybe it's just me. Maybe other people have a calmer approach to life.

I bring a cup of coffee to Paul, asking Dave if he wants a refill.

"Uh, sure. Thanks." He hands me his mug with a trembling hand.

Dave is polite enough, but he's likely nervous because he's in a strange house, trapped for the foreseeable future. And his wife is no doubt at her wits' end.

Setting a plate of cookies on the coffee table along with Dave's fresh coffee, I ask if he has children at home.

"One boy."

Knowing he's a father makes him less of a threat, but I'd rather he didn't know that Jake isn't here. "Well, hopefully you'll be able to get home soon. Make yourself comfortable in the meantime. I'm going to join Jake upstairs since there's nothing else we can do right now. He must have fallen back to sleep after taking a pill for his headache. Paul, are you okay to keep Dave company?"

My mouth opens wide, and I draw a deep breath in a fake yawn. Paul nods, tapping the bat into his hand. Russ's less-than-ferocious bark backs him up. We're usually more than hospitable in our rural community. But having a stranger in the house at night in the middle of a blizzard makes one wary. Especially since the last time an unfriendly man made himself at home in my family room.

Paul is aware that Jake and I have had some difficulties with unwelcome visitors over the last few months. He grabs the remote and clicks on an action movie. "We're good, aren't we, Dave?"

Upstairs, I leave the bedroom door half open so I'll be able to hear if Paul needs help. I text Jake and ask what's going on, then stare at my phone when there is no reply. For not the first time, I consider whether we should sell the farm and move back to the city. Join Jake's parents and Craig and Vicky in Brampton Heights. When we moved out here after our wedding, Jake assured me it was much safer than the city.

"We won't even have to lock the doors," he said.

The events of the past year have proven otherwise.

Chapter Nine

You're frickin' kidding me! Another body in the cornfield?

My grandparents never had to deal with bodies on the property. Not that I know of. Mal and I have had the cops out here so many times this year, they might as well make this their headquarters.

But…this body is alive. Barely. Turned on his side, legs drawn up to his chest, the man's eyes flicker, and his grasp on me loosens. Mouth open, snow covering his hair and beard, flakes dotting his pale face, his breaths come slowly.

"Get up. Come on." I nudge him with my boot. I pull on his arm. Roll him onto his back.

He's a dead weight. About to be deader soon.

Need to get him to the house where it's warm. The snowmobile lies overturned, not much chance of riding out of here. I tug at the tarp covering the farm implement, wondering whether I can hoist him onto it and drag him along, but it's frozen to the ground and rips when I pull at it.

How the hell do I get him out of this drift? My eyes flit toward the barn. Maybe there's another tarp or something in there that can help move him.

I brush the snow off the man, unfold the thermal blanket, and wrap it around him like I'm tucking him into bed for the night. "Stay here. I'll be right back." As if he's going anywhere.

I keep checking my compass, and the old red building becomes more visible as I tramp in the direction of the gangway. Weathered boards and a stone foundation still standing, snow blows across the ramp. I push my way up the gangway, the wind knocking me sideways. Removing my gloves to get a better grip on the rusty hook, I'm prepared for it to resist and for the double sliding doors to be frozen shut, but they slide along the track as my upper body strength pushes them apart, and access to the interior goes smoothly. A respite from the wind, but not the cold.

Illuminating the space is a bit rougher. The side of my hand scrapes a sharp edge as I flip the light switch, grateful we left the electricity hooked up. Snow has made its way in, scattered as though someone stomped it off their boots, not the narrow drift I expected to come through the crack where the doors meet. A swatch of red forms on my hand, blood welling, thanks to the protruding nail on the wall. Mallory's first aid kit would come in handy right about now.

Grandpa used to keep one here in case of an accident. Along the right wall, a wooden cabinet sits, having been given a second purpose when it was ripped out of the kitchen twenty years ago during renos.

One of the cupboard doors isn't completely closed. As I fully open it, hoping for a stray bandage or bit of gauze, my foot kicks something out from under the lip of the bottom cupboard. My eyes take in the huge emerald surrounded by diamonds. Reminds me of those rings John and I used to get in gumball machines when we were kids.

Junk.

I scoot it back under the cupboard with my foot and pull down the large first aid kit. Dirt covers the shelf, except for a swatch where the dust has been disturbed. As I unzip the bag, blood oozes down the finger of my other hand.

Well, this is a pleasant surprise, Grandpa.

A roll of gauze and tape, scissors, various sizes of bandages, antibiotic cream, a bottle of pain relievers, a stash of diamonds and gold. Typical first aid items.

After staunching the flow of blood, I stuff my coat and pant pockets with some of the costume jewelry and scan the interior of the barn for something of use amongst the antiques. A man's life is at stake.

Grandpa was old-fashioned; he liked the simple farm life he had when he was a kid himself. No monster machinery. Rectangular bales of hay, grain, hanging tools, a small tractor and the old wagon, farm implements, the snow blower Grandpa attached to the tractor…

Why the hell didn't I haul that out instead of pushing the snow thrower up and down the lane for the last three winters? What other treasures are in here? Tons of old stuff.

Luck's on my side. The sight of the old toboggans leaning on the left wall, a red plaid cushion on one and blue plaid on another, ignites a nostalgia for when my brother, John, and I raced down the back hill. Our grandparents bought them for Christmas. But now's not the time to go down memory lane.

I grab my toboggan, haul it out the barn door, latching it behind me to keep more snow from blowing in. I'll come back and explore another time, see what else Grandpa left behind. The compass and flashlight guide me back to the nearly dead dude. His eyes are closed now, lashes encrusted with snow.

"Hey, wake up!"

Shaking him doesn't get a response. I uncover my ears, pull off a glove, and lean down to check for signs of breathing, a heartbeat, or a pulse, while holding my own breath. Shallow, slow, faint, but he's alive. For now. My hand on his heart connects with something hard, and I pull the phone out of his shirt pocket. Not recalling my buddy Sam's number, I dial 911 emergency and explain I need paramedic Sam Houston from Idlewood at my house ASAP because there's a guy half-dead from hypothermia in my back field.

With a couple of pulls and shoves, I roll him onto the sled's cushion, securing the thermal blanket around him. I head westward, according to my compass, pulling the dead weight behind me. Every few minutes, I stop to rest and catch my breath.

I need to lift weights or join a gym. I'm getting mushy from all those years behind a desk. Before I know it, I'll have a dad bod. Meanwhile, Craig's got those biceps…

I stop myself from envisioning his arms around Mallory and remind myself she chose me, not him. Whatever might have happened between them doesn't matter any more than my relationship with Vicky before I met Mal.

Every once in a while, I see the light in the distance, and it encourages me to keep trudging along, no matter how much my muscles ache. Mallory and the baby are all that matter. And it might be good to get this guy some help before he croaks completely.

Move your ass, Jake. You can do this.

With each step and tug forward, the light at the end of the tunnel brightens until I can make out the house through the squalls. All the lights on inside and out, and the glow of Christmas bulbs, shed color on my grim situation. We're going to make it.

I turn sideways and tilt my head to yell at the guy, "Hang in there. Almost home."

As I straighten around, one shoe snags on the other, pitching me forward into the powder. Flakes fly onto my face, and I brush them from my mouth and nose, then use my arms to clear snow away and push up to a kneeling position. One foot struggles to get under my body, but the other one doesn't cooperate. The whistle around my neck brushes against the cold ground as I flail about. Even if Mallory did happen to hear it, what could she do? Maybe I should rest a while, gather my strength.

I use what's left of my energy to force air through the whistle in a series of short, sharp, frantic blows. Then I lower my head, close my eyes, and rest. I'll try again. In just a moment.

Chapter Ten

I*s that Jake?*

A dim light through my curtain prompts me to descend to the main level, mindful of my steps. Can't risk a fall.

"Russ! Get back here! What are you doing?" Something sends Russ bolting for the back door.

My attention is focused on the sound of an engine coming down the lane. Through parted curtains, headlights illuminate the slanting snowfall, squalls whipping up the bank along the driveway. Jake's home.

Thank God!

I rush to the door, yanking it open and pushing on the outer pane of glass. But Paul grabs his coat and boots, heading to the back door where Russ barks and scratches to be let out. He's probably just caught a whiff of Nellie or Lucky striding through the mudroom. The stranger remains rooted to the club chair.

The vehicle pulls up close to the house, and my heart drops to the floor. Someone exits a black pickup truck and stands beside it.

"Mallory! Come here!" Paul calls as the back door opens, and a blast whips through the house.

But I need to know if the truck has something to do with Jake. I remain rooted to the top step, straining to see who's out there. An emergency vehicle, sirens flashing, pulls up behind the pickup truck, and the passenger door flings open.

Please, please, don't tell me Jake is hurt. Or dead. I can't handle him being dead again.

The two people remove a stretcher from the back of the emergency vehicle and rush toward the porch. As the space between us closes, it's apparent that the stretcher is empty. "What's going on?" I shout.

"Jake called emergency. Said to meet him here." I recognize Sam Houston as he motions for me to go inside.

His wife, Jilly, also a trained volunteer paramedic, supports the other end of the stretcher as they follow me into the house. "Jake said he found someone in the back field suffering from hypothermia. He was bringing him here. Is that him?"

Jilly points to Dave, whose face is ashen, his mouth gaping open. I shake my head.

Stumped as to what Jake was doing in the back field, I rush to the back of the house and shove the screen door open. Russ' bark pierces through the wind, short whistle bursts accompanying him. Paul shuffles across after his dog, sinking into the drifts as he shouts for Russ to come back. In the distance, a light bounces through the driving snow.

Chapter Eleven

"Russ, old buddy! Am I glad to see you."

The Jack Russell terrier bounds through the snow, yaps up a storm, circles me and the toboggan, and stops to lick my face.

"You're right. I need to get up." I brace myself against one knee, trying again to pull the other foot beneath me while Russ tugs my parka.

My snowshoe slides into place. Russ yanks. And I'm upright. "Thanks, Russ. You're a great help."

I trudge forward, Russ forging the path to the house and Paul slugging toward me, waving both arms in the air. Mallory waits for me with the door and her arms wide open.

"Jake! Are you okay?" My wife is a vision of beauty in her red flannel robe, long blond waves, and round belly.

"I'm fine, Mal. But this guy needs help." I motion to the toboggan behind me and remove my snowshoes before stepping onto the tiles.

Sam and Jilly haul the stretcher into the mudroom, and I assist Sam in transferring the guy from the toboggan.

Sam checks his vitals. "He's hanging in. Good job, Jake."

"Thanks to Mallory for the emergency kit. And for keeping the lights on."

A new face appears in the kitchen, and if I thought the nearly dead dude was pale, this one'll give him a run for his money.

"Is he alive?" The stranger stares at the stretcher as if he's never seen a half-frozen body before.

"Yes. Do you know him?" Sam asks.

"Uh, no, don't think so. Is he going to be okay?"

"We'd better get him to the hospital."

Minutes later, Sam and I load him into the rescue truck, Jilly and Paul following as Mallory stands, arms crossed, on the porch.

"We'll need to hurry," Sam shouts. "But the corner's blocked. I'm not sure the truck can clear a path through."

Ah, right. It must have been Sam's truck that zipped past me on the side road earlier. Good Samaritan Sam. Idlewood's self-appointed snow removal service.

I, too, have my doubts about his truck getting through that mountain of snow. But Paul's snow blower has carved a nice path along the lane. "Hey." I turn to Paul, who stands shivering beside me. "What do you say you give Sam a hand clearing a lane up on the corner, so they don't need to circle around town? Two can do better than one."

"Sure, no problem."

The three vehicles back out of the lane, lights and sirens piercing through the blizzard. And that leaves me alone with Mallory and the pale-faced guy fidgeting with his fingers. Who the hell is *he?*

I pull off my parka and snow pants and hang them on the hooks by the back door, with Russ tagging along. As I remove my hunter's hat, I notice Russ's vest is also a red plaid, matching my headgear and the toboggan pad.

"Nice sweater, Russ. Looks like we're twins. Want to go tobogganing when this storm settles down?" The discovery of the toboggan has brought forth nostalgia for a simpler time. One without bodies in the cornfield.

Russ barks in affirmation, and we join my wife and her visitor in the living room, the wind howling through the front door cracks. The man stands by the window, looking out at the storm. Not much to see. The exterior lights showcase a landscape of white against the gray-black, the sky dumping snow, the wind driving it sideways. Past the first foot or two, it's a blur.

I raise my eyebrows at Mal, who sits on the sofa watching the man, and wave to get her attention. "Who's he?" I mouth.

"This is Dave. His truck got stuck, and he came here looking for help. I called Paul because Jake is sound asleep upstairs, and you know how hard it is to wake him."

I scratch my head, staring at her as she rolls her eyes toward Dave's back. Not sure what this game is, but I'd better play along.

"So, Dave, you're stuck."

Dave turns to me. "Uh, yeah. Truck got stuck in the ditch up past the corner. This young lady let me in to warm up. But I really need to get home to my wife. She'll be worrying about me."

"I get you. Wives are like that. Worrying about nothing."

Mallory shoots daggers at me. Dave slumps into one of the club chairs, and I join him on the other. "Any chance of getting a hot cup of coffee, Mal?"

"No problem, *John*." She rises, leaving us guys alone.

"How bad is the guy you brought in?" Dave turns to me, his voice quivering. "He gonna make it?"

"He's in good hands now. Sam will get him to the hospital; it's about ten minutes down the road. They'll take care of him till he gets there. I'm sure he'll be fine. He was conscious when I found him."

"Hmm. Yeah, he'll be fine." Dave parrots, his ghostly face turned toward me.

"So where were you heading in this storm when your truck went off the road?"

"Home."

I nod. That was a stupid question. He's already covered that. "From where?"

"Visiting a friend."

"Here in town?"

"No."

Mal returns with my coffee and passes it to me. The warmth of the mug penetrates my hand. "Thanks. It's going to take me a while to get that chill out of my bones."

"Strange night to be out tobogganing," says Dave. "By yourself? Out in the middle of nowhere?"

Good point. I shrug, not having an answer.

"John's here visiting his brother. He loves to go out back on the hill. It reminds him of when they were kids. Isn't that right, *John*?"

Nice save, Mal.

"Yes, that's right. Lucky for that poor schmuck. I found him on my way in. Snowmobiler. Hit something out on the barn lane and got thrown off."

"Yeah, damn lucky for him." Dave brings his palms to his face and drags them down, heaving a big sigh.

"You okay?"

"Yeah. Yeah, just thinking it could have been me lying unconscious out there. Nice of your wife to let a stranger in. I appreciate it."

"My wife?"

"I heard everyone calling you Jake. I get it. Your wife, Mallory? She was right not to let on that she was home alone. But I'm harmless. Just a guy trying to get home to his own wife. Shouldn't have been out in this storm in the first place."

"Sorry, Dave, but thanks for understanding," Mallory yawns, rubbing her hands over her round belly.

I sip my hot coffee and grab a cookie off the plate on the table. "You may as well stay here till this quits. We've got a couch in the den. You can get a few hours rest, and I'll help dig you out in the morning."

"Thanks." Dave rubs his hands on his knees. "But I'd really like to get out of here as soon as possible. Any chance you can give me a hand now?"

"I've had a rough night. I'm beat. My own vehicle is stuck down the other way."

Dave glances at Mallory as though she might push him out of a snowbank.

"You're welcome to stay in the den," she says.

"Thing is," Dave clasps his hands together, and his eyes shift between me and Mal. "My wife's expecting any time now. I need to be there. Especially with this going on out there." He waves toward the window.

Russ rises from his position at my feet and runs to the entrance, yipping for all he's worth. I join him and open the door. "What's got you rattled, Russ?"

Paul's snow machine blows up the lane, clearing a wider path next to the one he made earlier. He climbs out and scurries up the porch to meet Russ as he barrels toward his owner.

"Good boy, Russ." He ruffles his dog's hair and steps into the hallway. "Sam got through okay. He's clearing the road ahead of Jilly and the rescue truck. They said they'll let us know when they have news."

"Thanks for all your help, Paul."

"What are neighbors for?" He slaps me on the back.

Mallory rises from the sofa. "I'll get more coffee."

If I had known we were having a party tonight, I would have brought pizza and beer. Life on the farm is more unpredictable than the roulette wheel.

"Do you think you guys can shovel me out of the snowbank once you warm up?" Dave hasn't regained any color. Must be worried his wife's about to pop the kid out. I can relate to that.

Paul says, "I'm willing to give it a go. If Mallory doesn't mind watching Russ a bit longer."

I head to the mudroom to get my snow gear. Looks like the only one snuggling up to my wife tonight will be Russ.

Chapter Twelve

Vicky! I forgot to call her.
It's nearly one in the morning. Three hours after Jake shut down the warehouse.

Vicky answers my call immediately. "Is he home yet?"

"Yes, Jake's home. What about Craig?"

"I was just about to call you. Craig got home a few minutes ago."

"Oh, good. Glad to hear he's safe. Jake went to help dig out Dave. You won't believe what happened to him."

"Who, Dave or Jake?"

"Jake's Honda went into the ditch just down the road, and he walked the rest of the way. It's a good thing because he might have saved some guy's life." I recount what I know of Jake's rescue and how Paul and Jake are out with Dave right now.

"Sounds like both our husbands are heroes. Craig stopped to help a stranded motorist. But when he opened the driver's door, a woman was slumped over the wheel, unconscious. Craig called 911, followed the ambulance to the hospital, and stayed until the doctor checked her over. She had a mild heart attack and is going to be fine. I'm so proud of my husband." Vicky gushes about Craig as though following an ambulance in a car is a greater feat than trudging through a mile of snow and dragging a man several hundred yards on a toboggan.

"Well, I guess we can both rest easy now knowing that our husbands are safe and saved a life. Thanks for staying on the line with me earlier."

"No problem. Glad to hear Jake made it home, even if his car didn't."

After wishing Vicky a good night, I check the locks and head upstairs. Nellie and Lucky's snores greet me as I open the door to our bedroom. I need my rest. But come morning, Jake is going to hear an earful.

Chapter Thirteen

Mallory is sound asleep by the time I crawl under the covers. So much for a warm welcome home. Not that I'd have the energy now. It took a bloody hour to get Dave on his way, between widening out the road at the corner and digging his truck out and pushing it back onto the road. Barely a thank you as he waved and took off.

While downing a beer, I texted Craig one word.

Home.

His response shouldn't have been a surprise.

I know. Vick told me.

In the shower, my muscles killing me, I let the hot water do its job. Arms, legs, back, shoulders, neck. You name it, it hurts. 'Toboggan guy' better live to thank me.

* * *

The sun assaults my face, and I stroke Mallory's shoulder, hoping she's in the mood. She moves further to her edge of the bed. Guess not. Might as well grab a few more Zs. I roll over and close my eyes.

"You didn't call me." Her voice jolts me as I drift off.

"Hmm?"

"You didn't call to tell me your car was stuck."

"What?"

"Last night, you could have told me what was going on. Instead, you let me worry. I'm so tired of thinking you're dead all the time. How hard is it to send a text? How long does it take to make a phone call? Why can't you ever think of me?"

I roll onto my back. "My phone died. I couldn't call you."

"If you could call Sam, why couldn't you call me?"

"I used the guy's phone to call emergency."

"And you couldn't use it to call me?"

Shit. I'm in the doghouse again. And it's too flippin' cold to sleep in the shed tonight.

"Sorry, Mal. I guess I was focused on saving the guy. I should have figured out a way to contact you. Next time I'm saving somebody's life, I'll stop and let you know."

She crosses her arms. "Are you mocking me?"

"No, hon. I'm saying I was freezing my ass off and killing myself while trying to find the way home with a nearly dead guy on my toboggan. But my priority should have been to call you. I'm sorry."

Her silence always scares the crap out of me, like the calm before a storm.

I try to salvage the conversation from continuing on a sour note, pecking her on the cheek. "You know you and our baby are my priority. I just didn't know how much time that guy had left."

The silent treatment continues. And I wait.

"Well…" She caves. "Okay. I'm glad you're not dead. But next time, call me."

"So…you forgive me?"

"Well, you *did* save someone. And it's not your fault your car went into the ditch. Or your phone went dead. Is it?" Her tight lips tell me it *is* my fault.

"That emergency kit was really helpful. Maybe we could add a phone charger for next time."

"So it's *my* fault for not putting a charger in the kit?"

I can't win this one. "Of course not. If it hadn't been for you, I wouldn't have worn my new winter boots and hat or had my snow gear in the car. I would have frozen to death. And the emergency kit came in real handy. It shouldn't be your responsibility to equip the car for winter. I'm a grown man. I should be able to take care of myself. But I'm sure grateful you're looking out for me. I love you. And the little one here." I rub her belly and lean in for a more passionate kiss.

The rest of the morning is spent with the five of us snuggling—me, Mal, two cats stretched out, and a baby. It's a good thing we have a king-size bed. This is exactly where I want to be. I doze off after we make love and wake to the smell of bacon and coffee.

In the kitchen, Mallory is all domestic in her maternity top and jeggings, hair pinned up, pouring batter onto the griddle. "I thought you'd be hungry after trudging through the snow and digging out Dave."

"Thanks, hon. You're an angel." I kiss her again before making myself comfortable at the table. Then I jump back up. "Oh, did you want me to help with anything? You shouldn't be straining yourself with the baby coming soon."

"I'm fine. Some women work right up to delivery time, you know."

The sun dances across her beautiful face. Or maybe her glow brightens the sun. "Have I told you how amazing you are? I'm the luckiest guy in the world."

"I know. Just don't keep pushing your luck." Her lips turn up and she brushes a stray lock off her forehead. It's a good day to be alive. And not stuck in a ditch or freezing in a corn field.

"I better call Mike and get him to tow out my Honda and check it over." Our local garage is on-call 24/7 for emergencies, with the owner taking up the slack when his two guys are off-duty.

Mallory places two plates on the table and pours coffee. My stack of pancakes and bacon is three times the size of hers. She's forgiven me for not calling. I shovel in pancakes slathered in maple syrup (the real stuff).

"Mmm, delicious." Before I can swallow, my phone rings. It's Craig.

"Jake? Hey, man."

I'm still chewing.

"Are you there?"

"Mmmm."

"Everything okay?"

I swallow, wash it down with coffee. "Yep, just great. Mal made me a huge stack of pancakes and bacon."

"I was wondering if you're going ahead with Group tonight."

"Don't see why not. Sun's out, wind's died down. Plow's been down our back road. Like I said, the media always exaggerate. Weekend storm of the decade fizzled out pretty quick. Why are you asking?"

Our support group meets Saturday nights. A few guys from work and their wives, Mom and Steve, with Mal and I hosting. It's a place to communicate and work out our marriage problems. Our marriage counselor suggested it. She's full of shit. Nobody's marriage has improved because of Group. Mal and I are going strong because of our love, not counseling or Group. But everybody's still married, so there's that.

"Well…I…ah…Vicky says we should give it a try."

"You and Vick?" Barely married three months, and trouble in paradise?

"Yeah…I don't want to air our problems in public, but Vicky thinks it would be good for us."

"Problems? I didn't know you guys were having problems."

"Neither did I."

"Welcome to the club. Why don't you stay over? We can order pizza, have some beers, watch a couple of flicks."

"I'll check with Vicky."

I continue stuffing my mouth after talking to Craig. Poor guy needs his wife's permission to stay over at his best friend's house.

"What's going on with Craig and Vicky?" Mallory asks.

"They want to join Group. I figured we could make a night out of it." I set my fork down. "Only if it's okay with you, hon."

"Of course. I'm just surprised. They're so happy. What problems could they possibly have? Vicky was just bragging about how proud she was of Craig for saving that woman's life last night. But that was nothing compared to what you did." She takes my hand in hers. "You pulled that poor man across the field in a snowstorm. You're the real hero. Craig just dialed 911."

"Couldn't exactly leave him there. Anybody else would have done the same thing." I shrug and pick up a piece of bacon, toss a few crumbles to the cats, and pop the rest into my mouth.

"I hope he's going to be okay. I wonder what happened to the other two snowmobilers."

"Other two?"

"There were three out there last night before the storm got worse. Why did he stay after his friends left?"

"Huh. Guess he wasn't done having fun." I stop munching and scratch my stubbly chin. "Kind of weird, though. Dave had a sled in the back of his pickup."

Mal's mouth flies open. "So they could have been together? But Dave said he didn't know the guy you brought home."

"Must be a coincidence, then."

"Mmm. Must be. I was nervous having him in the house on my own, but he seemed like a nice guy, just worried about getting home to his wife."

"You're a hero, too. Giving a stranger shelter in a storm. I'm glad Paul was there for you, though."

Mal nods. "I only opened the door because I thought Dave was you. I don't know if I would have let him in otherwise. But, yes, Paul made me a lot more comfortable with a stranger in the house."

"Yeah, I owe Paul. More than one. And Russ." I polish off the plate and push back my chair. "Guess I'd better get cleaning for our guests tonight. But first, I've got something for you. Wait here."

In the mudroom, I pull out a diamond necklace and earrings to match from one of my parka pockets. I'll gift Mom with the gold chain and bracelet tonight. The rest will go in my safe for Valentine's, for when the baby's born, Mother's Day, and any time I need to sweet-talk my way out of the doghouse.

One fist clasped around my treasure and the other fist empty, I return to the kitchen. "Something good came from finding 'toboggan guy'."

"Other than saving his life?"

"Pick a hand. Any hand." I stretch out my arms.

She chooses correctly and gasps as I transfer the jewels to her hand. "Where did those come from? They're so beautiful."

The string of diamonds sparkles in the light coming through the window, but it doesn't outshine Mallory's smile. "I found them in the barn in the first aid kit. Grandpa hid stuff away for Christmas and birthdays, or things he didn't want Grandma to see. One time, John and I found a stack of car magazines in the cupboard. Grandma didn't like him wasting their money. But he went to auctions and came home with some great stuff."

"They look so real."

"Yeah, amazing what they can do with zirconia. I thought they'd go nicely with your bracelet. And I'm going to give Mom a couple of gold pieces. Grandpa would have wanted her to have them. There's plenty more. I'll give her another piece for Mother's Day."

"Aww, she'll like that." Mallory kisses me, and I'm hopeful for a trip upstairs where she can show her appreciation in full, but her phone rings. "Hi, Jilly. Really? That's great news. Oh, my. That's not good. Yes, I'll let Jake know. Thanks."

"What? Is it about 'toboggan guy'?"

"Do you have to call him that? Anyway, you saved a life, Jake. He's awake and recovering nicely. But they don't know who he is. No ID on him. They think he might have temporary amnesia from the trauma."

"Maybe I'll call him Lazarus."

Chapter Fourteen

Jake scrubs the downstairs sinks and toilets while I tidy up the kitchen and sweep, the classic rock radio station keeping us company. The weather forecast has done a 180-degree turn from last night.

"See, I told you," Jake says, heading toward the cleaning closet. "When you live in southwestern Ontario, the weather can change in a blink. You can't make plans based on the forecast. One day you need a snowsuit, the next a bikini."

When Jake pulls out Mr. Vacuum, Nellie and Lucky scoot off the window seat and disappear into thin air. Taking a break, I put my feet up on the living room sofa and open my romance novel while the vacuum roars. As Jake's Mom repeatedly suggests to Rod during Group, a man who cleans while his wife reads romance has a better chance of scoring points than one who doesn't.

A glance out the front window rewards me with a brighter scene than yesterday's. Paul was out early, our cleared lane evidence of his morning excursion. Linda says he enjoys riding his new snow blower, so it's no trouble to do ours when he has time. We've become closer to our neighbors this past year, since Jake's problems made headlines in the Idlewood Chatter paper, run by town gossip, Jilly Houston. I think they feel sorry for me.

"Whose turn is it for snacks tonight?" Jake asks as he straightens and dusts.

"Gail and Sid."

"There won't be a shortage of wine, then." Jake stops to wink. "Too bad you can't have any. Maybe you should make other arrangements for the food."

"I told Gail to bring cheese and crackers with the wine this time. But I can pick up some cookies at the bake shop. Hopefully, we won't have a repeat of the last time Gail was in charge of treats."

Poor Sid, how embarrassing to have his wife drink herself into a stupor when we're supposed to be supporting them with her alcohol problem. No one had the courage to tell her to stop drinking after Rod's comment.

"Yeah, Rod kind of stuck his foot in his mouth…" Jake says.

"More like Gail stuck her fist in his mouth…"

"When he said nobody likes to see a lady make an ass of herself."

"I don't think he'll make that mistake again."

Jake chuckles. "Knowing Rod, he *will*. Maybe we should order sandwiches, too, from the deli at the FoodMart. Let's keep everybody busy eating and hide the wine away after break to avoid the opportunity for overindulgence. I'll call ahead and go into town once I'm done here."

As the sun shifts to the front of the house, its warmth coming through the bay window, my eyelids grow heavy, and I set my book down, letting myself drift off.

My eyes spring open as the ringing of the doorbell rouses me from a deep slumber.

Who on earth could that be? It's too early for Group.

"Jake! The door!"

The ringing persists, but Jake doesn't answer, so I slide off the sofa and head to the front door. Jilly stands on my front porch, bundled up.

"Mallory, hi. I just happened to be out for a walk and thought I'd drop by."

"Come in. You must be frozen, walking all the way from town."

It's an odd place for a walk. We don't get much traffic down our back road. Nothing here to see. Paul and Linda's place, and ours, farm fields, and the woods. I usher her in, and she makes herself at home, handing me her puffy jacket, hat, scarf, and gloves before asking for a hot drink and heading to the powder room.

She's perched on the sofa when I return with a tray and two mugs of tea. In the driveway, my vehicle is missing.

"I thought I'd get the full scoop directly from you. Who is this guy Jake found? Does this have something to do with Jake's, you know, not-so-above-board friend at the casino? And that stranger from the city you took in last night, who is *he*?" Jilly pulls a notepad and pen from her purse, eager to record my version of last night.

"I don't think the whole town needs to hear about those poor stranded men." Jilly will put a sensational spin on a bad-luck situation, making it into some conspiracy, no doubt with Jake at the center of it.

"Of course they do. Your bravery and Jake's actions need to be celebrated. You saved two lives last night. This will be a Good Samaritan story. Everyone likes to hear good news, especially since so much is bad these days. And after what you and Jake went through this year, with his disappearance and his arrest, this will be the perfect article to start the new year."

Maybe she's right. And if I don't tell her the truth, she'll ask everybody in town what they might know about it, and the entire article will be fabricated. I provide her with the facts, bringing in Paul and Russ as heroes alongside Jake. "And don't forget your husband's role in this. And your own," I add.

Jilly blushes. "Oh, I didn't do anything. But, yes, Sam is amazing. Always thinking of others. And it's nice of Paul to be so neighborly. But I'd like to focus on you and Jake. You know," she lowers her voice, "some people in town still question whether Jake is completely innocent—not that *I* think he'd be capable of anything illegal—with his association with that Dom guy."

"Jake isn't associated with Dom. Dom runs a casino. Jake used to gamble. That's all there was to it, and now Jake doesn't gamble. Jake saved a stranger's life. That should be enough of a story." I rise, indicating it might be a good idea for Jilly to leave.

But she sips her tea and settles deeper into the sofa. "Come on, Mallory, of course I'll write a positive story about Jake. No need to rehash all that nasty business. But if I don't print anything, you know people will hear about what happened anyway and gossip behind your back."

I nod, sitting down beside her. Surely, Jilly won't be malicious and print lies if I tell her what happened. She prides herself on being a journalist, even if it's a self-appointed job title. Jake saved a life; she can't put a negative spin on that. "You're right. Some of the newcomers in town don't know Jake well enough. Thanks for offering to set them straight and show what he's really like."

"Yes, of course. Jake deserves a full front-page story, only this time it will be a heart-warming one."

After Jilly leaves, her full exclusive recorded on paper along with my interview on her phone, Jake pulls up in the driveway, unloads the groceries, and listens to me as I tell him about my visit with Jilly and how he's going to be the big story in the next issue of Idlewood Chatter.

Jake, modest about his actions, shrugs. "I've been the big story more than a few times."

"But this time you're a hero."

"It was no big deal."

The big deal is this time no one can question Jake's integrity. Nothing bad can come from saving lives.

Chapter Fifteen

"That was a helluva storm last night. Good call letting everyone out early." Rod greets me with a slap on the back and grabs a couple of hangers from the closet.

His wife, Janice, hands me a pan of freshly-baked banana loaf. "To make up for the last time when it was Gail's turn for snacks, and you know—"

"Thanks," I interrupt her before she lambasts Rod for speaking his mind about Gail's drunken behavior. The poor guy was just voicing what everyone else was thinking. Nearly got a broken jaw out of it. "Come on in. Rod, why don't you help me set up the chairs in the den?"

Halfway down the hall, the doorbell rings. I welcome Jason, a plastic-wrapped tray in his hands, and Beth, her belly as round as Mallory's.

"Canapés," Jason says, head tilting down to the tray.

Canapés? He's sure gotten fancy since he won that fifty million in the lottery this fall. He swore to Beth it was his last time gambling, but his new association with Dom as his silent partner in the under-construction Kingston Island Casino isn't going over well with his wife.

"I thought we should have something besides wine this time," Beth says, handing me her coat. "Especially for Mallory and me."

"We're just heading into the den to set up. I'll take those to the kitchen." I lead the way, dropping off the canapés and banana bread. Jason and I join Rod in the den as he stands at the window, gazing across the cornfield.

"Things are kind of quiet here in the winter, I guess. Nothing growing in the field," Rod notes.

"No corn, but things aren't exactly quiet."

"Oh? Why? What's been going on?" Rod narrows his eyes. "Something shady?"

"Snowmobiles, for one thing. All over the field."

"Snowmobiles? Any idea what they were doing out there? Just goofing around, maybe?"

I recount last night's adventure. Before I get to the nearly-dead dude, the doorbell rings again. "Mal, can you get that?"

I'm at the point in my story where someone grabs onto my ankle when Sid joins us. "Hey Sid. I was just telling Rod and Jason about the body I found in the cornfield last night."

Their mouths drop open, eyes wide. These guys can't take a joke.

"A body? Holy shit! Was there another gun involved?" Rod, first to recover, unfolds a chair and plops himself into it. "Like last time? Who's dead this time?"

"So, you're out on bail?" Sid asks.

Jason rubs his chin and nods as though it's to be expected.

Before I can explain, my supposedly reformed ex-drunk, ex-abuser, ex-jailbird biological father (Mom insists I call him Dad), Steve, barges in without knocking, as though it's *his* house. A pat on the back like everything's been forgiven, and he asks how I'm doing.

"Just dandy, *Dad.*" I click open a chair and smack it onto the floor with more force than necessary. "How about you and my mother? She had the sense to leave you yet? Again?"

He chuckles as though I'm joking. "Going strong, Son. We're just here to lend support to the rest of the group. Even though we've got lots of unpacking to do at the new house. Boxes everywhere, piled ceiling high. It'll take us a year to get through it all. Your mom still has some of your old stuff. Maybe it's time you hauled some of it out of there into your own house. You've got plenty of space here. No need to use our house for free storage."

Yep, just erase every last bit of me from Mom's life.

I clamp my mouth shut as the women enter the room. We men busy ourselves setting up the rest of the chairs.

"Did Jake tell you what he did last night?" Mallory asks, her face glowing with pride. "It's going to be the front-page feature in this week's local paper."

Sid shuffles his feet, Jason's eyes fall to the floor, and Rod whistles a 'not-so-innocent' tune as though I'm guilty of something and they're washing their hands of it.

"I was just in the middle of the story," I say. "So, there's this body in the cornfield…"

Steve narrows his eyes at me. Mom gasps, "Not again, Jake!"

"It's not the way it sounds. I…"

Vicky's voice resounds from the hallway. "Hellooo. Sorry we're late. Did we miss anything?"

Vicky and Craig join the gang in the den, and we all find a spot in the circle of chairs.

"I think Jake was just about to hit us with the punchline. Right, Son?" Steve says.

All eyes on me, I give them the short version of how I saved someone's life. Mallory adds how proud she is and how brave I am. Everyone breathes a sigh of relief upon hearing the body is alive. The meeting is off to a good start.

"As you can see, things are going really well for us." I smile at Mallory, then turn to Craig. "And we've got the honeymooners joining us for the first time. Why don't you share next, Vick? You've got husband bragging rights, too. I'm not the only one who saved a life."

Vicky tells everyone about Craig's heroic act, then adds, "But…"

Craig squirms in his chair as everyone's eyes shift to him. I stretch out my legs, cross my ankles and arms, and tilt my head toward him.

This should be good. For once, I'm not the one in the hot seat.

"Vicky's upset because I didn't call her. I *did* call to tell her what was happening, but I didn't call back, and she's mad I didn't answer my phone. But I was kind of busy, honey."

"Busy? Too busy for your wife? All you had to do was text a couple of words so I wouldn't worry so much."

"I said I'm sorry. It won't happen again."

"I just wish you'd be a little more considerate, especially now that—"

"I will, honey. I promise."

Our heads snap from Vicky to Craig and back like we're watching a ping-pong game. Mallory chimes in. "You should have called Vicky. I know exactly how she feels. How hard is it for a man to send off a text? It's not an Olympic sport. Don't you agree, Jake?"

Mom agrees. "Really, Craig. You should be ashamed of yourself, making Vicky worry like that. Now that you're married, you need to be more responsible." Her eyes flit to me. "Isn't that right, Jake?"

How did this end up coming back on me?

"To be fair, Craig *did* save a woman's life." I side with my best buddy. "And it's not like he didn't tell Vicky he was going to be late. A man's gotta do what he's gotta do."

Six pairs of female eyes glare at me, daring me to keep talking. I turn the meeting over to Rod. "What do you think? Do husbands need to check in with wives constantly? Do you text Janice every five minutes?"

"I never text Janice. Why would I do that? If I've got something important to say, I phone."

Janice redirects her glare to her husband. "You *never* call me."

"That's because I have nothing important to say to you."

Janice and Rod have been married the longest of any of us, but they may not be the best role models. Maybe Jason can be of some help. "What about you, Jase? How have things been going with the two of you? Texting all the time, with the baby coming, I bet. And it must be great having all that money."

Beth speaks for him. "Money's not everything. Having someone you can trust by your side is what matters. And I don't think this deal with Dom is going to build our trust. How could you sign that business contract without me co-signing? I'm your *wife*. I thought *we* were a partnership, not you and Dom."

At least Beth has changed the topic, but I'm not sure I want to go there. I glance at Sid, but he shakes his head as if to say, 'Don't bother involving me in this.' Maybe it's time to see if Gail has brought that box of wine. We could all stand a drink, except for Mal and Beth.

"And I don't see why you can't give Jethro a bit more to tide him over till he finds a new position," Beth continues. "He just needs a break."

Beth's cousin, Jethro, isn't likely to find a new job anytime soon. He didn't leave Dom's employ on the best of terms.

"A break? He's a bum. And a criminal." There's no love lost between Jason and his cousin-in-law. "I gave him plenty, considering he deserves nothing. Why do you keep defending him? I don't trust him as far as I can throw him."

That wouldn't be too far, with Muscle Man Jethro outweighing Jason by more than a few pounds.

Beth sighs. "I know you're right, but he *is* my cousin."

Jason has the good sense to get off his ass and take Beth into his arms, telling her she and the baby are more important than the money and he'll give it all away to charity if it makes her happy. I know a bluff when I hear one, but she buys it, hook, line, and sinker. I open my mouth to tell them to get a room, but Mallory speaks first.

"Aww, that's so sweet, you two. Not letting a silly thing like money get between you."

I raise my eyebrows, tilting my head toward my wife, eyes bulging. A silly thing like money? After all the shit she's given me for my gambling debts? "That's right, hon. Money's not important *at all*. The only thing that matters is love."

Mallory smiles at me. "Sounds like a good place to stop for a break. Jake, honey, can you help me in the kitchen while everyone else gets comfortable in the living and dining rooms?"

Everyone shuffles down the hall, and I help Mallory arrange the food on the counter. I cube the cheddar onto a wooden cheese tray while Mal slices the banana loaf. There's enough food here to keep everyone busy stuffing their mouths for a good half hour. Might cut down on the squabbling time available. "Gail actually brought cheese and crackers?"

"Sid did, I think. Was that supposed to be some sort of sarcastic comment about us or something?" Mal stops placing food on the silver tray and crosses her arms.

I haven't got a clue what she's talking about. I set down the knife, furrow my forehead, and turn my palms out flat, so she'll elaborate. "Which sarcastic comment are you talking about?"

"The money comment. Was that about us?"

"What? No, of course it wasn't. But our marriage *is* stronger than ever. Because we face everything together. You're what matters. You and our family." I pat her belly and take her in my arms, following Jason's lead.

She purses her lips. "As long as you don't forget that."

She's not likely to let me forget. But I love her all the more for it. Mallory has given me more chances than I deserve. "You know I won't. I'm the luckiest man in the world."

Mallory responds to my kiss, and I decide to call off the second half of the meeting and make it an early night after snack time. "Let's get these people fed and out of here so we can have some alone time."

"Vicky and Craig are staying, remember? You invited them."

Shit. What was I thinking?

Mom has the wine glasses, teacups, and plates set out on the dining room table, and I take a moment to tell her I have something special for her, and I'll give it to her later. Mal guides Beth upstairs to show her the nursery. People scurry to the kitchen to start diving into the food as soon as I announce it's ready. Tea and coffee are set out on the counter. Gail cocks her head and asks what happened to the wine as though Mallory and I may have already consumed three bottles. I indicate they're on the kitchen table, untouched so far, until Gail makes a beeline toward them.

As I predicted, peace and quiet dominate the house while food and drinks smooth over any marital discord. It's hard to be mad with a full stomach and a drink in your hand. People will always show up at a meeting when there's food involved. Speaking of which, is that Russ pulling Paul up our driveway? The exterior lights confirm it is.

"Sorry to interrupt your evening," Paul says as I open the door. "But we were out for a walk, and Russ found something. He insisted on bringing it to you."

Please don't let it be a gun.

Paul pulls a pen out of his coat pocket and shrugs. "Did you drop this sometime?"

I turn it over between my fingers. Russ barks, and I ruffle the hair on his head. "It doesn't look familiar. But thanks anyway, Russ."

"Hi, Paul, grab a plate and glass and join us," Mallory says, hand-feeding Russ turkey from her sandwich.

The rest of the gang greet Paul and Russ, no doubt thankful it was a pen they found and not something that could incriminate me in a crime.

"I don't want to intrude." Paul gazes over at the plates on laps, and his eyes light up when he notices there's wine. "But I could stay for a minute or two."

He hangs his coat in the closet and heads to the kitchen, coming back with a glass of wine and a plateful of food. "So did you hear anything more about the guy you saved last night?"

"He's going to be fine," I say. "Just might take him a while to remember who he is."

"Oh? Amnesia?"

"Temporary, they think. Trauma-induced."

"What about Dave? He make it home okay?"

"Don't know. He didn't leave his number. Didn't call."

The munching and slurping has settled down as everyone focuses on Paul and what secrets he might divulge about his colorful neighbors. But Paul gives them a glowing report of my actions last night.

There's nothing to see here this time, folks. Just a case of me being a good Samaritan.

Once Paul downs his glass and polishes off his plate, he and Russ wish us a good night and head out into the night. Jason, still glued to his wife, says they're going to head out early so Beth can get her rest. I yawn several times to encourage others to follow them and forget about finishing our meeting.

Rod, who has been quieter than usual, sneaks a glance at Gail, downing her third glass in the last twenty minutes, rubs his chin, and seems to decide it's best to leave before she wallops him for some inappropriate comment.

Tipping the empty bottle, Gail tells Sid to grab her coat since the party's over. The house empties, vehicles backing out of the driveway.

But Mom and Vick don't move. When Steve and Craig return from moving their cars, Steve eyes me suspiciously. "What's really going on here, Son? Are you in some kind of trouble? Dom again? You can tell us now that everyone's gone."

Just like my old man, assuming the worst of me. I mention a body, and he takes it literally. I shake my head. "You're unbelievable."

My best bud, Craig, supports me one hundred percent. Not. "You've got to admit it's strange this guy shows up in *your* field. Considering what happened this fall."

Mom and Vicky nod, with Mom adding, "Why is this the first I'm hearing about this? Is there something you're not telling us?"

"He was one of the snowmobilers I saw last night," Mallory explains. "We get them all the time, using our fields like a recreational trail. He probably couldn't see in the storm. Jake says he hit a farm implement in the lane. If Jake hadn't come across him, he'd be dead now."

That shuts everyone up. If Mallory says I'm a hero, then it must be the truth. Mom is gracious enough to know it's time to leave, but Steve scratches his head as if there must be something more to it.

"Well, if you need help with anything, let me know," Steve says, heading to the entrance. "I'm here for you."

I snort and Mallory whips me a look to let me know I should keep the retort in my head to myself. "Yeah, *Dad.* Goodnight, Mom."

Maybe Craig will sense it's not the best night for a sleepover and follow the rest of the crowd. No such luck. He undoes his belt buckle, grabs his overnight bag, and escorts Vicky upstairs, his arm around her waist. "Are you still ordering pizza? Those finger sandwiches and canapés didn't quite hit the spot. We'll be down in a half hour or so for the movie."

I'm finally alone with my wife. "I'll clean up, hon. You get into your jammies, put your feet up, and search for a good rom-com."

A comfortable evening with friends might be just what we need after the excitement of last night. I order a couple of extra-large pizzas and settle on the family room sectional sofa, waiting for Mallory.

"That was another good Group session," I say when she returns.

Mallory tosses her head back and laughs. "One of the better ones. No one got insulted, hit, threatened with a divorce, or drunk, and no weapons were to be seen anywhere."

"Jason and Beth seem to be happy."

"Yes, we had a nice talk in the nursery, and Beth is looking forward to giving the baby all the things she never thought she'd be able to afford, and they're talking about another baby after this one, maybe a third. And she's coming to terms with Jason's investment in the new casino."

"She doesn't seem keen on him working with Dom. How is she dealing with that?"

"She's not *real* keen. They're trying to compromise. I think Beth is so relieved he survived after that altercation at Dom's. The partnership pales in comparison to thinking your husband may be dead."

Altercation is one way to put what happened last fall. Murder might be more concise. "Are you equally relieved *I* survived the altercation?"

Mallory's lips touch mine, and I think I'm about to get lucky, but the doorbell rings. A peek through the front curtains tells me the pizza delivery guy is here. Before heading to the kitchen, I holler and let the aroma waft upstairs. "Pizza's here!" In case the doorbell didn't pry the lovebirds apart, the aroma of tomato sauce and cheese might.

I set the boxes on the stovetop and grab a six-pack from the refrigerator along with some sodas for the girls. The stairs creak, and Craig and Vicky appear in the hallway, ready for a pajama party.

"What about this one?" Mallory indicates the movie she's tentatively chosen. "Have you seen it before?"

It's like we're still in high school, having a party in our parents' basement. I'm overdressed. "I'll be back in a sec."

When I return, dressed in the red flannel pajamas Mom bought for Christmas, a match to the nightgown she bought Mal, everyone's staring out the back window. Mallory, Craig, Vicky, Nellie, and Lucky. It's pitch black, and I wonder what the hell they're seeing.

"What's up, guys?" I join them on the window seat.

"I think somebody is watching the house," Vicky says.

"Snowmobilers," Mallory explains. "Only one so far. It kept circling around the field before heading toward us. Then it disappeared around the side of the house."

"Damn idiots. I'm going to have to put an electric fence around the property."

"Look! There's a light over there. Oh. No, I don't see it anymore."

"Should you call the police and report them for trespassing? You don't want to be liable if someone else gets hurt on your property," Vicky advises. "You might get sued."

I bring my hand up to my forehead. "They're on *my* property illegally, and *I'm* going to get sued?"

Vicky shrugs. "They might try."

"By the time the police drive up the lane, the snowmobilers will be long gone. I called them once, and they weren't happy I wasted their time; the cops won't bother coming. Besides, I don't want to see cops on my property ever again." Had enough of that shit this year.

I close the curtains, and we turn our attention to pizza, beer, soda, and a chick flick. Whoever was out there, they've left the premises. Nothing but a blanket of snow, the town lights in the distance. How many acres of land does a man need to own to have his privacy?

Chapter Sixteen

"I'm pregnant," Vicky blurts as we sip tea, watching the guys widen the front walkway by another foot, following a late night's dumping of snow. After an early breakfast, they dug out a path at the back and side doors, then headed to the front.

"Oh, wow." She didn't waste any time.

"I wasn't going to say anything yet, but I need someone to talk to, and I knew you would understand."

"Well, congratulations. That's exciting. Isn't it?"

"Thanks, yes. Just a couple of months along. I didn't want to wait. Craig thought we should have some time to ourselves before starting a family, but I'm ready now. I just hope he can handle the responsibility."

"Craig? He's the most responsible guy I know."

Vicky sighs. "I don't know if maybe I'm pushing him into all this—marriage, house, a baby. We've only been together for a few months."

"You've been together on and off for three and a half years. And all that time, you were friends, no matter what else happened. Craig loves you, always has, anyone can see that. And he's happier than he's been since I've known him." I won't mention that he did stray before they committed to each other, because we all make errors of judgment, and there's no reason to let those mistakes interfere with everyone's happiness.

Vicky's face lights up, confirming that little white lies are sometimes the best choice. I don't for one minute doubt that Craig is not only in love, but deliriously happy with Vicky. The past is over and done. "Do you really think so?"

"Absolutely." Then something occurs to me. "Why? Has he done something that makes you think he's not happy about the baby?"

"He says he's really happy. Maybe it's hormones. I've been worrying more than I normally do." Her eyes well with wetness.

"Vicky?" I place a hand on her arm to let her know she can tell me whatever is bothering her.

"I'm so happy…but what if he decides I'm not exciting enough for him, especially once I'm a stay-at-home mom for the next while."

The idea that someone as smart and stunning as Vicky, her long auburn hair and to-die-for figure, could be not exciting enough for Craig is absurd. It's more a case of Craig having the jitters about commitment because he's as immature as my own husband. Maybe all men are just big babies.

"You have nothing to worry about," I say. "The only thing that matters is that you love each other." How many times have I told myself exactly this?

"You're right." She brightens again. "I guess if Jake can finally step up and be a man, so can Craig."

I ignore the fact that my best friend, Jake's ex-girlfriend, has made a jab at my husband. "They're both acting more responsibly. Less time in the bar after work, doing jobs around the house, working hard. Saving lives. They're mature adults. Just look at them, shoveling the snow like grown-ups."

"Are they…" Vicky stands and approaches the window for a closer look. "Having a snowball fight?"

I gaze outside alongside her and tap on the pane. "Not anymore. Now they're making snow angels."

Our mature, responsible little boys burst in through the back door minutes later, their raucous laughter traveling down the hall. The refrigerator door opens, and although I don't see him, I know Jake is grabbing a couple of beers. Vicky and I join them in the kitchen, the snow on their faces still showing evidence of the 'hard work' they've been doing.

"Taking a break," Jake says. "Are my old snow pants still around somewhere? For Craig? I'll ask Paul to blow out a path to the barn after lunch. Then we're going tobogganing."

"What about Vicky and me?"

"Are you sure that's wise in your condition?" He crinkles his forehead.

"No, I meant I thought we could do something together, the four of us."

"Sure, but first I've got a couple of things I need to do."

"Like tobogganing?"

"Yeah. But after we go to the hospital." When I raise my eyebrows, he adds, "To check on Lazarus. See with my own eyes that he's okay."

"That's such a responsible thing to do, Jake." I flash Vicky a look to bring home my point. They're a lot more mature than they seem.

"Yeah. Maybe while we're gone, you could dig out those snow pants." He tosses back the beer can to get the last swallow. "And you should check out the snow family we built out back."

Chapter Seventeen

I *know something Mal doesn't. Nana nana na nah!*

The silly rhyme sing-songs through my head. I'm on a high. Craig just dropped the mother of all secrets while we shoveled out the back door. Now, we're twins. Blood brothers. Tied by a bond for life. I'm not in this on my own.

"I'm not supposed to tell anyone yet," Craig confessed as he dug his shovel into the drift intruding on the back exit. "But Vicky's pregnant. The baby's coming in July."

My shovel stopped halfway in the air. "You work fast. You just got married."

"Do you think it's too soon?"

"I don't think you can reschedule it. Babies come when they're ready. Usually nine months or so. Sometimes sooner, not too much later."

"No, I mean, do you think we should have waited? Like you and Mallory?"

"What do *you* think?"

"I think it's amazing. I'm going to be somebody's dad. I just hope I don't screw it up."

"You won't. Congratulations."

"Thanks."

I throw the shovel down, give him a big man hug, and slap him on the back. "Welcome to the club. You'll be decorating the nursery soon, maybe doing some renos. Let me know if you need a hand. I'm sure Vicky would appreciate my expertise. Maybe rip a wall out here and there, rough-in the plumbing for a new bathroom."

"Uh, thanks, but Vicky's hiring a decorator."

I punch his shoulder, maybe a bit harder than I intended, thoughts of my buddy's skill at impregnating his woman reminding me of my suspicions about him and Mallory, even though she swears there's no way it happened. "I'm just kidding. My home remodeling skills need more practice on my own property before I destroy someone else's place. I'm sure Vicky doesn't want me anywhere near your home makeover after my bungling the plumbing and electricity in our house."

Craig laughs, steps back, forms a snowball, and whips it at me. "That and the smell in your house during your previous renos might put her off."

"Yeah, that was unfortunate. But it was a one-time thing." A body decomposing in the house overcomes the freshness of a coat of paint.

"I would hope so."

Maybe not the best time to bring up the job offer from Dom, what with the reminder of the body and the schmozzle that resulted from that, but Craig's going to need extra income if he's having a kid. As Dom's second-in-command at the River Grand Casino, I'd have the ability to hire and fire staff. Craig, as floor manager, would be my first personnel change. Dom's the one who suggested it. "Have you given any more thought to ditching your glamorous job at the warehouse for something more lucrative? Now that you're starting a family, the extra cash could come in handy. Especially if Vicky's hiring out all the house renos."

Craig shakes his head. "I don't know, man. I'm probably best to stick with moving boxes of car parts around. It's good, steady employment, and there's nothing illegal about it. When your wife's a lawyer, you've got to be careful about these kinds of things."

"Nothing illegal about Dom's job offer. The casino operation is all above board." I pack snow into a ball and throw it at him; he catches it. "The ball's in your court. Vicky, the baby, and you earning extra dough to support them. Give it more thought."

Craig aims the ball back at me, then reconsiders, bending down to roll it around the snow to make it bigger. "When was the last time you made a snowman? That seems like a skill we should teach our kids, not how to run a casino."

Our shoveling forgotten, we engage in a ball-building contest to see who can roll a bigger ball of snow. When we're done, three snow people lacking facial features stand guard several feet from the back door. Daddy snowman, Mama snowwoman, and Baby snowperson. Just a couple of macho guys playing in the back yard.

"You know what else our kids will love? Next winter, we'll be pulling them on a baby sled. We can take them on the back hill when they're older. I had a riot out there with my brother when I was a kid. What do you say we pull out the toboggans after lunch and take a few runs down the hill?"

"Speaking of toboggans, tell me more about that guy you saved." Craig picks up his shovel and continues creating a path from the back toward the side of the house, indicating we've got work to do.

"I don't know what else there is to tell. I stumbled over him and his overturned sled after my car slid into the ditch, took out my toboggan from the barn, called 911, and dragged him home. Which reminds me, I should give him his phone back. Do you want to drive me to the hospital? We could pick up my Honda at the garage on our way home and stop to get takeout for a late lunch. Kill three birds with one stone." I chuckle at my joke, following alongside Craig to widen the path.

"We'd better hurry if we're going to do all that in the next couple of hours."

Once the front walkway is cleared, we take a few more minutes to goof around before heading inside. I let Mal know we're picking up my Honda and lunch after visiting Lazarus in the hospital.

In Craig's car, he turns up the volume on the classic rock station, and we head down the country road toward our closest health center, in the town of Cal Waters. Fifteen minutes later, we approach the nurse's desk in the small hospital, and I explain who I am and my connection to the hypothermia victim with amnesia.

"How nice of you to check up on him. Did you happen to make an anonymous call last night and earlier this morning asking about the status of our John Doe? Sorry that we were only able to tell you he was in stable condition," says the young guy manning the counter. "Hospital policy, privacy, and all that."

"Hmm," I say, wondering who made the calls.

"Maybe seeing the guy who saved his life will trigger his memory. He's expected to recover. It's just a matter of time. He's in Room 109, down the hall."

We head to the right, in the direction he points, but he beckons us back to the counter, finger crooked. "Hold on a minute. I'll need to see some ID and have you sign in."

They got some sort of security check in the hospital? Do they expect visitors might off the patients when the staff isn't looking?

"Is that some new standard procedure?" I ask.

"For this guy, it is. After this morning's incident. I was told he had an unfriendly visitor. My coworker asked him to leave, and he wouldn't. Had to threaten to call security. He was badgering our patient. She ended up filling out a report and notifying the police."

"Badgering?"

"Kept asking him where he'd stashed the rest of it. And his voice rose every time he asked, as though that would get rid of the amnesia. He could be heard down the hall. Used some colorful language when the patient said he didn't remember. So he might still be a bit upset. Try to keep him calm. Amnesia patients can get anxious. They can't be forced to remember."

"We won't stay long. Just want to see how he's doing."

In Room 109, a guy around my age sits propped up on the bed, flipping through a magazine. Seeing us enter, his eyes narrow. "Who are you? What do you want?"

I guess it's a normal reaction considering his last visitor wasn't exactly friendly. "My name is Jake Shelton. I'm the one who found you, out in my field. This is my friend, Craig Dunsmere."

His demeanor changes, and he holds out his hand to shake mine. "I'm really glad to meet you. The paramedics told me about you. Said you saved my life. Thanks, Jake. I owe you."

"I'm glad to see you're doing well, except for the memory thing."

His eyes shift to the door. "Yeah, that sucks. But it's supposed to be temporary."

"I bet you'd like to know who you are. Maybe this will help." I hand over his phone.

Recognition flashes in his eyes. "Thanks."

"We won't keep you. Hope that reminds you of who you are." I point to the cell.

He nods. "I won't forget this. What you've done for me. Like I said, I owe you one. I'll reach out when I remember who the hell I am."

Craig interjects. "What about the visitor you had this morning? Who was he? Was he any help in spurring your memory? We heard he was asking you where something was."

The guy shakes his head. "Never saw him before. He didn't leave a name. No idea what he was talking about."

"What did he look like?" I ask.

"Youngish. Muscular. Couldn't make out his face. It was covered with a scarf and his parka hood."

"Would you know him if you saw him again?"

"Not likely. But I doubt he'll be back. One of the nurses escorted him out. Maybe he's one of the psychiatric outpatients. Anyway, thanks for saving me. And for the phone." He settles back into the bed, closing his eyes.

"No problem."

Craig and I stop at the Idlewood garage to pick up my Honda. No damage from what I can see as I examine it from every angle. I was assured it's in running order. The snow has been brushed off, and the keys are under the visor. Car theft isn't a concern with our local mechanics.

At the diner, we order a couple of burgers with fries and onion rings, along with a couple of pasta dishes and side salads for the girls. Leftover bakeshop cookies and banana loaf should take care of dessert.

When we get home, the girls are in the nursery discussing the color scheme. Mal chose aqua and cream because it reminds her of our honeymoon in Jamaica, and it will work if we have a girl next. I insisted on adding some navy nautical accents to make it more masculine for Jakey.

I holler up the stairs. "We're home. Lunch is here. Come get it while it's hot."

In the kitchen, I lay the bags of takeout on the counter and reach up to get plates out of the cupboard. Craig settles himself at the table as though he expects me to hand-serve him. I grab my own food and leave him sitting with an empty plate. He clues in and serves himself.

"Sorry, man. I'm not your wife," I chuckle.

My joke doesn't go over well. Mal and Vick join us at the table. Mal passes me both their plates. "We're starving. What's for lunch?"

"Chicken penne, mushroom fettuccine, and salad."

"Do you want some of each?" Mal gets a positive response from Vicky, then turns back to me. "Fill them up, half of each. And a couple of ginger ales."

"Beer for me," adds Craig.

The cats show up from somewhere, tripping me as I spoon the pasta onto plates and deliver them. I grab the chicken pâté from the refrigerator and scoop it into their bowls, adding a few pieces of sliced chicken from the pasta.

Only after ensuring everyone has been properly served do I return to my own meal. I'm sure that's a smirk on Craig's face, but I ignore it. He'll have more than his share of kowtowing to Vicky and the baby.

"The Honda's good," I say between mouthfuls of ground beef sirloin. "Not a scratch on it."

"That's good. What about the poor guy in the hospital?" Mallory is always thinking of others. "Is he going to be okay? What about his memory?"

"He seems good. The amnesia is supposed to be temporary, and now that he has his phone, it might jolt a few memories. Which reminds me, I need to give Paul a call. See if he'll come over and clear a path out to the barn and the snow hill."

Paul says he and Russ will be right over. The early afternoon sun is above the house, shade filling in behind it. Before you know it, it'll be dark. Winter in southern Ontario has only so many hours of daylight. If I didn't need to work, I'd just hibernate for four months.

"We'd better not stay late tonight," Vicky says. "I've got work in the morning, and I'm tired."

"We'll just be out for a couple of hours. Then you guys can head home." That's fine with me. The sooner they leave, the more alone time I'll have with Mallory.

I watch through the back window as Paul plows across the field, heading to the red barn in the distance. Craig and I finish our meals, then bundle up in the mudroom. Toboggan hill, here we come. "Be back soon," I promise as we head out.

"Make sure you text if you're going to be late," Mallory shouts out the door.

I pull my old toboggan along behind me, much lighter without the hypothermic dude. Craig and I follow the trail Paul has carved out for us, our boots crunching in the snow. More of a three-minute walk without the extra weight, no wind, and a cloudless view. How I ever thought I was lost out here beats me. But it does look a lot different now than it did Friday night.

Paul's machine sits by the barn. Paul exits as we approach, pulling out a toboggan. Russ circles him, yipping. "Hope you don't mind. I thought I'd join you. I haven't done this in years. I just watch the grandkids when they're out tobogganing."

"No problem, Paul. I need to drag out John's old toboggan from the barn for Craig."

The gangway to the barn doors is still slick, the wind having blown across it to form an ice rink. We ease ourselves up the ramp, the tread on our boots gripping the layer of snow. The latch on the door isn't properly hooked. I must have left it that way in my hurry to get help for the guy dying in the snow. Inside, snow lies scattered on the wooden floor, more of it than before, blown in as a result of an unlatched door. John's toboggan stands upright along the wall where I left it Friday night. But something's different.

I can't put my finger on it, but things seem...messier. Maybe it's my imagination. I didn't get a thorough look when I was in here Friday night, but even the hay bales appear skewed now. I've been doing my darndest to keep my OCD under control, letting things get a bit untidy at home. Mal says it's going to get a lot messier with the baby, so I'd better get used to it. I'm still aware when things are out of place. And something is definitely out of place here. I tell Craig to grab the toboggan.

"I want to take a quick look around, see if Grandpa left any more treasures behind."

Paul asks what kind of treasures.

"I found some jewelry last time I was in here. Diamonds, gold."

"Real diamonds? And gold? In a barn? That's quite the place to keep valuables." Paul's eyes widen. "Good thing there are never any break-ins out in the country." He reconsiders. "Well, I guess *you've* had some trouble recently. You're lucky no one thought to look in this old barn. Guess they wouldn't think there's anything valuable here."

"They aren't valuable. Zirconias. Gold-plated jewelry. Grandpa loved going to estate auctions and buying what he thought were treasures. Grandma had a jewelry box full of stuff, none of it genuine. He couldn't afford the real stuff."

Another glance around confirms things aren't where they belong. The first-aid kit sits on top of the cupboard, not in it. I'm sure I put it away. When I bend down to replace it on the upper shelf, I spy another box sticking out on the bottom shelf. Was that there before? More jewelry?

A cardboard box, the flaps folded over, slides out when I tug on it. Gloves removed, my fingers sift through the contents as my mind assimilates what I've found. Craig, noticing my shock, approaches. "Hey, man, you okay?" He glances over my shoulder. "Hmm. Why would your grandpa keep that in the barn?"

I shrug. "I have no idea. I'll have to ask Mom. Maybe she knows."

It's a conversation I want to have in person so I can see her reaction. Because it appears Grandpa had a secret life.

Chapter Eighteen

"Isn't it great? They'll only be five months apart. Our kids will grow up together like twins or siblings or cousins," Vicky says.

Her comment hits almost too close to the truth. That one mistake with Craig could have had life-long consequences, but by some miracle of fate, I was already pregnant with Jake's baby. I assured Craig that that was the case, and we agreed that Jake and Vicky need never know we messed up.

We're searching online for nursery decor ideas when Gloria calls. "Hi, Mallory, I just remembered Jake said he had something for me, and last night we left in such a hurry, he must have forgotten. I called Jake, but he's not picking up. Would you happen to know what it was?"

"I do, but I should leave it to Jake to surprise you."

"Can you give me a clue? Is it a pleasant surprise or more of a shock? We've had plenty of those."

"Oh no, it's nothing bad. Jake found something in the barn when he was getting his toboggan out Friday night, and he wants you to have it." When Gloria doesn't respond, I ask if she's still there.

"Yes…yes, I'm just curious. How…um…how did Jake seem when he told you about it?"

"He was excited, thinking he'd found a real treasure. But I don't want to give it away, so I won't say anything more. He'll give it to you the next time he sees you. It's nothing that can't wait."

After our phone call, Vicky stands to stretch and gazes out the window at the snow family Jake and Craig built. "That's so cute. The four of us will have so much fun raising our kids together. One big happy family."

I smile at the thought. My happy family vanished the day my parents perished in the house fire. Until Jake came along, I thought I'd always be alone, except for my aunt and uncle. But my family has grown over the last few years—Jake, his mom, his brother and wife, and their kids, and then his dad came back into the picture. Craig and Vicky are family, too. Blood isn't the only thing that ties people to each other.

"Is it okay if I tell Jake about your baby?"

"I wouldn't be surprised if Craig has already told him. But, other than the four of us, let's keep it quiet for now."

I watch the beautiful woman standing at my window with a sense of awe. If she hadn't broken up with Jake, I wouldn't be married to him now, having his baby. He and I may never have crossed paths. That chance encounter with Vicky, my childhood best friend whom I hadn't seen for ages, and her boyfriend Jake, changed everything. I suppose I owe her my life—the life I have now. Vicky has become more than my friend. The realization that our bond surpasses that strikes me, along with a sense of guilt. She's my sister; she confides in me. And I've betrayed her with one moment of stupidity triggered by jealousy. Vicky had Jake once, and I worried she could have him back with a snap of her fingers.

"Things have worked out perfectly," she muses, her face glowing. "You and Jake have had your share of problems, but they're all behind you now. And you two are responsible for getting Craig and me together."

"Yes," I agree. "Everything is perfect." Just the way I've always wanted things to be. Everything is absolutely perfect.

The doorbell rings. I jump, wondering who ventured out to our isolated farmhouse unannounced on a Sunday afternoon. When I open the front door, that all-too-familiar wave of panic courses through me. We haven't heard from Jake or Craig for the last couple of hours. Gloria said Jake wasn't picking up his phone.

And now the police are at my door.

Chapter Nineteen

I'll deal with it later. I have no idea what it means, no idea if Mom knows about it, and no clue if it really matters now that Grandpa's gone.

But holy crap, the things you find out about your grandparents after they're dead. Makes me wonder what the hell my *parents haven't told me, thinking it was none of my business.*

If he hid it in the barn, he probably didn't want anyone to know about it. I'll have to be careful how I approach Mom about this. If she doesn't know, maybe she doesn't need to.

If Paul wasn't here, I'd probably share what I discovered with Craig. If I could trust him with the body fiasco this past fall, I can confide my thoughts about this. But it's not something my neighbor needs to know.

"It's nothing." I shove the box and the first aid kit back where they belong, out of sight and out of 'What the hell is *that* about?' I indicate Craig should grab John's toboggan, and we'll head out onto the hill.

Paul, who has wandered off to explore the barn, gasps. "Hey, Jake! Come take a look at this."

What now?

Craig and I rush over to see what's got Paul's attention. He stands above the open hay chute, staring down, his phone illuminating the barn floor below.

"Careful, Paul. It's a long way down." Especially for someone his age. "John and I used to jump down on a pile of loose hay when we were kids. Had a riot. Except for the one time I landed on a half-pile of hay and broke my arm."

"You sure you didn't crack your skull?" Craig quips.

"Ha ha."

"There's something down there. And it's not hay," Paul says.

Craig and I lean over the chute, peering into the hole. Light reflects off an object, a glint shining upwards.

"Glasses," Paul says, narrowing his eyes. "Any chance there's a body connected to that eyewear?"

"A body? Come on, Paul. Those must be Grandpa's. Probably fell out of his pocket, and he didn't get a chance to retrieve them."

Please don't let there be a body.

"Yeah. Yeah, you're probably right. It's just with your history of finding… things…on your property…"

"There are no bodies on my property. Let's go down and pick up the glasses and have a look around."

"You mean jump?" Craig asks, his face ashen.

"Of course, I don't mean jump. There's a concrete floor down there. And we're not fifteen. We'll go around back to the main door, where the stalls are."

Our boots sink into the snow as we circle the barn. The rusted latch doesn't resist, sliding open with unexpected ease. Inside, the smell of manure, old straw, and cattle lingers throughout the empty stalls. Below the open chute, the glasses lie on the concrete, cracks in their lenses.

"Garbage," I say, picking them up. "But…they were Grandpa's, so maybe I'll hold on to them as a memento."

"Did your Grandpa slaughter the animals here?" Craig asks, his face only slightly rosier from trudging through the snow.

"No, of course he didn't slaughter them here." What kind of stupid question is that? Craig's been living in the city too long. A good three months. He's forgotten everything he knew about country life. I shift my eyes to where Craig and Paul stare at the floor.

That is NOT blood on the concrete.

Paul strolls through the barn, peering into all the stalls as though he expects to find a body, while Craig and I stand dumbfounded by the stain on the floor.

"Nothing else here," Paul reports back with a look of relief on his face.

"We'd better head out to the hill before it gets too dark," I suggest, thanking God there are no bodies in the barn.

We head back to the gangway where we left our toboggans and trudge over to the hill, the climb up a lot longer and tougher than I remember it being in my youth. Out of respect for Paul, I stop now and then to catch my breath. At the top, we line up our sleds several feet apart, ready to race to the bottom. I'm not sure the effort of reaching the crest is going to be worth the thrill of sliding down. My memories may be colored through a kid's lens. It won't hurt to get back in practice. Someday I'll teach Jakey how this works.

"On the count of three. Ready? One, two, THREE!" I shove off, grab the rope, and bump along at a slower speed than I expected.

Craig's ahead of me, zipping along. Paul must be pulling up the rear. A quick peek backward tells me he's having trouble steering, his toboggan veering to the left. Craig hits a bump, his sled flying, and loses control. He's tossed off like he's a lightweight. I whiz by him, my arms up in victory.

Until I, too, plow headlong into a semi-solid mass.

What the...?

Snowdrift. I'm thrown off, landing hard on my side, the toboggan overturning close to me. Paul slides along next to me, half on and half off his sled, Russ jumping off, yipping up a storm as Paul lands on the snow.

We should have brought the first aid kit along. I pull myself off the ground, brush off the snow, and check on the old guy.

"Think I should leave the tobogganing for the grandkids. But that was fun," Paul says as I pull him up.

Craig has managed to haul his butt off the ground to retrieve his toboggan. Standing frozen, he stares at something on the ground, then his foot brushes the snow off.

His scream pierces the crisp air.

By the time Paul and I reach Craig, his face is as white as the powder blanketing the hill. He points to the shape huddled beneath a layer of the fluffy stuff.

No. No friggin' way. No, no, NO.

This time, there's no question. The body in my cornfield won't have a heartbeat or pulse. The only breaths we hear are our own.

"Another snowmobiler?" Paul asks.

I turn 360 degrees. "But where's the sled?"

"Better let the police sort this out." Paul pulls out his phone.

"No. No police. Just give me a minute to think." I pull off my gloves and hat, rake my fingers through my hair, trying to come up with a solution.

Body on my property. Again. This can't be good.

Craig has recovered enough to speak, although he looks like a zombie. "There's...a body...in the snow."

"Huh. Yeah." I scratch my head.

Paul holds his phone, his eyes shifting from me, to the body, to his cell.

"Let's not do anything rash here," I say, watching his thumb about to press 911. "We need to get our story straight."

This ain't my first rodeo.

"Call the police," Craig says as Paul's thumb hovers. "We haven't done anything wrong."

My palm up in the air results in Paul tucking his phone into his coat pocket. "What *have* you done, Jake?"

"Me? Nothing. But let me check with Dom. Maybe we don't have all the information we need."

"What information would that be? There's a dead man in your cornfield. He's not going to disappear. Somebody is going to find him sooner or later."

I hit Dom's number in my contact list, hanging up when it goes straight to voicemail. "Shit."

And here I thought we were friends. I consider him more of a father figure than Steve. Family-oriented. Looks out for his own. Keeps the economy running. His casino employs a lot of people. A few questionable business practices aside, he operates mostly on the right side of what's legal. There are enough higher-ups in his back pocket to ensure that the law works for him.

Our personal relationship goes back to the day I turned twenty-one and my best friend, Terry, dragged me into Dom's casino to celebrate. Dom was kind enough to advance me the funds to play—to the tune of tens of thousands of bucks and more. The problem was, he wanted the money back with interest. Dom continues to use my cornfield for his weed operation as collateral on future loans, should they be necessary to pay for body disposal or some similar service. But we worked through all that. Dom has offered me his left-hand-man position, second only to his right-hand man, Nick. Dom respects Mallory. Mal and I have been guests at his cottage up north. Dom is looking forward to being a godfather to Jakey. I don't want to mess with my good standing. A good beating to knock sense into me would be the least of my punishment. A trip down a well would seem pleasant. A fall from a helicopter, not so pleasant.

I call the desk at the casino. "Jake Shelton here, looking for Dom. It's a matter of life and death. Emphasis on death. I'll wait for his call."

Pulling my sled under me and telling Craig and Paul to sit till we get instructions, we keep vigil over the dead guy. Neither of us looks at him, our eyes cast down to our gloved hands as though in prayer.

Minutes later, my cell goes off.

"This better be good. You pulled me out of a meeting." No affectionate greeting from Dom. He gets right to the point. "What do you want, Jake, my boy?"

"There seems to be a person lying in my cornfield."

Silence on the other end.

"Did you understand me, Dom?"

A snort. "Get to the punchline. I've got serious work to attend to."

I repeat myself, adding the details of how we came across said person, without adding that he's dead. Dom will get it. "So I'm just…ah…checking… in case this item happens to belong to you, and you want to pick it up? Our lost and found department will be closing shortly."

"I don't recall losing anything recently. Does it appear to belong to me?"

"Well, it's not in the best condition, and I know you've misplaced similar items before."

"It's winter. My field workers are on vacation. Can't imagine they dropped anything while harvesting the corn."

"So you won't mind if I call in the authorities on the matter?"

"I'd say you'd be safe to do so. Now, if there's nothing else, I'll let you get back to the lost and found." He hangs up.

My next call is to the Brampton Heights police department. No point in calling 911. This guy's not going anywhere. This is the worst day ever. Right up there with a trip down a well or a car explosion.

Or at least a close second. Everything's relative.

Chapter Twenty

"Mrs. Shelton. Are you okay?" Officer Heinz supports my weight. "Do you want to sit down?"

"Jake? Is he dead?"

"Jake called us. Specifically asked for me and Officer Rombough. Said we'd understand the situation better than anyone."

"Situation?"

"We have a team heading out to your back field." Officer Heinz motions to the vehicles pulling up in the lane. "To retrieve a body from the snow."

"A body? Oh, no! Is Craig okay?"

"Craig?" Hearing his name, Vicky joins me at the door.

"Mr. Shelton and his friends found a body out back. Possibly another snowmobiler. This one didn't make it," Officer Rombough explains.

The shock reverberates through me. I saw three snowmobilers out there Friday night. Jake found one, now another. Where is the third? Through the window, I observe as several people exit emergency vehicles with their tools. A stretcher, cameras, crime scene protection, and forensic equipment I can't identify. Vicky stands next to me, touches my arm, and assures me there's nothing to worry about.

"Just tell the officers what you know. It's an accident, but it's routine to investigate a suspicious death," she says. "Poor Craig and Jake, finding the body."

When Officer Heinz asks if they can speak to each of us separately to get our statements, I indicate the den is available. He is familiar with the layout of our house, having visited on numerous occasions. Officer Rombough stays behind in the living room with Vicky.

My statement is brief. I don't know anything about the body Jake found, other than I saw the snowmobilers, and Jake rescued one of them Friday night when he stumbled upon him on his way home after his car slid off the road. Officer Heinz takes notes, pausing to ask questions I honestly can't answer.

"Why don't you ask the man who survived? He's in the local hospital. Jake and Craig visited him yesterday."

Officer Heinz twirls his pen, not responding to my question. But he does have one more for me. "Did anything else unusual happen Friday night?"

"The storm."

"Yes, and did you see anyone else besides Jake and the victim?"

"Well, there was Dave."

"Dave?"

I explain how Dave got his truck stuck and came here for assistance, including Paul and Jake's roles in getting him unstuck after Sam and Jilly rushed the snowmobile victim to the hospital.

"You had a busy night."

I nod. "It's a shame Jake didn't find the other two bodies in time."

"The other two bodies?" The officer raises his eyebrows. "What makes you think there were *two* other bodies?"

"Well, if there were three snowmobilers, I assume there's one more somewhere, and it's probably too late for him or her."

The officer radios a team member on scene and tells them to search for another body, a possible snowmobile casualty. He and I join Vicky and his colleague in the living room. The back door opens, and Jake calls out, "Honey? We've got a problem."

When he and Craig enter the living room, Vicky speaks first. "You didn't text. You didn't call. The entire emergency team showed up in the driveway. Did you give any thought to us at all? What were we supposed to think when we hadn't heard from you, and the police came to the door?"

The only thing I have to add is, "Jake?"

"We were kind of busy, Mal. But, you're right, honey. We should have called you in between checking the dead guy, phoning the police, and getting over the shock."

Craig closes his eyes, shaking his head. "I'm still in shock. I'm sorry."

Vicky sighs, like a patient parent putting up with the antics of her toddler.

Officer Rombough turns to my husband with a smirk. "Well, Jake. Another day out on the farm, another body on the property. Maybe two? Must be hard to keep track."

Jake doesn't find it funny, his eyes showing regret that a man died.

Officer Heinz follows Vicky's lead with a heavy sigh in a 'been there, done this' kind of way. "We'll need to take your statements."

When they're done with Jake and Craig, Officer Heinz heads out to the crime scene while Officer Rombough remains with us. Vicky asks when she and Craig can leave.

"I don't think it will be much longer. Seems like an open and shut case. Tragic, but accidental." He pauses and glances at Jake. "Wouldn't you say, Mr. Shelton?"

"I wish I could have saved him."

"Don't beat yourself up about it. They chose to go sledding off the trail in a blizzard. Trespassing on your property. You saved a life. Concentrate on that."

A radio call comes through for Officer Rombough, asking to speak in private. The officer excuses himself, indicating he's going to the den. I escort him there and press my ear to the closed door.

Officer Heinz's voice is faint over the radio, but his words are clear. "We're calling in homicide. Blood was found inside the barn. And the hospital just reported the rescued snowmobiler missing. They have no ID and no idea where he might be. The medical examiner has declared our victim officially dead. Head injury. But here's the real kicker. We all know him. I don't know why Jake didn't mention it. It's Detective Swarovski."

Chapter Twenty-One

Shit. Shit. Triple shit.

I knew he looked familiar, but it's hard to tell for sure when somebody you're not expecting to see buried and frozen in the snow in your back field turns up. With the beard and without the glasses, snow encrusting his face, it was impossible to know for sure. And besides, what would the detective who arrested me this past fall be doing trespassing on my property, ripping around on a snowmobile?

Now, Officer Rombough tells me the accident is being considered a homicide, and we may be asked to go to the station for more questioning.

"I believe we told you everything we know. So unless you have cause to detain us, we'd appreciate getting back to our lives." Vicky takes over as my attorney, although I'm sure I won't need representation.

I haven't done anything. Except probably save the wrong man. The guy in the hospital is likely the suspect. He was probably trying to get away from the scene of the crime when he smacked into that farm implement in the laneway. Although, what the detective and Lazarus were doing in my field, I have no clue.

I've got nothing to hide. So I repeat the story I've told several times, adding, "To tell the truth, I *did* think the victim looked familiar, but I couldn't quite place him. Dead bodies in snow drifts look different than live bodies. Did he have some sort of makeover or something? Detective Swarovski looked a bit rough around the edges. Of course, I suppose being dead will do that to a person."

Keep your cool, Jake.

This cop knows me; he'll see right through any fibs I tell. We've danced around the ring together before. Seems like he's having trouble processing what's going on here. His expression shows exasperation that I'm not telling the whole truth, and disbelief that his colleague is the accident victim, which it turns out, may be a homicide.

"So you're telling me it's a coincidence that the detective who arrested you a few months ago has been found murdered on your property?" He leans forward, hands clasped in front of him. "Why is it that nearly every crime in this small town seems to connect to you?"

Something tells me this isn't the time to insert a joke here. I look him directly in the eyes. "I honestly don't know what is going on here. I've told you everything I know. Why would I call you if I was involved? And I'm very sorry for the loss of your colleague."

I know this isn't the last I'll see of these guys, but the officers seem to have had enough of me for one day. With dark setting in, the crew out back is packing up, too, taking the body with them, leaving the crime scene tape around the toboggan hill and snowmobile field, as well as the barn where Grandpa's secret remains hidden.

The four of us breathe a collective sigh once the cops and their paraphernalia are gone. Vicky says it's been a long day, and the upcoming days are likely to be longer yet. "It's too bad you couldn't have saved Detective Swarovski instead of the murderer. Now there's a cop killer with amnesia on the loose."

Chapter Twenty-Two

"I'm sorry," Jake says once we're alone.

"For what?"

"For wrecking your holidays. You're supposed to be resting up from school, getting ready for the baby. Not dealing with this." Jake covers his face, then rubs his temples.

"It's not your fault. You did the right thing rescuing that man. How were you supposed to know he might have killed someone? And, if you hadn't brought him home, they may not have found him or Detective Swarovski's body until spring."

"You're right. It's not my fault. I couldn't very well leave that man out there to die. And when we found the body, I called the cops, just like any normal person would do." His eyes meet mine, but the slight twitch tells me he's keeping something from me.

"Except most normal people don't find dead people on their property. Especially homicide detectives who recently arrested them," I point out.

I don't want to put the blame on Jake because I know he's not responsible for that poor detective's death. But I'm not so sure about Dom. As nice as he is to us (or pretends to be), I think he might be capable of anything, including murdering a member of the police force. "What about Dom?"

"Come on, Mal." He shakes his head. "What possible reason could he have for dumping this on my lap?"

Jake doesn't deny the possibility that Dom could commit murder, simply that he wouldn't leave the body on our property. But I'm not so sure. Dom knows he's losing his grip on Jake. I wouldn't put it past him to take drastic action to bring him back into his fold.

"I have a headache coming on. I'm going to make tea." In the kitchen, I boil water and set a peppermint tea bag into a mug while Jake grabs a beer.

"What do you want me to do, Mal?"

"Nothing. I don't know. Maybe it will all blow over. If they find the guy you saved, if he regains his memory, maybe he'll give the police the answers they need."

"Yeah, you're right. It'll all work out." Jake tips back his beer can, flops onto the sofa, and grabs the remote. "What do you want to watch?"

"Something that doesn't involve murder."

Chapter Twenty-Three

In my office. ASAP.

Dom's text comes through at seven a.m., rescuing me from a nightmare where I toboggan into a pile of corpses, and they rise up and stalk me through the cornfield, arms outstretched, chanting, "Brains. We want your brains."

As if I had any to spare.

Mallory stirs next to me. "What is it?"

"Dom wants to see me." I jump out of bed, throw on my jeans and rumpled shirt from yesterday, and head to the bathroom to brush my teeth. "Gotta go, sorry, honey."

Mal groans.

The main highway is clear; you'd never know there had been a storm. The white on the road is from an excess of salt, not snow. Such a difference from the back roads, which are passable, but still snow-covered. During the thirty-minute drive to the River Grand Casino in Brampton Heights, my mind goes through every possible scenario, but I know it doesn't matter. Whatever Dom wants, Dom will get. Eventually.

I've repaid my gambling debt. Dom has released me from further obligations. He's offered me a genuine, legit job at the casino, which I've declined. We're on friendly terms. Dom loves Mallory, and he's excited about the baby. He's a family man himself, a good guy. I've seen the crack in his tough guy act.

I keep telling myself Dom wouldn't hurt us, but when I pull into the casino complex parking lot, I'm nowhere close to being convinced. My hands tremble as I turn off the ignition and step onto the sparsely populated concrete space. Snow has been not only cleared, but taken away in trucks to allow for as many spots as possible in the evenings when the place lights up with action.

The massive entrance to the hotel and entertainment complex, with its wood and stonework, is a natural oasis, complete with fireplaces, fountains, waterfalls, ponds, and greenery surrounding the leather seating. A playground for the rich and wannabes. A world-class hotel with all the amenities, live entertainment, and unique shops. But what it's best known for is the casino.

How Dom affords all this, I have no idea. It brings in a ton of money, but how did he get to this point? He must have been born a multi-millionaire. Inherited. Somebody handed him the keys to the kingdom. No man builds this kind of empire by the time he's in his mid-thirties. And that's how old Dom was when I met him. Already a big shot. And he's offering me a spot in his empire. Which I'm turning down because Mallory forbids it. What a man won't do for love.

I'm met at the casino entrance by Nick, Dom's number one man. Tall, dark, mysterious. Gets his point across in as few words as possible. He nods and locks the glass doors behind us, escorting me to Dom's office as though I've never been there when in reality I know it as well as the interior of my own shed.

"Jake." Dom sits behind his massive mahogany desk, actually looking up at me when I enter. "Hope you and the little woman are doing well."

Nick lowers himself onto one of the chairs facing Dom, motioning for me to take the other. I slide into the leather and nod. "All good. Except for the uninvited visitor in the back field."

Dom clasps his hands together and sits back. "I understand you have a problem. And any problem of yours becomes mine."

I fidget in my seat, thinking of an appropriate response. "No need for you to take on my problems, Dom. I'm sure this will all blow over quick."

"The police questioned me last night." Dom leans forward, elbows on his desk. "Of course, I assured them I know nothing about your unfortunate situation. But it makes me look bad. You understand what I'm saying, Jake?"

I nod, although I have no idea. Best not to ask questions.

"It's bad for business. We've barely recovered from the rumors this past fall. It's the holiday season. People want to enjoy themselves. Bodies turning up aren't conducive to enjoyment. They're best disposed of where they can't be found."

I bob my head up and down again.

"So, do you mind explaining to me why one showed up in your back field? A respectable homicide detective? One who put you behind bars. It doesn't look good."

I cross my leg over my knee, trying to look casual, although I'm sweating bullets. "I don't…"

Nick kicks me in the shin. "Show some respect. Dom's talking."

I set both feet firmly on the floor and sit up straight, all ears.

Dom continues. "I can't have someone with even a shadow of doubt about their integrity fronting for my operations. Any scandal, and I may need to rescind my offer of bringing you on board."

"No problem, Dom, I—"

Nick's foot connects with my calf, eliciting a shout from me. "What the fu—?"

"Respect, Jake. Dom's not done."

Dom rises and strides to the bar, pours scotch into a whiskey snifter, and hands it to me, gripping my shoulder. "Family is everything, Jake, my boy. You're either family, or you're not. I consider you family. And I look out for my family."

He pours a glass for Nick before returning to his desk with his own drink. "So I'm sure you don't want to put me in a position where I have to kick you out of the family. I've invested a lot of time in you, Jake. And I realize you may not be up for the job just yet, but I need you to keep your nose clean."

I nod again, keeping my trap shut, the pain shooting up my leg.

"Which is why I'm prepared to assist you in making sure the person responsible for the deceased is brought to justice as quickly as possible, clearing your good name."

Not sure what specifically that means, I keep nodding. Dom raises his glass, Nick and I follow suit, and the liquid gold burns my throat.

"I don't put my complete trust in many people." Dom's eyes move from Nick to me. "So consider yourself lucky. What I need from you is your assurance that you will stay loyal to me no matter what. Do I have that, Jake?"

"Of course, Dom."

Dom raises his snifter again, and the glasses clink against each other. "Good. I'm glad to hear that, Son. Welcome to the inner circle of the family."

What the hell did I just agree to?

"Keep me posted on your situation. If you need anything, give me a call." Dom rises, slaps me on the back, and tells me to have a good rest of the day.

As Nick escorts me back to the entrance, I risk another kick in the shins. "Did I miss something? What does Dom want me to do?"

"Dom likes you." Nick smirks. "I don't know why. Although you can be entertaining. But you don't want to cross him." Every once in a while, Nick manages to string a few sentences together.

"I have no intention of doing that."

"Good. Because he doesn't put up with shit. He'd probably feed *me* to the wolves if I gave him half a reason."

"You been with him long?"

"You could say that. All my life. He's my brother."

I stop walking so abruptly, I nearly fall forward. "Brother? Like a *real* brother?"

"Yeah. Half-brother. Same father."

Nick continues striding toward the glass exit doors, giving me a few last words of advice. "Prove yourself. Find a solution to your body problem. And keep the cops from sniffing around your back yard."

Chapter Twenty-Four

I t's quiet. Jake left for work early, saying he was going to drop by the hospital to see if he could get any information about what happened to the man he rescued. Lunch consisted of a bowl of soup and toast. He wasn't in the mood to eat. Although he spooned it in, I don't think he tasted it. I wish he wouldn't blame himself. Jake had no way of knowing he aided and abetted a criminal.

There's no evidence in the back field as far as I can see. The sun reflects off the snow, a sparkling of diamonds. I'm tempted to go out and enjoy the beauty of nature; if it weren't for the baby, I'd tromp back to the barn and look for clues. Instead, I clean the kitchen, start the dishwasher, and pop in a load of laundry. Jake texts to say he made it to work, and he loves me.

Immersed in my paperback novel, a romantic thriller, I drop it onto the family room area rug as the doorbell startles me. On my front porch, Jilly rubs her arms, shivering. The weather has changed from an hour ago. Flakes now fall from a gray sky, the wind driving them at an angle.

"Jilly, I'm surprised to see you again. It's gotten a bit blustery out there."

Once we're comfortable on the family room sofa, Jilly gets to the point. "I hear you had a lot of action out here yesterday."

"Oh? What did you hear?"

"Well, you know how news travels in a small town. Myrtle's son was driving out of town after his visit yesterday, and he came across several police vehicles heading into Idlewood. He pulled over to call his mom and told her there must be something big happening in town, like a murder or something. Myrtle called Trudy, and Trudy called Helen, and Helen's husband, Hank, drove out here to have a look because…well, everyone figured it must have something to do with Jake. But Hank thought it would look suspicious if he hung around, especially if someone *did* get murdered, so he didn't stay around to find out. Helen called me, and I said I would come around to see you to make sure you're okay." Jilly stops for a breath.

"I'm fine. Everything's good."

"So…Jake's at work? Because we wondered, you know, if maybe he'd be in jail. But he's out on bail already? That's good. It is good, right? Jake didn't try to hurt you? Because if he did, I hope they keep him locked up for a long time. I did an article once about abuse, and I know how hard it is to come forward and admit there's a problem. You're so brave, Mallory."

"Jake didn't do anything. He—"

"I'm glad to hear that. I didn't think he would hurt you. But everyone knows about his dad, and it's hard to break a cycle of abuse."

"Well, Jake has broken it. And Steve has reformed and is repenting his poor behavior and bad choices, trying to do better with his life."

Jilly purses her lips. "That's good."

"Yes."

"So, what happened yesterday?"

"An unfortunate accident, I'm afraid. Jake found another snowmobiler in the field. But this one didn't make it."

Jilly sits up straighter, her mouth open. "Oh, my. How awful."

"Jake feels bad. He wishes he would have found him in time."

"At least he saved one life. He should look on the bright side. This will put a bit of a damper on that 'feel-good' story I'm writing, though. And I'm afraid we'll have to cancel the life-saving medal award ceremony I was planning to organize."

Jilly sips her coffee, blinking before speaking again. "Was the victim anyone Jake knew?"

"Mmm, I don't think so. Just some guy out snowmobiling." I'm not sure how much I'm allowed to divulge about the police investigation.

"And that's all there is to it?"

I shrug. "It's unfortunate, but accidents happen."

Jilly's eyes flit to the window. "Is there…is that somebody out there?"

"Just the snowmen Jake and Craig built. I know…they kind of spooked me, too."

Jilly rises and moves to the window. "No, not the snowmen. Way out there, past the shed."

The lone figure strides closer, into the back yard, past the shed, toward the back door. With their parka hood covering their head, and the now steady snowfall obliterating my view, I can't identify the person approaching. Jilly asks if the door is locked, rising from the sofa to check, even though I assure her it is.

"Should I call the police?" I ask.

"Let's wait and see what he does. But given the circumstances, we should take precautions. Do you have anything we can use as a weapon? There are two of us and one of him."

"Jake's baseball bat is upstairs. And there are power tools in the basement."

Although Jilly assumes it's a male, she seems to think we can overpower him. She searches the kitchen, spies the wooden block on the counter, and removes two sharp knives. I grasp mine tightly, ready for the intruder.

"Go fetch the bat. I'll search for some tools." Jilly opens the basement door. "Stay upstairs and let me deal with him. I don't want to put the baby in danger. Call 911 if it sounds like he's a threat."

Obeying her orders to some extent, I climb to our room to remove Jake's metal bat from the closet, then return downstairs and wait at the bottom of the steps. Bat in one hand, knife in the other, phone in my pocket, I listen for any sign of trouble.

The doorbell startles me as though I expected him to break down the door without waiting for an invitation to come in. Jilly shouts, loud enough to be heard outside. "What do you want?"

To hear his reply, I slink down the hall toward the back exit, lean the bat against the wall, and remove my phone, ready to call 911. Jilly jumps and turns around when the bat clatters onto the floor. Along with the knife, she is now armed with the cordless reciprocating saw. "Mallory! You scared me to death. I told you to stay upstairs."

The man pounds on the door, then shouts, "I'm a friend of Jake's."

Jilly and I stand still, our eyes meeting in a question. Do we let him in?

"What do you think?" Jilly turns from me to the door as the knocking continues, interspersed with the chime of the bell.

Considering that I had another stranger at my door in the last few days, and he didn't try to harm me, I still bend over to retrieve my bat. Clutching my weapons and phone in a balancing act, I nod to indicate I'm ready for battle. Jilly herself is a frightening sight with the sharp blade of the knife pointing straight ahead, the saw poised midair. She unlocks the door with the hand holding the knife and eases it open, telling him to stay where he is.

"What do you want?" Jilly repeats.

"Like I said, I'm a friend of Jake's. Is he home?" He removes his hood, giving me a clear view of his head and face.

If he's a friend of my husband's, he's not one I recall. Nor is it Dave or Lazarus. This is a new stranger. Spotting the knife and saw in Jilly's hands, he takes a step back. "Are you…cutting something?"

"Who are you?" I ask.

His eyes flit to me, and he raises his eyebrows, seeing my round belly, the knife pointed in his direction, and the bat poised to swing. Shaking his head, he says, "What the fuck, Mallory? Did I catch you ladies in the middle of woodworking or something? Shouldn't you be knitting or making a quilt for the baby instead?"

Even with the parka, I can tell that this stranger, somewhere in his thirties, has a solid build. His snide comment and off-kilter sense of humor, combined with the fact that he knows my name, leads me to suspect he *is* acquainted with Jake.

"What's your name? I don't recall meeting you." My bat remains ready to strike.

"Jethro. I used to harvest your crop. My car stalled on the side road." He nods to his right. "Alternator's bad. I figured Jake could come out and give me a boost."

I *do* know this man. Not personally, but enough to know he's not above criminal activity. Jethro worked for Dom before he got fired. He's also

CHAPTER TWENTY-FOUR

Beth's good-for-nothing cousin.

"Jake's not here," I say. "So you better call someone else."

Jilly attempts to shut the door in his face, but he holds up his hand to block it. "Can I at least come in to warm up while I wait for someone to come? It's freezing out here."

Snow clings to his eyebrows and lashes, his cheeks rosy. I instruct Jilly to allow him in. "It's okay. I know who he is."

I also know he's not in Dom's good books, nor Jake's, nor Beth's, or Jason's. At least he's not a total stranger. Jethro knows our property well, has been in our home, and is familiar with Jake, if not with me. I show him where to hang his parka and invite him into the kitchen to sit on one of the dinette chairs, where Jilly takes a seat and keeps her eyes peeled on him, weapons still in hand, while I call his cousin to deal with him.

"Hi Beth. Is there any chance Jason can come pick up Jethro at our place? He's had car trouble, and Jake's not home."

While I wait for her to check with Jason and get back to me, Jethro shakes his head. "He won't come. He'd just as soon see me freeze my ass off in a ditch than help me."

"I'm sure that's not true. But it could be that you expect too much of him." Like handing over a million or two from his lottery win. "Maybe he thinks you should be able to take responsibility for yourself."

"You've been talking to Beth, haven't you?"

Minutes later, Beth calls back to say Jason will be there within the hour. Family is family.

"Can I get you a coffee?" My hostess instincts kick in, watching him rub his hands together, a few drops of snow melting down his face.

"Got anything stronger to add to it?"

I put the coffee on and slip out to the dining room to retrieve the bottle of Jack Daniels that Jake keeps on hand for the times stress becomes too much for him. We settle in at the table with our hot coffee, minus the Jack for Jilly and me, and wait for Jason. Having overcome her distrust of the stranger with us, Jilly drills him for information.

"How exactly do you know Jake? And what were you doing out here?

Why didn't you call someone from your car and wait there? Wouldn't that be wiser in this weather?"

Jethro shrugs. "I just figured I'd pop in and see my buddy, Jake, since I was next to his property. Who are *you*, anyway?"

"Jilly Houston, Mallory's friend."

His eyes pop. "Are you the Jilly that puts out the local paper in Idlewood? I've read those articles you wrote about Jake. Fake news. Jake never killed nobody."

"I didn't say he did. I simply reported about the police investigation. They thought Jake was guilty the last time a body showed up on his property. And now it's happened again, so it's only natural they might be suspicious."

That much was true. But Jilly may have drawn some conclusions that weren't factual.

Jethro nods. "Yeah, I noticed the police tape. But what the fuck do the cops know about anything?"

It seems like a rhetorical question. In any case, neither Jilly nor I answer, continuing to sip our coffee. Nellie saunters into the kitchen, meowing for treats. I grab the bag from the top of the refrigerator and toss a few morsels on the floor, which she devours, then tilts her head up looking for more. Lucky, hearing the bag open again, darts in for his share, rubbing his silky black fur against my leg. After scarfing down his yum yums, Lucky jerks his head as he notices I have company. A quick hiss, baring his fangs, followed by a growl, Lucky bolts for the laundry room, Nellie on his tail.

"Friendly cats," says Jethro, his tone not matching the words.

"Lucky was a stray we took in a few months ago. He's still a bit wary of strangers."

"I'd just as soon have a dog. You can take a dog for walks. On car trips. Take him hunting. Fishing. A dog will protect your property. Dogs are man's best friend."

Following his endorsement of dogs, Jethro stands and stretches. "Mind if I use your john?"

I point to the back bathroom, next to the laundry room, but Jethro says he'd just as soon stay clear of the cats, seeing as they're none too friendly, so I wave in the direction of the powder room down the hall. As he heads there, Jilly whispers, "Are you sure you can trust him?"

"He'll be gone soon."

Jethro takes his time in the bathroom, leading Jilly to question what he's doing in there. As she rises to check on him, the doorbell rings. Before we get to the front door, Jethro has let Jason in.

Jason greets his cousin-in-law. "You and that clunker of a car of yours. I gave you money for a new one. What happened to that?"

"I'm still shopping around, trying to get the best deal."

"Hi, Mallory. Thanks for putting up with Jethro. I'll get him out of your hair now."

Jilly brings his parka to him, and Jethro reiterates Jason's thanks before heading out with his cousin-in-law to his new Hummer. Their winter vehicle, according to Beth. The AWD drive convertible BMW is their all-season vehicle. Since his lottery win a few months ago and partnering up with Dom in the casino/hotel business, the Bartletts' lifestyle has made a 180-degree turn. Beth no longer worries about going to work at the makeup consultant boutique to ensure the rent is paid.

Once the Hummer pulls out of the lane, Jilly turns to me, her eyes wide. "Wow. Is that *the* Jason, the one who won the lottery? Tell me all about him."

I'm happy to comply. A good-news story about Jake's friend beats another article about Jake being questioned by the police about a murder. Once Jilly has the full scoop, she asks if I don't mind giving her a lift home.

Although it's only five o'clock, it seems later. Darkness settles in quickly. Ten minutes later, I'm back home, the security lights illuminating the front of the house. Another long night ahead of me, waiting for Jake to come home. Sometimes I wish he had a different job, one that didn't leave me so lonely.

With the exterior lights on, the scene through the front window is picture-postcard perfect. The snow has quit, the maple trees dusted with powder, the laneway and road with banks to the side, and the woods casting shadows, gaps where leaves have abandoned the trees. Once I extinguish the lights, they will become menacing, darkness obliterating the light. What is magical and expansive during the day transforms to an unknown and claustrophobic terror by night.

But this is Jake's home. My home. Our home. Maybe, once the house is filled with children and laughter, the old farmhouse will maintain its magic through the dark and the storms. Tonight, I could use some peace and quiet. The end to a nightmare of a weekend.

Winters are particularly hard out here in the country. I can't sit outside, tend to my flower gardens, or go for a walk. Even driving into town for groceries is an ordeal, getting dressed and brushing off the car, lugging in bags through the snow. Jake has stocked the house with supplies, so I won't need to worry about going out in my condition. If it weren't for my books and the television, I'd go stir-crazy.

The street lamp blinks on, illuminating specks that look like dust. I rise from the sofa to take a closer look.

It can't be snowing again. I thought it was over.

Jake always says the weather out here is unpredictable, being in the snow belt, and I've seen that myself the last three years. My life in the city, only a half hour away, didn't prepare me for the open countryside. No shelter from the wind, no warmth from surrounding buildings, nothing to stop the drifts from blowing in.

A winter storm advisory pops up on my weather app, confirming that it is indeed snowing, and squalls with localized snowfall amounts of up to five inches are expected. Once again, I will worry about Jake getting home safely. It makes me wonder how I will cope with a baby in these circumstances. The city offers safety, with services and amenities, with neighbors and family close by. Would Jake even consider moving now that our finances are in better condition? Could we find jobs in Brampton Heights? We would never need to leave the city in the winter.

Nellie and Lucky meander in and out between my legs, indicating I should head to the kitchen and prepare supper. From a lower cupboard, I remove a tin of cat food and scoop it into their bowls before heating a plate of ham, scalloped potatoes, and corn in the microwave. With a flick of the switch in the mudroom, the back yard becomes visible, figures standing not far from the window.

Who's out there?

Snowmen. Nearly causing me to jump out of my skin.

A cute little family that Jake and Craig built. We didn't get a chance to talk about it, and I wonder whether Jake knows about Vicky's pregnancy. Do men confide these things to each other?

The television tuned to the local station, my plate on a tray, I wait for the weather forecast. Outside, flakes descend, further powdering the walkway Jake and Craig cleared yesterday. I'm glad we had a white Christmas, but now that it's over, the thought of months more of this brings on melancholy.

Gloria and Steve, John and Deb, and their two kids joined us for an old-fashioned family celebration on the farm. Jake, John, and Gloria reminisced about Christmases spent here with her parents. Even Steve recalled their happy moments, Jake allowing him to share their warm and fuzzy memories. A genuine truce, maybe something more, transpired between father and son. John, like Gloria, has forgiven his father. For Jake, the process is taking longer.

A piece of corn sticks in my throat, the coughing startling Nellie and Lucky next to me. I reach for my glass of apple juice, eyes on the screen where a video of our back field, surrounded by yellow police tape, plays as news of the murder becomes public. The reporter gives no details, stating that the police investigation is ongoing after a body was discovered in a local farmer's field. The story will be updated as more information becomes available.

Thanks for the ham and potatoes, hon. How are you doing?

I respond to Jake's text, telling him I'm good. No point in mentioning the news. My phone rings as I load my dishes into the dishwasher. The caller ID indicates I'm not the only one watching our local station.

"I just saw the news. Please tell me that's not your field."

"I'm afraid it is."

"I thought Jake saved that snowmobiler."

"He did. This is another one Jake found yesterday."

"What do you mean, another one?" Steve's voice booms over the phone, indicating I'm on speaker.

I recount the facts surrounding Jake's discovery. When I mention the victim's identity, Gloria's gasp is audible. "Detective Swarovski? What was he doing there?"

"Was Jake questioned?" Steve asks. "Did he have his lawyer with him?"

"Yes, and yes. We were all questioned. Vicky and Craig were here at the time. Craig, Paul, and Jake discovered the detective lying in a drift on the snow hill when they were tobogganing."

A moment of silence is followed by a barrage of questions, not many of which I have an answer for. No doubt Steve and Gloria are wondering if Dom is involved and how deep Jake has been pulled in. I assure them it's a coincidence that Detective Swarovski was found dead on our property.

The snowfall and snow family in the back yard create a wonderland illuminated by the exterior lighting, beckoning me to sit on the window seat once our call is completed. With my book in hand, I fluff the pillows, pull the throw over me, turn on my reading light, and prepare to lose myself in the story. The gentle flow of white crystals from above is hypnotic, and I spend more time gazing out than reading. It's so pretty, I envision myself strolling out in the yard, boots scuffing up snow, twirling as flakes land on my tongue. Next year, we'll be out there, the three of us, building another snow family.

My eyelids grow heavy, the steady snow lulling me to sleep, I lie curled up on the bench, happy thoughts keeping me company along with the two cats at my feet. The bliss doesn't last long, interrupted by a roar. A light bobs in the field, the source of the revving intruding on my peace.

I pick up my phone. Surely, the police will come this time. Someone could be disturbing the crime scene. By the time the police get here, the snowmobile could cover any tracks or evidence they might need to re-examine. Although the snow and wind will do that anyway.

Maybe I can discourage them from staying. In the mudroom, I flip the switch up and down several times, hoping they'll notice and understand they're not welcome on our property. Sometimes, that works. Sometimes, they ignore it.

This time, they do neither. The headlights in the distance turn in my direction, glowing like eyes through the screen door glass as the snowmobile zips directly toward the house. Door closed and locked, I scurry off to the living room, closing the hallway door after me.

I need to call the police.

But the sound grows fainter as my finger taps the emergency call button, and a dispatcher says, "911. What's your emergency?"

"I…uh, I'm not sure. There's a snowmobiler in my back yard."

"Are you in danger?"

Returning to the back door, phone to my ear, I check for the location of the intruder, but everything is quiet, the headlights no longer visible. "No. I think they're gone. Sorry, but our back yard is a crime scene, and I don't think they should have been there. But it's okay. They left."

After I provide my name and address, the dispatcher says to call immediately if they return. I don't think they will. I've scared them off. With the back exterior lights left on, I retreat to the living room to watch TV until Jake comes home. The wind has picked up, the streetlight showcasing the flurries visible through the open curtains. I grab the remote and start flipping. Nearly eight-thirty. Only a few more hours.

Headlights shine through the glass into the house. It's too early for Jake. Too late for visitors. A door slams; a shadow strides toward the porch. Parked outside is a pickup truck.

Could that be Dave coming back to thank me for giving him shelter? Why now?

The knock sounds tentative, then louder as I ignore it. The doorbell rings. Taking a deep breath, I open the door a crack, then slam it shut upon seeing who is on the other side.

Chapter Twenty-Five

No sooner do Craig and I settle down to the fresh-out-of-the-microwave meals our wives lovingly packed than the metal steps clank with heavy footsteps, a loud knock following.

"Come in," I shout, wondering who has the nerve to disrupt my short-enough-already supper break.

Rod and Sid burst through the door, red-faced and grim-looking. Either climbing the stairs was too much for them, or they're embarrassed, maybe pissed off about something.

"Janice just called. I thought it was because of all that crap talk during Group about texting, and she was trying to start up some new 'call me from work every day' shit. Then, I worried that maybe she'd had an accident or something, so I decided to pick up when she called again. Turns out she was calling about you being on the news."

Sid joins in. "Gail called me, too, right after Rod's call. Started prattling on about the body in your cornfield. I reminded her you saved the guy, and she said the local news reported a *dead* body was found in a local field."

"What the hell, Jake? Was he alive or dead?" Rod asks.

"He's alive and doing well. But I found another body yesterday." Not sure if that came out right, but it is what it is.

Craig provides more details, probably more than they need to know.

"Well, that's not good," Sid says. "I hope you understand we don't want to be involved in whatever's going on. We think it would be a good idea if you don't mention we were at your place this weekend."

"That horse has already left the barn. The police questioned us, and we all told the truth because we have nothing to hide. Isn't that right, Craig?"

"You didn't happen to mention that you told us about the first body, did you? Because if they're connected, that might make us accomplices or something. We don't want that added to our record after what happened this fall." Sid makes it sound like they were guilty then, and they're guilty now.

I'm pretty sure these guys don't have a record of any kind unless having a miserable marriage is a criminal offense. "I don't think there's anything to worry about. The cops know you weren't anywhere near my back field this weekend or any other time. Craig and Paul were there when the body showed up, and they can attest to the fact that I was as shocked as they were. I'm sure the police are looking for a suspect unconnected to me, so you guys are off the hook. Somebody must have had an issue with Detective Swarovski and decided my property was as good a place as any to dispose of him."

Sid and Rod's expressions change again as their jaws drop. Rod sums up their feelings on the issue. "Detective Swarovski? The guy who put you behind bars? They didn't mention *that* on the news report. *Somebody* disposed of him? We weren't born yesterday. You're in deep shit, Jake, and we're not wading into it with you. So keep us out of this and clean up your own manure pile."

What are friends for? "I wouldn't expect anything more from you, Rod. Thanks for standing by me."

Sid apologizes for them both. "We *do* stand by you. But it's getting to be a bit much to deal with, never knowing what will show up on your property. Maybe we should hold off on coming to your place for Group or getting together at the bar until things die down."

I clear my throat at the word 'die', but I nod.

"This isn't going to affect our jobs here, is it? Nothing personal against you," Rod says.

"Nothing personally taken," I assure him with a wave of my hand. "We're all good. But I'm not extending supper break, so I'd suggest you eat while there's still time."

As they clank back down to the main floor, Craig says, "You can't blame them. I wouldn't want to be associated with you, either. Too much chance of ending up dead or charged with murder."

"Very funny." I dig back into my ham and scalloped potatoes.

Both our phones ping with an incoming text. Our eyes meet as we look up from the message. Dom has invited us, along with our wives, to his place tomorrow night for a celebration to ring in the new year. Craig shakes his head. "No way. Vicky will never agree."

Neither will Mallory. But Dom doesn't take no for an answer.

Chapter Twenty-Six

The doorbell keeps ringing. I can't call the police again just because someone's at my door. Although it's not someone, it's *the* one. I remember him from Friday night when they carried him away on a stretcher. This man that Jake saved, the one who lost his memory, the one Jake visited in the hospital yesterday, and who is now missing. Here he is at my door.

I hit redial on my cell. The same police dispatcher answers my call and tells me to keep the door locked and hide in the house until the police arrive. Knowing the man can see my shape through the sidelights, I consider where to hide. Upstairs in the closet with Jake's baseball bat? I'd be trapped. The kitchen with the steak knives? That would give me a chance to escape through the back or side doors, but he'd see my tracks and outrun me.

Paul. He'll get here quicker than the police. After calling him and explaining the situation, I head to the basement. It's a place I've only been a couple of times. Not only is it claustrophobic with the windows bricked in and no second exit, it has housed dead things—mice being among the least of them.

It's also where Jake keeps his power tools. Drill, saw, grinder, sander…I scan the tool bench looking for something I can handle, spot the cordless nail gun, and remove it from the charger. With my left hand, I reach for a hammer and screwdriver from the pegboard. Securing them low on my hip in Jake's toolbelt, I search for more weapons. The reciprocating saw Jilly used has my attention, but I grab the more manageable box cutter.

My plan to hide under the stairs and lunge out at my attacker if necessary sounded better in my head. Now that I'm down here, the walls press in, the smell suffocates, and the shadows play tricks. I need to get out.

Left hand holding the box cutter and the railing, nail gun in my right, I ascend the wooden steps, mindful of the creaking. Every couple of steps, I stop to listen. The doorbell rings again. He's still outside on the front porch. Not going away, but not breaking in either. I ease open the basement door, step into the kitchen, and consider what to do next.

My phone pings. A message from Paul.

I'm in your driveway.

It makes me brave enough to approach the front door again, open it a crack, and peer out. The man stands there, snow-covered, his head turned to the driveway where Paul exits his vehicle, shouting. "Hey! Can I help you?"

"Yeah, I'm looking for Jake. I wanted to thank him."

Paul strides toward him in the dark, a shovel in one hand and a snowbrush/ice scraper in the other, as though the man might need assistance backing his truck out of the driveway. Then it occurs to me they may be masquerading for their real intent as possible weapons. Armed myself, I open the door wider, greeting Paul, then answering the stranger. "No need. I understand you already thanked him."

"I also wanted to ask him a question." The man tilts his head, eyes on my tools. "Are you fixing something?"

Stepping onto the porch, I point the nail gun at him and pull out the hammer. "Yes, things break around here all the time. I can relay your question to Jake."

"Oh, okay, then. Jake returned my phone to me. I wondered whether he found anything else of mine."

"Did you lose something?"

"Possibly. Or misplaced it. I'm just starting to remember things. Anyway, if Jake does find something more on the property that doesn't belong to him, it's probably mine. And I'd like it returned."

"I'll let him know. If he finds it, what's the best way to contact you?" If I can get some information from him, it may help the police. If they ever get here.

"I'll reach out to him again. Thanks. I'll be on my way now."

Paul steps aside from the stairs leading off the porch to allow the man to leave. "Call first next time."

"Oh, wait!" I say. "I just remembered. Jake said he'd be home early tonight. If you don't mind waiting in your truck, he should be here shortly." Maybe I can get him to stay till the police come and arrest him.

"Sure, sounds good." He passes Paul on the way to his truck.

I motion for Paul to come inside. "Thanks for coming over again. I hope the police get here before he decides to leave."

We watch through the screen door as the truck idles in the driveway. Paul turns to me and points at the toolbelt and tools as I set them on the entry table. "Doing more renovating?"

Minutes later, a police vehicle pulls in behind the man's truck, and the man exits with his hands in the air. I can't tell what they're saying, but the two officers who responded to my 911 call escort him to the back of their car. One of them comes to my door, and I let her in, recognizing her from this past fall.

"Thank you for coming, Officer Chen."

"Just checking that everything is okay. We're taking the suspect in for questioning. Any other intruders on your property?" Her eyes flit from mine to Paul's and back to mine.

"No, just my neighbor, Paul. I called him, and he was nice enough to come over until you got here."

She nods, satisfied that I'm safe, and Paul says to call anytime I need him. Once they're gone, I head upstairs to bed. Too much excitement has left me exhausted. On the third step, a text comes through from Jake.

Hey hon, how you doing? Did you see the news?

I not only saw the news, I may have made new headlines by apprehending the suspect. I call Jake so he's up-to-date on what's happening and doesn't worry.

"Hi honey, I'm fine, but I've had a busy day. You'll never believe this, but the guy you saved, the one who probably killed the detective, came to the house tonight."

"What? Are you okay, honey?" Jake shouts in my ear, and I hold the phone further away. "What happened? Did he get in? Did he hurt you? I'll *kill* him if he touched you."

"I'm fine. No, he didn't come into the house or hurt me. He seemed pretty harmless and said he wanted to thank you and ask if you found anything that might belong to him besides his phone."

"Like what?"

"I don't know. He didn't say. Anyway, the police have him in custody. I called them, and then I called Paul to wait with me till they came. So I think it's all over now. Case solved."

"Just like that? The murderer returned to the scene of the crime and got arrested? That seems too easy."

"Sometimes it happens like that in books I read."

"Oh, okay then. Did the police say anything? Do they know why he killed Detective Swarovski and left him in our field?"

"No. They didn't say."

"But, you're safe now? I could come home early."

I assure Jake I'm fine and just want to get some rest. Nellie and Lucky scoot past me on the stairs. Too tired for anything, I slip into my nightgown and slide into bed with them, drifting off to sleep and putting aside the stress from the last few days.

It's all behind us now.

Chapter Twenty-Seven

Well, that's a relief. Case closed. Maybe now they'll take down the police tape, and I can get back to the barn to take a closer look at the things Grandpa stashed away, hidden from his family. And what do I do if my suspicions turn out to be true? Does Mom have the right to know? He was her dad. What kind of man cheats and lies and hides things from the people he loves?

The faint reflection in the glass as I stand overlooking the warehouse floor gives me my answer. My genetic makeup leaves a lot to be desired. I'm half my father. A waste of space. And if my mom's father wasn't the man I thought he was, what percent of a decent human being does that leave me with? Twenty-five? The part that is my mother, handed down from her own mother? My mom is a good person, but she doesn't know how to walk away from evil. She's too kind, too forgiving, too easily manipulated and controlled by her loving nature. Her judgment is impaired. Mallory and the baby deserve better than me and the crappy life decisions I've made and will likely continue to make. They need someone who can balance genetics with a proper environment to grow up in. An honest, hard-working, dependable husband and father. They deserve someone like…

Craig clanks up the stairs to my office and bursts through the door. "They caught the man who escaped from the hospital? Vicky just called. Mallory told her the guy came right up to her door. Thank God she's okay. She must have been terrified."

"Mallory said he seemed harmless. What if he's not the killer?"

"They took him into custody, so they must have some evidence that proves he is. And that puts you in the clear. I tell you, man, it had to look suspicious that the detective who arrested you wound up dead on your property. No matter how innocent you are."

Am I?

Rod and Sid pound up the stairs and burst through the door as if in response to my question. "Well, that was a lucky break," Rod says. "I heard they made an arrest. What do you say we go out after work and celebrate your innocence?"

"They reported it on the news already? That was quick."

"No. Janice called again. I hope she doesn't make it a habit. Anyway, she texted Mallory to let her know we won't be attending Group until this whole murder thing gets wrapped up, and Mallory said they just arrested the guy at your place."

Sid chimes in. "Sorry we doubted your innocence. It's just that this kind of thing seems to happen to you a lot. Bodies and stuff. Let us buy you a couple of drinks tonight so there's no hard feelings."

"We're all good. I'd better get home to Mallory, though. She'll still be shaking."

"I don't know about that. Janice said Mallory scared the guy with a nail gun and detained him until the police got there. Pretty gutsy." Rod compliments my wife, adding, "For a knocked-up broad."

Craig beats me to defend my wife's honor. "Don't talk about Mallory that way."

"What way? I was just saying she's a lot ballsier than I thought." He addresses me. "Bet that puts a damper on your manhood. Or maybe you find it a turn-on?"

Sid saves Rod from a clip to the jaw. "We'd better get back to work."

"Yeah. Anyway, glad they caught the killer," Rod speaks for us all.

Chapter Twenty-Eight

"Hey, sleepyhead. You were sound asleep last night when I got home." Jake's kisses trail from my forehead to my nose, to my chin, and back to my lips.

"Mmmm." I smile as his lips move to my neck. "So tired."

He lifts his head and gazes into my eyes. "Too tired?"

"No. Not that tired."

Being apart from Jake when we're working is hard. Some couples seem to enjoy time on their own and even take separate vacations. But Jake and I aren't like those couples. We want to do everything together. I miss him so much when he's not with me.

We lie in each other's arms after making love, Jake gentle with me like I'm a china doll. He rests his hand on my belly. "The baby okay?"

"He's good. I'm good. But I had a busy day yesterday. Your friend Jethro's car broke down on the side road. He walked across the field, thinking you could give him a boost. I called Beth, and Jason came to collect him."

"Jethro? I haven't seen him since Dom fired him." Jake scoops me in his arms, kissing my forehead. "Listen, hon. There's something I need to ask you. And I'll understand if you say no, especially with that guy showing up last night scaring you like that. The last thing you need is more stress. But Dom has invited us to his place tonight to bring in the new year."

"No." I move Jake's hand off my belly and roll over, my back to him.

"Okay. No problem. I'll call and tell him you're not feeling well."

"No."

"No, we're not going, or no, I shouldn't call because you changed your mind? Which is it?"

"We're not going, and I feel fine. Tell him we have other plans. I wanted to spend tonight with just the two of us. It's the last year we can do that. So call Dom and tell him no."

Jake's sigh is so heavy it bounces off the mattress and into my ear, magnifying his disappointment. He must have known what my answer would be before he asked. It can't be a big surprise. But it *is* a shock when he picks up his phone and calls Dom to tell him he appreciates the invitation but sends his regrets.

I roll back to face him and kiss his cheek. "Thank you for putting me first."

As he leans in to start another round of kissing, my phone rings. "Mallory, how are you?"

I recognize the deep, smooth voice immediately. Like a dark chocolate almond melting in my mouth, Dom can be both charmingly sweet and hard as nails. I haven't been able to ascertain which is the real him and which is the facade, but I have my suspicions.

I tell him I'm fine and repeat Jake's regrets about the New Year's Eve invitation.

"I understand completely. You two lovebirds want to be alone to celebrate. But perhaps you would consider stopping by for a short while. No need to stay all night. It's a small, informal get-together, just family, come and go as you please."

"Thank you, Dom, but..."

"I'd be honored if you would join us. My wife is eager to meet you. And of course, the little ones are excited they get to stay up past bedtime and join in part of the fun. Come early, stay for an hour or so, say hello and grab a bite to eat, some non-alcoholic wine, and you'll be home in plenty of time to ring in the new year."

"I don't..."

"Come now, Mallory. We've been through a lot together this year. Since our initial meeting, you've struck me as the kind of woman who puts family first. I consider you and Jake part of my family. Don't disappoint me.

Cocktails and snacks are at six, dinner buffet at eight. We'll look forward to seeing you."

"Um…"

"Good. Thank you, Mallory. Your presence means so much to me."

Dom ends the call before I can explain that we will not be attending. Jake raises his eyebrows, his blue-green eyes wide. "How did he take it?"

"I guess we could stop by for fifteen minutes. Just to make him happy."

"Seriously?"

"We'll make an appearance. We won't know anyone there. I'm not feeling up to making small talk with strangers."

"We'll keep it real short. Thanks, hon."

Jake insists on making breakfast and bringing it to me on a tray. He says he wants to make a head start on the new year and get off on the right foot. I lounge in bed, wondering what on earth I'm supposed to wear to this party. Not the flannel plaid nightie and red robe Gloria bought for Christmas. Not leggings and a stretchy maternity t-shirt. And certainly not any of the clothes I wore pre-pregnancy.

Twenty minutes later, Jake returns with a full plate of scrambled eggs, bacon, and toast with jam, along with orange juice. He joins me in bed with his own tray, turns on the romantic pop station, and we enjoy our meal. I wouldn't mind starting every day like this, but I can't help but wonder if Jake doesn't have an ulterior motive.

He carries the trays back down when we're done, telling me to relax so I won't be worn out for tonight. From the family room sofa, I watch as he cleans up the kitchen before sitting next to me. "There's something you should know, Mal."

Uh-oh, here it goes.

"I don't want anything to ever come between us again. I know I haven't been the best husband, and believe me, there are times when I wonder whether I should step aside and let you find someone worthy of you." He kisses my belly.

"So you're breaking up with me?" I chuckle because I know he's joking. He'd never leave me.

"Seriously, Mal. I love you so much. I'm not sure I can be the man you need me to be."

"Jake, what's going on?"

"You know what kind of role model I have for being a father."

"You're not your dad, Jake."

"I'm trying hard not to be. And then there's Dom. He says I'm family. I don't know what to do with that." Jake covers his face with his hands and shakes his head.

I take his hands in mine. "We'll deal with Dom together. But if you're gambling or borrowing money or doing something illegal, you need to tell me. Now. Before things get any worse."

"No, I swear I'm not. I just don't know what Dom is expecting from me. The job offer? Or something more? But there's something else bothering me. And I don't want to lay this on you, being seven months pregnant and all, but I don't know what to do about it. And I want to be honest with you about everything from now on. You deserve at least that much."

"You're scaring me, Jake. Just tell me."

The doorbell interrupts our conversation. Jake heads to the front door and returns with a large, white rectangular box. "A courier dropped this off—for you."

I remove the wide blue ribbon and bow, open the lid, and run my fingers over the contents. A gift? A bribe?

Chapter Twenty-Nine

"This is gorgeous. Thank you, honey. Even though it means you assumed you would convince me to go to the party." She holds up a fancy dress from the white box. "Oh, there's a card."

My dearest Mallory, Please accept my apologies for the late invitation to tonight's party. I hope one of these will be acceptable. If not, please call the boutique and let them know what you'd like, along with any accessories. Have them charge my account. Warmest regards, Dom.

If that man thinks he can steal Mallory from me, he's got another thing coming. "He's got a nerve. Thinks he can have any woman he wants because he's filthy rich and powerful."

"I really don't think he meant it that way. I think he's just being nice."

Dom, nice? Mallory admires the low-cut royal blue dress, then sets it aside and picks up the red lacy one with a less-revealing collar. She tries them on, modelling for me, asking what I think. I think I'd like to know how Dom got my wife's size right. Has he been ogling her?

"They're both good. I like the red."

Mal sets the box aside, grasps my hands, and gazes into my eyes. "Tell me what's bothering you. Whatever it is, we'll face it together."

I tell her what I discovered in the barn. Besides the jewelry.

"Oh, Jake. I'm so sorry." She takes me in her arms. "That must have been such a shock. If only your grandpa were here to explain…"

"Explain what? That he led a double life? A secret one? Jeez, Mal. I don't know if Mom knew about this. And if she did, why would she not tell me?"

"I don't know. But I think you should talk to Gloria, and maybe the two of you can make sense of it. Not right away, after the holiday. Let's not ruin that. And there's nothing you can do about it at this point, anyway."

I nod. Mallory is right. She always is.

With seven hours to go till Dom's party begins, we settle in to binge-watch a series Mal says is great. She's seen the first five episodes. "This has everything in it—romance, obsession, addictions, abuse, betrayal, secrets, organized crime, murder. And the picturesque scenery is nice, too."

"So…like real life."

She raises her eyebrows. "I guess."

We watch the series from the start, with Mal commenting on what's happening because she's already viewed it and must think I won't be able to figure things out for myself with all the flashbacks. Too complex for my brain to handle. After the first couple of episodes, I hit the pause button and prepare a quick lunch. Boxed pasta and chicken nuggets. Not the fancy fare that Dom will have catered in.

I notice Mal's yawn. "Should you have a nap before we head out tonight?"

"No, I'm too wound up about it to sleep, but promise me we'll be home by nine? I need to get some rest. We'll have a busy day tomorrow, and I don't want to disappoint Gloria by cutting it short because I'm too tired."

Mom will prepare a big meal for noon, then we'll play board games in the afternoon, followed by a family movie in the evening. John and his family will be there. It's always good to see them. But this is the first year in over a decade that Steve will be joining us in our New Year's celebration. If I had my way, it would be his last.

"Nine is the absolute latest, but I don't think we'll be there that long," I agree. Hobnobbing with Dom's criminal connections isn't my idea of a good time. I'd rather be in bed snuggling with my wife.

When four o'clock rolls around, Mallory heads for the shower, leaving me with Nellie and Lucky and the remote. I flip through the selections, not finding anything of interest. My mind is too preoccupied with Dom and what he wants from me.

Outside, dusk sets in, no snowfall to wreak havoc on the roads. I would have insisted we stay home had there been any call for bad weather. Getting stuck in the snow with my wife and unborn child isn't something I will risk. The forecast for tomorrow also sounds good. So much for that storm of the decade prediction.

Mallory's voice travels down the stairs and through the hall. "I'm out of the shower. Maybe you should get ready."

Since Dom didn't send *me* any formal attire, I root through my closet to the back and find the one suit I own, then hop into the shower while Mal dries her hair.

It's dark by the time we're dressed, but too early to leave. We stand in the entry hall, and I admire my wife in her red dress and long, blond waves. She's wearing the new necklace and earrings I gave her, along with the zirconia bracelet I bought for her birthday. Just the right touch of makeup—classy yet sumptuous. I'm tempted to say the hell with Dom and take her back upstairs to the bedroom.

"What are you staring at?" Mallory tilts her head.

"My gorgeous wife. How did I get so lucky?"

She smiles, making her even more beautiful.

"Let's go see if there are any stars out tonight," I suggest.

"It's too cold out there."

"We'll sit in the car and stargaze through the sunroof. Wish on a star."

"That's so romantic."

My arm around my wife, the heat cranked up, heated leather seats on, love songs on the radio, we sit back and feast our eyes on the sky. New Year's Eve starts out perfectly—me, Mal, the baby, our home, the stars, a wish for a long, happy life with my family.

I have everything I've ever wanted right here in the car with me. It's going to be a great year.

Chapter Thirty

"That's some fancy house." Jake drives up to the gated property, a glimpse of the stunning mansion ahead, the treed driveway leading to it.

"Yes, I've been here before."

Jake turns to stare at me as he pushes the button to gain entry. "You've been here?"

"When you were in jail."

"Oh, right. This is my first." Jake is not inclined to discuss that further, pushing the bad memories aside. He announces our arrival, and the gate swings open, Jake cruising toward the brick-paved circular drive, a snow-covered fountain in the center of a large white flower bed. I bet it looks spectacular in the summer. Jake pulls up in front of the door. Several vehicles line the driveway, with more off to the side.

A valet opens my door and helps me out. Jake tosses him the keys and takes my arm, leading me up the steps to the two-level sprawl of a modern mansion that Dom calls home. It's not what I would call home. Most people would be impressed by his wealth, but I wonder how many people have suffered so that Dom and his family can live like this.

The double doors are unlocked. A man greets us in the expansive marble-floored entry hall with its twin curved glass staircases, takes our coats, and motions for us to continue into the great room. Vaulted ceilings with wooden beams, floor-to-ceiling windows overlooking a lake, and a roaring fire in the huge stone fireplace complement the off-white walls and dark chocolate leather sofas arranged throughout the vast space. The splashes of color indicate a decorator's touch, and the artwork and sculptures look like they came from a gallery, not the dollar store. On one wall, a fully-stocked bar with a bartender serves guests. I didn't get this far during my previous visit. Although he did invite me in, Dom and I spoke in the doorway, my words to him short and concise. He got the message. If Jake went down for murder, so would he.

Twenty people or so stand in groups or sit on the expensive furniture in the airy, but cozy, room. Dom spies us out of the corner of his eye and excuses himself from the group surrounding him. He takes my hand and kisses it, then shakes Jake's hand. "Mallory, so glad you could make it. And Jake. Welcome to our humble home. Let me introduce you to the family."

Dom leads us to a woman in her thirties, a young boy and girl, about six and four years old, respectively, fidgeting on a sofa next to her. The woman's wavy dark brown hair hangs loose around her shoulders, her face striking with high cheekbones and emerald eyes that match the jewels around her throat. "This is my wife, Isabella. And our children, Dante and Angela."

When she rises to hold out her hand to me, her smile is genuine, although I'm not sure about the hair and eyes. Her face doesn't appear heavily made up, her beauty natural. I'm not surprised. A man like Dom, with his dark good looks, would have a beautiful wife. A trophy on his arm. And a good-looking boy and girl to round off his millionaire family.

"It's lovely to meet you, Mallory. I'm glad to see you liked one of the dresses I picked out for you. I hope you don't mind. I know how hard it is to find the right outfit when you're expecting. You look amazing. And those diamonds are spectacular."

"Thank you. Jake gave them to me a couple of days ago." I smile at my husband. The fake jewels have fooled Isabella. Not everything that glitters is real. It's the thought that counts.

"Jake. Dom has told me so much about you. He has great respect for you." She extends her hand to Jake, who grasps it, saying how nice it is to meet her.

"Thank you for the dresses. That was very considerate of you." My eyes take in the off-the-shoulder emerald dress that hugs her curves, and the well-behaved, cute kids next to her. "And what lovely children you have."

"I'm four," Angela says. "I'm in kindergarten. Dante's six. He's in grade one."

"You're in JK," Dante clarifies. "Still a baby."

"Am not." Angela crosses her arms.

"Are too," Dante insists, sticking out his tongue.

They bicker back and forth several times until Dom puts a stop to it, addressing them with one word, speaking calmly. "Manners."

Isabella's smile widens. "Ah, children. They're such a joy. You must be looking forward to your little one coming soon."

"Yes, we're very excited." I smile at the children, who nudge each other playfully, continuing their argument in silence. Just normal kids.

"Can we go play now?" Dante asks.

"Yes, go on now." Dom excuses them to join their nanny and cousins in the family room, and they dash off.

"They're very excited," Isabella says. "Getting to stay up late and having their cousins stay over."

"If you'll excuse us, my dear, I'd like to introduce Jake and Mallory to the rest of the family, and then you and Mallory can get to know each other." Dom steers us to a group of people standing by the window.

"You know Nick, of course," he says. Nick nods in response. "His girlfriend, Adele. And these are my cousins. Mario, his wife Lena, Aldo, his wife Sofia, Carla and her husband Tony. The rest of our family still lives in the old country."

"Old country?" Jake asks.

"Sicily. Our parents and siblings, aunts, uncles, cousins. Isabella and I visit at least once a year. I came here with my father on a business trip when I was nineteen. He went back home, and I stayed, went to college, got a job, made my own way in the world."

Dom continues escorting us around the room, presenting us to the upper echelon of staff who manage his hotel complex and casino. People continue to stream in, and Dom makes the rounds, welcoming them and introducing us along the way. No one I know. Maybe Jake has met them before; some seem familiar with him. But one couple stands out above the rest when they make their entrance.

A gorgeous redhead in a glittering skin-tight peacock-blue dress with a plunging neckline enters on the arm of a good-looking guy who appears uncomfortable. Whatever unease he feels, she makes up for with her confident stroll into the room full of people.

I tear my eyes away to glance at Jake, his eyes glued to her. And the jealous rage flows through me. Why does my best friend have to be so drop-dead gorgeous? And why does she still get this reaction from my husband?

Chapter Thirty-One

"Well, that's a shocker." I stare at my best friend and his wife, wondering how on earth he got her to agree to come. Then I turn to Mallory. "Did *you* know they were coming?"

Mallory doesn't respond. Something's bothering her. "What is it, hon? What's wrong?"

Dom's eyes are on Vicky as he saunters toward the couple, then escorts them over to us. "How nice your friends could join us, Jake. And I see Jason and Beth have arrived."

My head whips backward, and sure enough, Jason and Beth, all done up to the nines, make their grand entrance. I nudge Mal, whose lips are tight and eyes narrowed. Is she pissed off about something? "See, we know people here. Loosen up. It's not so bad."

Jason and Beth join our group, and Dom suggests we get a drink from the bar while he and Isabella check in with the caterers. A glass of alcohol-free wine in one hand and a scotch in the other, Jason, Craig, and I weave through the crowd back to our wives, who have perched their pregnant selves onto a sectional. Everyone scoots over and squeezes in together, leaving me squished like Play-Doh between Mallory and Vicky. My arm slides over Mallory's shoulder, the glass in my other hand to my mouth, and Mallory tenses.

Between the noise of thirty or more people and the Italian rock music in the background, I have to raise my voice to carry on a conversation. I don't dare turn my head because Vicky and I would be nose to nose. "So, Vicky. I'm surprised to see you here."

She also looks straight ahead. "Dom can be persuasive. And, you know the old saying: Keep your friends close and your enemies closer. I'm not sure which Dom is, but he *did* play a big role in getting you out of trouble this fall."

"And getting him into it." Mallory leans over my lap to talk to Vicky. "But you're right. If you keep people close to you, you know what they're up to. Right, Jake?"

"Right, Mal." Always best to agree with my wife. I down the rest of my glass and extricate myself from this Mallory and Vicky sandwich, choosing a more comfortable position on the arm of the sofa, next to Craig.

"Why do you think we were invited?" Craig scans the room, watching others mingle. "We're not family, not friends, not employees."

"I don't know about the rest of these people, but Dom is a friend."

"I hardly know the guy."

"You're friends by association, I guess. With me."

Craig scratches his head. "Not sure I should be associated with you, much less him."

"Let's just enjoy the free booze. Wanna go for a refill?"

Craig and I grab Jason on our way over to the bar, leaving the sofa to the women. We join a conversation about the wacky weather we've been having. Alfie, or whatever his name is, says we should be in Sicily, where they don't have to put up with this snow shit. "And the scenery there…magnifico."

"So what made you move here, to boring Brampton Heights?" I ask.

He chuckles. "Have you never wanted to get away from your family? See something different in the world? I met my wife here when I was on vacation one summer, trekking across Canada. We're here to stay."

"Yes, Aldo decided to move to Brampton Heights. For me," says his wife, hooking her arm into his. "But we make frequent trips back to see his family. Aldo is a pilot with Italia Airways, so he's back and forth between Canada and Italy all the time."

I've never seen any part of the world other than where I can drive from the Brampton Heights area in a few hours. Except for our honeymoon in Jamaica. Maybe we should go on another trip. I bet Mal would love Sicily. I wonder how hard it is to travel with a baby. Can't be that tough. We could practically put him in a carry-on, just tote him along wherever we go.

"I'll have to suggest a trip to Sicily to my wife." I turn to Jason. "You can afford to go wherever you want, anytime you want. Maybe *you* should go to Sicily."

"We'll be busy with the baby for the next while, so I'm sticking close to home except for a few trips to Kingston to check on the new casino. I want some hands-on experience in the project, even though I'm a silent investor."

"Dom's trying to convince Mario to move there and run things," says the woman attached to Mario. What's her name? Lisa? Lena.

"I think I'm better with the hotel management side of things," he says. "Which leaves you, Tony."

Seems like everyone is turning down the job Dom offered me a few months ago.

"Or me," speaks up the chick with Tony.

"Of course, Carla." The men nod, although I'm sure they're thinking, 'A woman running a casino?'

Dom slips into the group and puts his arm around my shoulder like we're best chums. "Glad to see you guys getting to know the family. Looks like dinner will be served shortly. Buffet-style in the dining hall in a half-hour or so."

He moves to speak with other groups of people scattered throughout the room. We've been here for over an hour, and Mal hasn't tried to drag me out. Looks like we've got a free meal ticket tonight. Wonder what's on the menu.

Craig, who has been silent the whole time, says we'd better get back to our wives to escort them to the dining room. When we get to the sofa where we left them, only two women remain seated.

"Where's Mallory? Bathroom?" I glance toward the wide doorway leading to the hall.

"No, she's in the kitchen with Isabella," Vicky says.

Huh. She's made herself at home.

Chapter Thirty-Two

Isabella fusses in the designer cream-colored kitchen, even though the caterers are in charge of preparing the food. She oversees each dish, checking one oven then the other, stirring pots on the stovetop, observing food chopped and arranged on the dark brown granite counters, and discussing the various dishes. She thanks the head chef, apologizing for intruding on her domain. "I love to cook, and usually I prepare meals for my family. But my husband insists it's too much for me when we have guests. I just like things to be perfect."

Her candor and interactions with the catering staff take me by surprise. She appears so polished and refined, yet here she is in the kitchen chatting with, and assisting, the help. I stopped in after using the bathroom (which I took my time admiring—I have some ideas for our next renovations) and was mesmerized by Isabella interacting with the caterers.

Satisfied when everything is ready to be served, Isabella turns to me. "Do you enjoy cooking, too?"

"I do, but nothing fancy." I can't even name some of the dishes I see being arranged on serving trays. I do recognize various pastas, risotto, seafood, prosciutto, sausages, and vegetable dishes, mixed with indeterminate fare. When the food is wheeled to the dining room, Isabella announces to her guests that dinner is served, and everyone is welcome to make themselves comfortable wherever they wish—in the kitchen as well as the dining and living rooms.

I join Jake and our friends, and we follow others to the dining room where plates are stacked at the head of the large table with the self-serve meal set out on it as well as on top of the dining buffet cabinet.

"Quite the spread," says Jake. "Hope you and the baby are hungry. What is all this stuff, anyway?"

"I'm not sure. Sicilian food, I guess."

We return to our spot, left vacant as though we were expected back. Crammed together on the sofa makes using utensils difficult without jabbing someone in the stomach, but it seems the six of us are most comfortable sticking close together. We're the outsiders here.

But then, Dom and Isabella approach with their dinner plates and sit on the sofa adjacent to us, Nick and his girlfriend following, as though we're part of their clique. Dom addresses us, his eyes on me. "I hope everything is to your satisfaction."

"Delicious," says Jake. The others join him in expressing their approval.

Our conversation revolves around home and family. Vicky compliments Isabella on their lovely home and asks about her decorator. Isabella offers to give a tour of the house when we finish our meal. Beth says she'd love to get some ideas for their new home, which is in its planning stages. When I say it's a beautiful home in which to raise their family, Dom wraps his arm around his wife's waist and speaks of his son and daughter like a normal doting father, telling us about their talents. Dom's pride in his children is evident as he speaks, his smile wide. Piano lessons and drums, art and dance classes, gymnastics and karate, soccer and T-ball—the list goes on. These children have a busier schedule than I do.

Isabella switches the topic to us. "Mallory and Beth, you must be getting excited with your babies due soon. Do you have your nursery ready?"

Ever the gracious hostess, Isabella also draws Vicky and Adele into the conversation. "I hear you just got married. Our Nick and Adele have set a date for this summer. Tell us about your wedding day."

The men join in with an occasional comment or nod as we discuss home decor, babies, and weddings. With the cloth napkin laid out on my lap, I still manage to slop sauce on my chest, leaving tomato smeared on my red dress.

I wave my hand over my front. "Oh no! This is going to stain. I'd better get cold water on it before it sets in." I set my plate on the square stone coffee table and wiggle off the sofa.

Isabella says not to worry; she has done the same many times. She rises and invites me to come with her. I follow the glass staircase to the master bedroom.

"I have something that should work on that sauce." Isabella opens her walk-in closet, exposing racks of designer clothes and dressers. "Here, put this on while we get the stain out."

She hands me a plush white robe and closes the door to allow me privacy. When I hand her the dress, she takes it to the ensuite bathroom where she applies cold water to the red sauce, then treats it with a spot stain remover and blow dries it on the cool setting. "See. I told you I've done this many times."

I don't know if I'm more in awe of her stain-removing skills or her masterpiece of a bathroom, which rivals her bedroom in its magnificence. Adele enters the room with Beth and Vicky, and we continue the tour of the house together. I find myself considering whether I would want to live this kind of life. Beth has found the adjustment from lower middle-class to multi-millionaire status overwhelming. Vicky isn't wealthy, but has a career that puts her in the upper-middle class. Where do I fit in? Just an ordinary working woman, an everyday wife, soon to be a mother. No nanny. No caterers. No mansion. No professional decorators.

Isabella has a perfect life. The perfect home, the perfect husband, the perfect children. It's what I've always wanted. And I have that with Jake, the man I love. Or I imagined I did. But *this* kind of life is one I could get used to. The question is: at what cost?

When we return to the living room, the men, who seem to have been deep in a serious conversation, stop talking and lift themselves off the sofa until we are seated.

"Did you enjoy the house tour?" Dom asks, paying particular attention to my response. "What do you think of our humble home?"

"Absolutely amazing. I love it," I say, with Vicky and Beth expressing a similar sentiment.

At some point, I hope to speak to Isabella in private. To get to know her better. To get a real picture of her life. To see if she's as happy as she pretends to be. To see if she's trapped. To see if this is all a facade.

If it looks too good to be true, it probably is.

Chapter Thirty-Three

With just the men left in our group, we turn to more important topics like the Toronto Maple Leafs' loss to the Philadelphia Flyers, the upcoming Canadian International Car Show, projections for the Toronto Stock Exchange, and dropping interest rates, and how the government sucks, but there are no viable alternatives.

Typical guy talk, except this is my first time shooting the breeze with Dom and Nick in a social situation. Beats the usual intimidation, threats, or sucker punches.

Having come to a resolution about the political state of our country—we need new blood—Dom says he's been thinking of throwing his hat in the ring by running for regional council. "That means I would be very busy were I to get elected. My family is my priority, of course, and I won't take time away from them. I'd like to have things in place should my political aspirations come to fruition. I'm hoping Mario will step up to look after the new Kingston operation, with Jason taking on a more active role than originally expected. Our private copter will ensure that you're back home with your family in the evenings, as we discussed. That will allow you to keep an eye on your investment." Dom turns to Jason for confirmation that he's on board with this increased responsibility, and Jason nods.

My eyes wander around the room, and I imagine myself living like this. Nick shoots me a look to indicate I'd better listen, or he'll reach over and smack me to attention.

"And perhaps Tony and Carla can oversee the hotel end of things here at the River Grand if Mario and Lena move to Kingston. As you know, I've hired new muscle along with a pilot since Adam's…departure. Staffing isn't an issue. The River Grand is one of Brampton Heights' largest employers." Dom pauses.

I pick up the lull in the conversation with a change in topic. Hiring, staffing, employees—not exactly a titillating topic. "This is a great place you've got, Dom. Did you do any of the work on the house yourself, or did you hire out all the renos?"

Nick motions for me to shut up, but Dom goes with the flow. "I hire *everything* out. It gives me more time to enjoy life with my family. Which brings me to your role, Jake."

I gulp. My role? I've already turned down managing the Kingston casino and taking over Adam's role at the River Grand. How many times do I have to say no?

"Nick will be in charge of the entire operation when I'm not available. And I'd like you," his eyes hold mine, "to be second-in-command, working side-by-side with my brother, as we've discussed on numerous occasions. You're the only one who's not blood or married in, or not investing a fortune, but the thing is, I like you, Jake. You're young. I see your potential. I trust you. Like a brother."

I put my hand up to stop him and indicate I've already told him I'm not interested in working for him, with him, or taking charge in any capacity.

That's a bunch of crock. I want this position. Mal *is holding me back.*

"I realize you don't see yourself as ready to take this on, but you'll get hands-on training from myself and Nick. And if you fall out of line, Nick will set you back on track. Isn't that right, Nick?"

Nick nods.

"I appreciate all that, Dom. But I have a respectable position with the Auto Supply Warehouse. And Mallory…"

"Mallory will come around. *This* will be a respectable position. I won't ask anything of you that I wouldn't ask of my own son when he reaches an age to work alongside me in another fifteen to twenty years."

"I'm sure you can find someone better suited for the position. I don't have the exper…"

This time, Dom puts his hand up, and I have the sense to *shut up.* "You know the casino, Jake. Inside and out. As a good customer, as well as a client who has been on the outs. You're a player, and you know the game well. You've had the strength to overcome your addiction, and you've demonstrated responsibility by paying your debts. You're also familiar with my position and role as owner of the entire operation, having frequently found yourself on the opposite side of my desk. I'd say you're already privy to the dealings of my business. The Auto Supply Warehouse has provided you with valuable supervisory experience. Now, it's time to use your skills for something bigger. Time to reap the rewards commensurate with your abilities. How does the title Director of Casino Operations sound? You'll report directly to me, and to Nick in my absence."

It sounds damn good. But Mallory will kill me.

"Like I said, I don't think…"

"I suggest you start thinking. I don't offer these types of opportunities lightly. So decide soon, Jake, my boy. Do you want to be part of the family or not?" Dom turns to Craig. "And, of course, as Jake's right-hand man, we'd offer you a supervisory position. Lower management training for starters, in the casino or elsewhere in the hotel complex, wherever your interests lie."

Craig shakes his head. "I'm more interested in car parts."

"As lucrative as that may be, I can offer better monetary compensation and prestige along with opportunities for advancement."

From the corner of my eye, I notice Mallory in her red dress. Along with the other four women, she reclaims her spot on the sofa.

"What have you men been discussing?" Isabella touches her husband's shoulder. "I hope it wasn't business."

"We were talking about the importance of family, my dear." Dom raises his glass, prompting everyone to join him. "To the family. And to a prosperous new year."

Chapter Thirty-Four

I t's nearly ten o'clock, and I want to suggest we head home, but Jake seems to be enjoying himself, not only with Craig and Jason by his side, but also making the rounds again and chatting with Dom and his family members. He's right at home in this setting, a glass in one hand and gesturing with the other as he talks, a smile pasted on his face and laughter erupting, no doubt stemming from some silly joke he's telling. Once in a while, he checks in my direction to make sure I'm okay, and I smile, not to appease him, because I really am enjoying the evening.

A beautiful home, upbeat Italian rock music, great food, pleasant company, a lit-up winter wonderland through the wall of windows, and a relaxed atmosphere make me forget that not long ago, Dom was a scary entity. Seeing him and his wife play the gracious hosts, welcoming us into their home, his eyes full of love for Isabella and their children, shows me another side of him. I had considered him a thug, a mobster, a criminal, possibly a murderer. Maybe I was wrong.

Vicky and Beth share the sofa with me, immersed in a conversation about the house and ideas for their own upcoming building and renovations, while I observe Isabella floating around the room and engaging with her guests. When Beth pushes herself off the sofa, saying she needs to use the bathroom, I tag along.

"This house is amazing," I say as we walk side by side down the hall.

"It sure beats that crappy little apartment Jason and I called home."

"Would you want to have that back? Not the crappy apartment. The simple life you had before all the money? When it was just the two of you and no money and no business to worry about?" I ask because I know she's had reservations about Jason's involvement in Dom's business, and the money has caused conflict between her and her husband.

Beth takes a deep breath of air and lets it out with a whoosh, hands on her belly. "The money has changed everything overnight. It's a lot for us to deal with. But, honestly? No, I wouldn't go back to our old life. Jason is happier than he's ever been. That makes me happy. And knowing I'll never again have to do other people's makeup makes me even happier. Now, I can do what I *want* to do, not what I have to do. I'm thinking of starting my own cosmetic company once the kids are in school, and Jason's new casino venture gets off the ground."

On our way back to the living area, we encounter Isabella and a small group of children of various ages, along with a woman who I assume is the nanny.

Dom's voice rises above the rest. "Everyone, if we could have your attention."

The room quiets down, and Dom continues. "The children will be saying goodnight before heading off to bed. But first, I promised them we would end the year with fireworks. Come."

He gestures for the children to stand by the windows, makes a call saying it's time to begin, and sets a hand on each of his children's shoulders as they prepare to watch the show.

The interior and exterior lights are extinguished as if by magic. Minutes later, the sky lights up and the children, not to mention adults, gasp and exclaim at the bangs and colorful patterns above the dark lake.

How do I reconcile this considerate and loving family man with the attractive, wealthy casino owner who instills terror with his intimidation of those who don't adhere to his rules? Is this the kind of man Jake wants to become? Is it the kind of man I want him to be? One who runs a tight business and commands respect out of fear, but has a gentler, loving side?

Jake's arm is around me as we enjoy the festive display, the music cranked up. "This is the life, isn't it, Mal?"

I thought the life we had was *the* life, as fraught with disasters as it was.

Our love, our home, our family, our friends, our work, our hobbies. Is Jake not happy with what we have? He is *so* in his element tonight. His admiration for Dom and the life he has built radiates from Jake.

When the show ends, Isabella taps me on the shoulder and asks if I want to accompany her to put the children to bed. "They won't go easily," she laughs.

The nanny gathers the kids and marches them up the glass staircase. She leaves Angela and Dante with Isabella and escorts the others to guest rooms. Following their bedtime routine, Isabella asks me to read tonight's story, then she tucks the children in and plants a goodnight kiss on their foreheads. Soon, I will be doing the same with little Jakey.

Isabella motions for me to join her in the master bedroom. "Dom wanted me to speak with you."

"Oh?'

She closes the door. "He senses that you are against Jake taking Dom up on his offer to work with him at the casino."

This takes me off guard. "I...I'm not sure it's the best move for Jake, with him being a recovering gambler." I don't mention my concerns about the legality of Dom's business policies.

"Dom believes that will make Jake a stronger leader—his connection to the clientele. Do you have doubts about your husband's capabilities?"

"I...no, of course not."

"That's good. Because a woman should stand side by side with her man. That's the only way he can succeed. I can't imagine where men would be without women propping them up. What Dom has achieved and continues to grow is largely because of me. He knows that, but doesn't widely advertise my contributions. Male ego." She tosses back her hair and laughs.

"I didn't know you were involved in the business."

"Very much so. Dom and I are a team. Don't get me wrong. Dom is a self-made man, even though his family money and the funds from my trust fund were used for his start-up. I work behind the scenes mainly, especially since the children were born. The hotel and entertainment complex are of more interest to me, but he keeps me in the loop where the casino—and his other business ventures—are concerned."

"Oh. I didn't know that. I thought Dom was solely in charge."

"In charge, yes. Dom is absolutely in charge. Solely? No. Dom and I rely on our family and their unconditional support in running the business smoothly. Family is everything." She smiles.

"Have you been married for long?"

"Nine years, but we've been together for seventeen. I have known Dom since I was a kid. His parents and mine were friends back home in Sicily. We moved to Canada when I was seven years old. Dom relocated here not long after. I had a silly schoolgirl crush on him, even though he was eleven years older. I knew Dom was my soulmate at a very young age. We started dating when I was sixteen, but Dom insisted we wait till I completed my schooling before getting married. We both have our MBAs."

"Oh, that's so romantic. I didn't meet my soulmate till I was twenty-four."

"A power greater than ourselves decides when these things happen." Her eyes flit to the portraits above their king-size bed. Jesus and Mary flank their framed wedding photo.

"Yes, I suppose so." To say I'm surprised by Isabella and Dom's religious ties would not do justice to the disbelief coursing through me. My own beliefs have been a roller-coaster the last several years, and Jake isn't outwardly religious, though he uses Jesus' name frequently.

"Getting back to business…Dom would like nothing better than to have Jake work with him. But, not without your approval, naturally. And you should know," she says, placing her hand on mine as we sit side by side on the bed, "that Dom doesn't extend these kinds of opportunities frequently or lightly. So I hope we can count on you to support Jake's career advancement."

"Yes, I fully support Jake—"

"Good. I no longer have siblings or cousins in this country. I look forward to sharing a sisterly bond with you, Mallory. Dom speaks so highly of you and Jake. We would love to welcome you to our little family." She startles me with a hug, then rises, taking me by the hand.

When we join the rest of the guests, Jake is off in a corner, deep in conversation with Dom. My husband is a pro at hiding his feelings, but something Dom says concerns him. I know Jake, every twitch and cue that something is off. At the same time, I'm uneasy about my own conversation with Isabella.

Did I just agree to Jake joining forces with Dom?

Chapter Thirty-Five

I let Mal take the wheel. She's in charge. I've had a few too many to drive. She concentrates on the road, and I keep my eyes open as the back-seat driver, but riding shotgun. We don't speak, other than to say we enjoyed the evening.

I mull over what Dom told me when he cornered me on my own. Somehow, he knew all about Mal's visitor last night and how she managed to get him into custody.

"I heard your wife's handy with tools," Dom had chuckled. "I bet that poor guy didn't expect her to be carrying when she opened the door to him. Hammer, box cutter, nail gun? That's one scary woman you married, Jake. Maybe I should hire her as a bouncer at the casino."

By the time we pull into our driveway, it's ticking over to one o'clock in the morning. In the entry of our house, I kiss Mallory. "Happy New Year, honey. I've got a good feeling about this year. It's going to be a lucky one for us with the baby."

The mention of luck brings both Lucky and Nellie to greet us, looking for a midnight snack. "I'll feed them. You go ahead and get into bed. I'll be up in a minute."

A handful of cat treats on the kitchen floor, door locks checked, I climb the stairs. Mallory is still struggling to get out of her dress and asks if I can help with the zipper. I'm more than happy to undress her.

"That was interesting," she says. "Isabella is nice. And the children are lovely."

"You sound surprised."

"I am. It's like a whole other side to Dom's life."

"Yep. I know what you mean." Having eased Mal's dress off, I work on getting out of my monkey suit. She assists with the tie and my belt.

I fall into bed, too tired to brush my teeth. Mal joins me, forgoing removing her makeup. I'm not sure who falls asleep first.

* * *

Mal is the first to wake. She nudges me, saying it's nearly ten o'clock. "We're expected at Gloria and Steve's by noon."

"I'm up." I roll over, hearing myself snore.

The smell of coffee brewing wafts up the stairs. I'm going to need a few gallons to be ready to face Steve playing host in my mom's house. Maybe a couple shots of rum mixed in. I pull on pajama pants and stumble downstairs.

"You're extra tired," Mal says, sitting opposite me at the kitchen table.

I down a cup of coffee and pour another, then pick up a piece of toast with jam. "Hobnobbing with the rich and powerful is exhausting. Not my usual night out."

"You seemed to be enjoying it."

"I was. What about you?"

"Yes, it was fun. But, when I came back downstairs after the children were put to bed, I noticed you were speaking to Dom privately. Did he say something to upset you?"

I suck in a deep breath and let it out. "Yes and no. He didn't upset me, but I was surprised. We're sort of back to square one with that police investigation. And Dom wants it dealt with."

"Oh? What happened? I thought they arrested the man you rescued."

"They didn't. Dom said that according to his sources, the man was released. He had nothing to do with Detective Swarovski's death. He was actually another victim. Only survived because of me. That means the killer is still out there. Dom said I'd better get my shit together and figure out who's dumping bodies on my property."

Mallory shakes her head. "He can't seriously expect you to do that. It's up to the police."

"Dom isn't a big fan of the police, but he did say he's willing to work with all parties involved to resolve the situation. Something else he said is bugging me."

"What's that?"

"Dom said you looked absolutely beautiful, and I was damn lucky to have you for a wife."

"Aww, that's so nice of him."

"Yeah. He also wondered how the hell I could afford those rocks around your neck."

Chapter Thirty-Six

Jake seems lost in his own thoughts as he maneuvers the Honda past snowbanks, eyes on the road. I finger my 'diamonds', which I've chosen to wear again as it's a special occasion, along with the blue dress Dom sent (I mean, really, what other opportunity will I get to wear it). Wouldn't it be nice to have a wardrobe full of designer clothes and places to go?

It's the first day of a new year destined to be wonderful.

When Jake told me about Dom's compliment and his comment about the necklace, I gasped. "He thought they're real?"

"Unless he was mocking me, knowing I can't afford to buy you what you deserve, thinking he can shame me into taking the job he's offering. I explained they were zirconia, handed down from my grandparents, and had sentimental value. He just smirked."

I assured Jake I didn't need 'real' diamonds; I was happy with the zirconia, which matched the bracelet he had given me for my birthday, and besides, there were better uses for money than frivolous jewelry. But I know Dom struck a nerve with Jake, parading his wealth and how much he has been able to provide for Isabella and their children. I haven't told Jake yet about Isabella's trust fund or her role in Dom's success.

I turn to him as he stares out the windshield, his jaw set. "You know I don't need a big fancy house and all that 'stuff', right? I know it's impressive, but Dom and Isabella's life isn't what I want." My words drip with envy, even to my own ears.

Jake adjusts the volume on the car radio, his muttering telling me Dom got under his skin. "Still playing Christmas music, milking it for all it's worth."

Seeing he's not in the mood for communicating our feelings, I relax back onto the headrest and close my eyes. The last thing we need on the first day of a new year is an argument about whether or not Jake should accept Dom's job offer.

When we open the door to Gloria's new home, the smell of home cooking wafts through from the back of the house. As much as Jake refuses to call this Steve's home, the fact is that the money he inherited when his father passed away has paid for it. The modest bungalow they sold held some good memories, but the years of Steve's alcohol addiction and the ensuing abuse he inflicted on his family had seeped into the walls.

"Mallory, how are you and the baby doing?" Gloria greets us in the entryway, sweeps me up in her arms, then pulls away to examine me from head to toe, deciding I'm doing well before I can answer. "I see Jake is taking good care of you. What a gorgeous dress! You're positively sparkly. That's a beautiful necklace and earring set."

Having worked for decades as a nurse, Gloria can spot sickness in people's eyes. "You're looking a bit peaked, though, Jake. Have you been getting enough rest? You'll need all your strength once the baby arrives."

"We're both good, Mom. Just had a late night out ringing in the new year with some friends," Jake says.

He doesn't mention Dom. To keep the peace on this family holiday, it's best to steer the conversation as far from Dom and the casino as possible. Gloria has no use for Dom and his associates, who set Jake on a destructive path, taking advantage of his gambling addiction.

Steve bellows from the kitchen. "Come on in. And shut the door. We're not heating the outside."

Jake narrows his eyes, then turns to press the door completely closed against the draft. The amount of time this takes indicates he's struggling to keep his cool. I follow Gloria into the kitchen, leaving Jake to grit his teeth.

"Mallory, so nice to see you again." Steve closes the oven door and touches his hand to my stomach. "Won't be much longer now."

Whether he's referring to dinner or the baby, I return his smile, though mine isn't totally genuine. The issues my husband has had to cope with are the direct result of his father's failure as a human being. But Gloria says everyone deserves a second chance, an opportunity to make up for things they regret. Because of Gloria, I bite my tongue and give Steve the benefit of the doubt. I only hope he won't disappoint us all. Gloria doesn't deserve any more pain in her life. And it would crush Jake.

"Two more months. And baby Jakey will be here." I don't add that it's round two for Steve and he'd better earn the title of world's best grandfather, or I just might kill him myself before Jake works his way up to it.

I offer to assist in the kitchen, but Gloria says it's all taken care of. "We're having a buffet-style meal. Steve's got the beef tenderloin, roast potatoes, and carrots under control. The salads are in the refrigerator. And I baked a couple of pies and loaves of bread."

Gloria waves toward the kitchen island, where plates, cutlery, and napkins are stacked next to a cutting board, the bread fresh out of the oven. Then she indicates the recliner and tells me to put my feet up.

The ruckus arising from the front hall tells me there won't be much resting happening for the remainder of the afternoon. John and Deb's two young boys bound into the room, nearly knocking over Gloria. "Grandma!"

Steve opens his arms, and they run to him. "Grandpa! Do you have candy?"

Grandpa Steve chuckles and fishes out a couple of snack-size chocolate bars from his pocket. Children don't hold grudges. It's as if Grandpa Steve has always been a part of their lives, not just dropped into their world several months ago.

John, Deb, and Jake spill into the kitchen with as much zip as the boys. Their laughter tells me Jake is putting on his best show, joking about the weather forecasters and their ineptitude.

"Storm of the decade, ha! That was nothing compared to some of the winters on the farm when we were growing up. Remember walking on the banks, the power wires within reach? It's a wonder we survived." Jake's chuckles come to an abrupt stop when his eyes take in the boys clambering up Steve's legs, begging for more candy.

"Sorry, boys, don't want to spoil your lunch. But there's ice cream and pie later." Steve scoops up one, then the other, and spins them around.

Deb, John, and Jake sink into the sofa, with Steve and Gloria on the loveseat, while the three and four year old boys head to the toy chest in the corner and pull out their vehicles. Their 'vroom vroom' and 'beep beep' occupy the space left quiet by the adults.

Deb breaks the silence. "It looks like you still have lots of unpacking to do. Maybe we could help after lunch."

"No, no," Gloria waves away Deb's offer. "I know it's a mess, but we'll have plenty of time this winter to settle in. Today is about family. I dug out a couple of games from when John and Jake were little so the boys can join in."

"Those were the good old days, playing Hungry Hippos and Kerplunk," Steve reminisces. "Do you boys remember Trouble? You loved popping the dice."

"I remember plenty of trouble," Jake responds.

Deb nudges him. "Jake…"

Jake plops onto the area carpet, joining the boys in a car race, adding a few 'vrooms' of his own punctuated by a 'wee woo wee woo' as his police car catches up with a speeder. "Pull over to the side of the road. You are under arrest for driving too fast," Jake jokes.

"Speaking of arrest, what's new with that situation in your back cornfield?" Steve leans forward, oblivious to the fact that Jake is doing his best not to kick him out of his own house.

The timer dings, signaling a postponement of the conversation. Steve rises to remove the food from the oven while Gloria sets the salads on the counter.

It's a first. The first day of a new year. The first time in years that Steve has celebrated this day with his family. Seeing Steve lay his filled plate on the dinette, Jake opts to dine on the sofa. John, Deb, and I follow Jake, leaving Gloria with Steve and their grandsons.

"You know what we should do next Christmas?" Jake turns to his brother. "We'll take the kids on the snow hill out by the barn. Remember how

Grandpa used to plow a path from the house to the barn and over to the hill? We'd spend hours out by the barn, then head back to the house for Grandma's hot cocoa and homemade chocolate chip cookies."

"The kids would love that," John agrees.

Jake nods, stuffs his mouth with tenderloin, and avoids glancing over in Steve's direction. No mention of the body in the cornfield or what he found in the barn. I know it's tough on Jake. New house replacing his childhood home. Steve, playing the role of loving dad and grandpa. As if he could erase Jake and John's childhood trauma.

"Oh!" I cry out and rub my belly. "The baby's kicking. I think Jakey wants to let us know he's here, too."

Jake's mouth turns up, and it's genuine this time. No jokes, no fake smile, no pretending he's happy. His eyes meet mine as our fingers entwine.

The past doesn't rule our present. The future is ours.

Chapter Thirty-Seven

I f it weren't for Steve, this would be a great family day. Although I've got to admit the roast was done to perfection. Which, according to Mom, was Steve's doing. The boys' attention span makes short work out of the games, and before long, we're onto Scrabble for the adults while the kids run circles around us, high as kites on the ice cream and additional candy 'Grandpa' has pumped into them. Deb's as tolerant as any woman can be, gotta hand that to her.

Mom suggests we should stay overnight and make a fresh start home in the daylight. "I shoved aside the boxes in the bedrooms to make space for everyone. I'm sorry for the mess, but you should be able to get in and out of bed. And the bathroom's not in too bad a shape."

Three extra bedrooms (just in case everyone stays over sometimes), Mom had insisted when they were house shopping. So here we go, one day out of the year, our rooms ready for us as though we live here. Deb has brought along pajamas for the kids, anticipating a sleepover. Mom offers Mal one of her oversized nightgowns so she can get out of the fancy dress she chose to wear.

As Steve flips through the family movie selection on the big screen, I ask Mom if I can speak to her for a few minutes. If she knew Grandpa's secret, Mom's got some explaining to do. If not, she's in for the shock of a lifetime.

"I have something for you. Happy New Year." I pull the gold necklace from my pocket and hand it to her.

She holds the gold chain in her palm. "Oh, Jake, it's beautiful. Thank you."

"Thank Grandpa. He left some jewelry in the cupboard in the barn. I guess he didn't get around to gifting it before he died."

Mom tenses, her smile dissipating.

"Sorry, I didn't mean to upset you. I know you still miss them."

It's been eight years since he passed away, with Grandma following the year after he was gone. I've heard of this before—couples who die within a short time of each other, not able to live without their soulmate. Mallory and I will be the same. We won't survive without each other.

Mom hands me the necklace and turns around, asking me to help with the clasp. "I do miss my parents. But we have so much to look forward to with the next generation. Is the barn where Mallory's new necklace and earrings came from?"

"Yes, I hope you're okay with that. I know the jewelry was meant for Grandma and you."

"I can't believe he left a stash behind. I guess it wasn't worth much to him. Nor were we." She faces me, moistness seeping into her eyes.

I haven't a clue what she means by that. It's not like he died intentionally and left them behind (not just the jewels, but his wife and daughters). The man had a heart attack.

"Thank you," Mom says again. "A gift from my dad and my son. I'll treasure it. And of course, Mallory should have the diamonds. It's all yours now, Jake. Yours and Mallory's. The house, the farm, the barn, anything that came with it." She pauses before adding, "Did you happen to find anything else in the barn?"

I can't tell her what I found now. Not when she's so emotional. "Our old toboggans. That's why we were out on the hill when we bumped into Detective Swarovski. Otherwise, he'd be out there till spring when the corn gets planted."

It's the first time I've mentioned the body in the cornfield to Mom. Not something you want to discuss with your mother. She draws in a long breath and breathes it out as though she's practicing a relaxation technique. "Mallory told me all about it. I can't believe this is happening. Again."

Again. Neither can I. How the hell do bodies keep turning up in my cornfield?

"Is it Dom?" Mom whispers, as if afraid to say his name in case he might hear.

"No, Mom. It's nothing to do with Dom." Just in case her mind goes there, I add, "Or me."

"The detective who arrested you for murder a few months ago was found dead on your property, and it's nothing to do with you?"

I shrug.

"And there was nothing else found on your property?"

This is definitely not the time to tell Mom about Grandpa's little secret. She's got enough on her plate with a son who attracts murder victims and a reminder that her parents are gone. I shake my head and suggest we get back to the family room before we miss out on the start of the movie.

Steve spies the gold around Mom's neck. "I see you've been flying through your share of my dad's inheritance. You'd think you would have learned that money doesn't grow on trees. Sounds like you're back to your old ways of blowing through money. If you're smart, you'll invest the rest of my dad's hard-earned money for your family's future."

Mom shoots him a look to shut him up. "It was very thoughtful of Jake to give us something nice to start off the new year. Thank you, Son."

"Better jewelry for your mom and wife than gambling it away, I suppose." Steve's face falls, telling me he wasn't thoughtful enough to give his wife a New Year's gift.

Score one for me. And it didn't cost me a cent. Neither Mallory nor Mom nor I mention that they're costume jewelry Grandpa found at an estate sale.

Deb admires the gold and diamonds, her eyes widening. "Wow, are these real, Jake?"

Shit! I left out my sister-in-law.

I fumble in my pocket and pull out the gold bracelet I'd considered giving to Mom, along with the necklace, and hand it to Deb. "I thought all the women in the family should have something new and shiny to make a bright start to the new year."

Her jaw drops. John thanks me and clasps it onto his wife's wrist. "Thanks, but it wasn't necessary," he says.

I can't keep lying. "Actually, it's not just from me. It belongs to all of us.

Gifts from Grandpa."

Once the kids are settled in front of the TV to watch a Christmas movie, I motion for the adults to head over to the dinette table. And I confess the truth about what I found in the barn and in the field. No more secrets. No more lies.

Except for the photographs.

Chapter Thirty-Eight

"I'm glad you told your family the truth. They deserve to know."

I respect this new Jake, open and honest. I would have expected him to confide in Gloria, but to tell everyone, especially Steve, is groundbreaking. He's learning to trust in his family. Of course, he didn't tell them everything. But some things are meant to be kept secret.

"They'll find out soon enough anyway, once the gold tarnishes, that it's not real, and I'm not as generous with my money as they thought. And now they won't toss it, knowing it's a keepsake from Grandpa. It seemed like the right thing to do."

Jake doing the right thing isn't shocking. He's a good man. One who has had a history of glossing over the truth with whatever suits his purpose. A man with a side to him he would prefer to keep hidden because it's not pretty. But deep down, he has a heart of gold. You just have to dig down far enough to mine it.

"And it's good you were able to talk openly about Detective Swarovski and tell them that the suspect was released. It was kind of the hidden elephant in the room until you brought it up."

"Yeah, you're right. It's best to talk about things, get them out into the open."

I don't mention the photos Jake found. I know he didn't tell Gloria.

We're against the wall, tucked into the double-sized bed with boxes piled at the footboard, next to the headboard, and flowing out of the open closet. As Gloria promised, a path to the door and access to the bathroom has been cleared. I roll off the bed to make my second trip to the toilet since we settled in.

As I tiptoe across the hall, the glow from the nightlight guiding my way past the kids' room, I hear John and Deb arguing. Once I realize they're talking about Jake, I move closer to their door and listen.

"You can't seriously believe that story Jake made up about your grandpa leaving a pile of jewelry in the barn. Didn't you wonder why he only mentioned that after Steve lambasted him for spending money?"

"Grandpa used to hide gifts all the time. Jake and I would find stuff when we were kids, goofing around in the barn. Why would he lie about it now?"

"Because he's gambling and had a big windfall but doesn't want Mallory to know yet? And he's trying to butter her up with diamonds? And he thought it would be a good idea to bribe his mom and sister-in-law and keep himself on our good side?"

"Jake wouldn't do that. He's not gambling, and he's not bribing anyone."

"Just like he has nothing to do with that detective's death?"

Silence follows Deb's accusation.

John swings open the bedroom door, pillow and blanket in hand, and comes face-to-face with me. "Mallory. Did we wake you? Sorry if we were too loud."

He sidesteps me and makes his way toward the family room sofa. Deb exits the bedroom in an attempt to stop him at the same time Jake steps out of our room, wondering what's taking me so long in the bathroom.

"We had a fight," Deb says. "About you."

"Me? What did I do now?" Jake throws his hands up in the air, his raised voice eliciting a 'shhh' from Deb.

Deb heads down the hall. I follow, and Jake tags along, muttering, "What? What?"

John lies on the sofa, his shape visible with the glow coming through the window. He sits up, asking what we're doing.

"What are *you* doing?" Jake demands. "Arguing about me? What the hell did I do? I played with your kids, brought your wife a gift, and kept the peace with Steve."

"Keep your voice down," Deb warns.

"Keep my voice down? Who are *you* to tell me to shut up? This is my mother's house."

Steve rushes out of the master suite adjacent to the family room, flips the light switch, and glares at Jake. "What's going on here? Jake?"

"That's right. Blame me."

Oh, boy.

It was too much to hope for Jake to get through an entire day and night with his family assembled in Steve's house. Christmas was different. Jake ruled the roost at our farmhouse.

But Gloria joins us, making it clear who is really in charge here. "Steve! Jake! Sit down."

John gathers up his blanket, making room for Steve and Jake, who do as Gloria asks. Deb and I sit on the loveseat while Gloria remains standing, her eyes flitting between all of us.

"Who wants to explain what's happening here?" Gloria turns to John. "Maybe you can tell me why you're sleeping on the sofa."

"Jake started it. He barged in here, hollering at me and Deb."

"*I* started it? I was in my room. You two woke Mallory with your arguing." Jake motions to Deb. "About me, for some reason. What the fu—?"

Steve doesn't make the situation any better. "Keep a lid on that temper of yours, Son."

Jake rises, but plops back onto the sofa when Gloria holds up her hand. "I don't care who started it. It's going to end now. What's this about, John?"

Gloria crosses her arms, waiting for an answer. John relays his wife's comments about Jake, saying he doesn't for one minute believe that Jake is gambling or making up stories about where the jewelry came from. He's one hundred percent behind his brother. All eyes turn to Deb, who squirms uncomfortably next to me.

"Well...I just wondered...you know I love you, Jake. And it's out of love and concern that I'm questioning what's going on with you. The jewelry, the detective found on your property. I'm worried you might be involved in something again with Dom and the casino and your..." Deb trails off, turning to me for confirmation that Jake is in trouble with gambling and loan shark borrowing, as per his usual.

"Jake isn't gambling. He's not involved with Dom or the casino. And he found the jewelry in the barn." Two truths and a lie.

Gloria takes me at my word and shakes her head at her other daughter-in-law. "I appreciate your concern for Jake, Deb, but are you suggesting he might have something to do with the detective's death?"

"Of course not." Deb shrivels into the sofa, outnumbered, and I sense she wishes she had kept her concerns to herself. "I'm sorry. Like I said, I'm worried. Thank you for the bracelet, Jake. I didn't mean to imply you were up to no good."

"It's fine. Apology accepted. I understand. I don't exactly have a great track record." Jake's magnanimity comes as no surprise. He really does like Deb.

As long as Steve keeps quiet, Jake will leave it at that and allow us to all get some sleep. I yawn, hoping they'll get the hint. Unfortunately, Steve doesn't have the sense to put the topic to rest.

"Your track record does leave a lot to be desired, Son. It's not the first time you've stumbled upon a body. If you've had a relapse or gotten yourself into a situation, you need to be straight with us. We're here for you."

You'd think Steve had said something hilarious. Jake roars, slapping his knee, shaking his head. "Wow. That's rich, *Dad*. *I've* got a bad track record. And *you're* here for me."

John places a hand on his brother's shoulder. "We're on your side, Jake. We know you had nothing to do with that cop's death. And if you say you're done with Dom and the casino, that's good enough for me."

Gloria nods. "And just so you know, Deb, what Jake said about the jewelry is true. My dad was a collector. He loved antiquing and going to garage and auction sales." She turns to Jake. " It's beautiful. Thank you. Whether it's real or not, it's a treasure."

One more glare that could kill directed at Steve, Jake says, "If we're done with the accusations, let's get back to bed before we wake the boys."

A blow-up diffused, Jake manages to remain calm. His family is more important to him than his animosity toward Steve. This is the man I love.

The boy Gloria has raised. The brother who has a bond with his sibling. This is the man Jake truly is.

But in the light of the early morning, the boys rousing us from sleeping in, doubt seeps into the family room where we gather for a big breakfast. Morning television grabs our attention as the news anchor reports last night's crime.

"The first murder of the year in Brampton Heights is being investigated in connection with a robbery. Business owner, Leonardo Zervos, was found in his living room, a single bullet through the head, following a break-in at his home. His wife, Tiffany Zervos, was asleep in the upstairs master suite at the time of the murder. Police are stressing that there is no danger to the public. Zervos' store, *Tiffany's Jewels,* was also the target of a break-and-enter during the night. No signs of forced entry were found. The alarm had been disabled. Over eight million dollars in jewelry was taken. Police are labelling it as a professional heist. This follows a series of smash-and-grab jewelry store thefts over the last year. Anyone with information should contact their local police station."

The clatter of forks and knives stops, our meal interrupted as mouths gape open and brows furrow. All eyes tilt toward Jake.

Steve utters the first word. "Jesus."

Chapter Thirty-Nine

If Steve could keep his trap shut, we'd be able to enjoy the pancakes, bacon, and eggs Mom prepared. Then we'd all head home with a warm, fuzzy feeling. For Mal's sake, for Mom's sake, for John, and for his family, I've put up with Steve. Keeping my anger under control is tantamount to trying to stamp out a forest fire. No chance of it fizzling out if Steve keeps throwing fuel onto the flames.

"This has Dom written all over it," he declares, as if he knows Dom intimately.

I stand up for the man who has treated me with more respect than my biological father, who thinks he should be forgiven because he's sorry for his abusive behavior.

"Why the fu…" I rethink my response, seeing the boys whip their heads in my direction. I know they've heard colorful language before. Having it come out of their Uncle Jake's mouth isn't an image I want stuck in their heads.

"What makes you think Dom would be involved?" I keep my voice calm, my eyes flashing resentment toward my so-called father.

"Anything that happens in Brampton Heights revolves around Dom. His hotel complex, *especially* the casino, his money—everyone knows he runs this city. Got half the politicians and cops in his back pocket. The other half are too scared to question his business practices because he employs *half* the city and brings in a shitload of tax revenue." Steve picks up his fork, waves it in the air to emphasize his point, and resumes shoveling in pancakes.

Even I know that's not true. Sure, Dom's got money and some clout. His way of running a business may not be entirely legal. That doesn't mean he's behind everything rotten in the city.

"Dom runs a respectable business. Hotel, entertainment, casino, personal financing. He's got his hands full without robbing jewelry stores and killing their owners." I don't bring up the marijuana grow op, and God knows what else Dom does as a sideline.

"It's not what Dom does or doesn't do that concerns me. It's whether you're still involved with a criminal. No son of mine is going to prison. Take my word for it—it's not something you want to experience. And if you got dragged into some scheme of Dom's again, we're here to help you get out."

I push back my chair and stand, hands clenched around the table to keep myself from lunging at him. "I don't need your, excuse my language, friggin' help. And if I ever do need help, you'll be the last person I'll come to, *Dad.*"

Mal's elbow to my gut rivals the memory of Nick's kicks to the shin in pain intensity, causing me to double over and sit. "What Jake means is he appreciates everyone's concern, and he doesn't want to be a bother to his family, but he is in no way involved with Dom, or the casino, or Detective Swarovski's tragic death. Jake feels terrible about it. He wishes he could have saved him, too."

"No one's blaming Jake," Mom says. "He's a hero. And we're all proud of him. The food's getting cold. Eat."

My appetite is gone, but like everyone else at the table, I pick up my fork and do as I'm told. Mom changes the TV channel to a Christmas movie so we can watch the happy family on the screen, putting an end to further conversation about me.

Breakfast over, Steve clears the table and fills the dishwasher. As he collects my plate, the man has the nerve to put his hand on my shoulder and squeeze it. "I *am* proud of you, Son. Don't doubt that for one minute."

I contemplate grabbing the knife from my plate and stabbing him—nothing fatal, just an accidental nick to inflict pain—but he chokes up with his next words. "You're more of a man than I ever was. I'm proud of all my boys."

Mom steps in between us, further squashing my stabbing fantasy. "Steve, why don't you take the boys out and pull them around on the sled? I'll finish tidying the kitchen."

Good move, Mom. Get Steve out of my way before I kill him.

Deb and John bundle up their boys in puffy snowsuits, hats, and hoods pulled over their foreheads, scarves wrapped around their necks past their noses. No one would be able to identify them if it weren't for their eye color, three-foot stature, and wobbly gait. I'd tell them not to rob any jewelry stores, but Steve wouldn't get it.

Once they're out the door, Mom tells me she'd like to speak with me in private. Great. Steve gets to go out and play while I get a talking-to from my mother.

She leads the way down the hall to 'my' bedroom, leaving the others to watch TV, and we sit side by side on the bed. "Is there something bothering you, Jake?"

I won't spoil Mom's day, her hopes for the new year, her dream of a perfect ever after with Steve. Or her memory of her beloved father.

"It's just this thing with the detective and knowing there's a killer out there. I'm sure the police will figure it out." Partly what's bugging me, but not all of it.

"I know it's hard for you, having Steve back in our lives."

Understatement of the century.

"But at least he had the courage to come back and apologize and try to make things right," Mom continues.

Lips pressed together, I fight the impulse to break her bubble by voicing my opinion of Steve trying to make things right. Six months back, after a twelve-year absence. How long can he put up a front, pretending to be a reformed man? I've spent the last five months doing my best to be the husband Mallory deserves. Fighting my gambling addiction, staying out of debt, keeping a handle on my jealousy, no more secrets from my wife, keeping my cool. I'll spend the rest of my life doing my damndest to be a good husband and father. I won't be the man my biological father was and will be again, given time.

"He hasn't had a drink in over a decade."

I guess that excuses all the DUI charges and scaring us half to death as we sat in the back seat and the car wove back and forth between lanes, Steve refusing to let Mom take the wheel.

"And he hasn't shown any signs of depression or violence."

Let's give him a medal, then.

Has she forgotten how he used to smack her when she suggested he didn't need another drink? How he gave John and me 'a good spanking' when we dared talk back to him? How he cried and promised 'never again' once he sobered up?

John and I never blamed Mom for any of it. She protected us the best she could. But in spite of my counselor explaining that women stay in abusive marriages for a myriad of reasons, and they're the victims, I can't for the life of me begin to understand what the hell she's thinking, letting him back into her life.

"Why, Mom? Why would you take him back? You know he's no good and never will be. It's just a matter of time till he shows his true self. Must be hard on him putting on a show about how sorry he is."

A heavy sigh as her body trembles makes me regret my words. "Oh, Jake. You don't remember the good times. Before he fell into a deep depression and the alcohol changed him. Maybe I should have left him when it started."

"Maybe you should have."

Mom wrings her hands, and I worry she's about to break down and sob. Mom is a strong woman. She's endured more hardship than most people. But she wasn't strong enough to leave her husband. Not until I made it clear his staying was no longer an option.

"How can I explain? I don't know if I understand myself. I love him. We were happy. I kept hoping that we'd get that back. I thought I could help him if I loved him enough and stood behind him through it all. I didn't want to raise my children without their father."

"Humph. We'd have been better off." My hand goes to my mouth, too late to stop the words.

"You're right. And I'm sorry I didn't make better decisions then. But *I'm* not better off without him."

My turn for a deep sigh that shakes the bed. Now that John and I have families of our own, the chances of me successfully kicking Steve out of Mom's life are nil. "You're old enough to do what you want, Mom. I just hope Steve doesn't make you regret giving him a second chance."

I lift myself off the bed, but Mom pulls me back down. "There's something else I want to talk to you about. You and John. But I want you to hear it first. It's about my own father. And I expect you might already know. If you found the jewelry, you must have found the photographs."

Chapter Forty

Whatever Gloria said to Jake, it hasn't improved his mood any. The anger has dissipated, turned into something morose. Jake forgoes sitting next to me on the loveseat, choosing the recliner instead. Gloria joins Deb and John on the sofa, her eyes on Jake as he stares out the window, thumb and forefinger supporting his chin. Steve heaves the rope attached to the sled, transporting his grandsons across the back yard. I can't read Jake's mind. Gloria rubs her arms as if to warm herself, biting her lower lip, opening her mouth occasionally, but saying nothing. The movie plays in the background. John's eyes, along with Deb's, flit back and forth between Jake and the TV.

No one speaks. My phone rings, interrupting the awkward silence. I don't recognize the caller and answer with a hesitant, "Hello?"

"Mallory? It's Isabella. I just wanted to thank you for joining us to celebrate the new year. It meant so much to both Dom and myself. We hope to have you visit again soon, maybe after the little one arrives. I would love to host a baby shower for you."

I don't know how to respond. I expected a baby shower at some point (maybe Gloria, or my aunt, or Vicky would organize something). But this woman I just met leaves me grasping for words. Why would she do this for me?

"Perhaps I'm being a bit too presumptuous."

I recover from my shock. "That is so thoughtful of you, but really, it's not necessary."

Jake looks in my direction, eyebrows raised. I wave my hand to let him know it's all good, mouth 'excuse me' to everyone, and head to the living room to continue the conversation in private.

"Perhaps we could go on a shopping trip together, then. My treat. Wouldn't that be fun? It's been a while since I've had the pleasure of splurging on cute little baby stuff. There are so many things a new infant needs, especially when it's your first. We can make a day of it."

I don't want to be rude, but I don't know how to respond. "Yes, that would be fun."

"I'll let you check your schedule and get back to you in a few days so we can set up a date, and I'll have my driver pick you up. By the way, I just want to say again how happy I am at the prospect of you and Jake working with us. I hope we can make it official soon."

I bite my lower lip. The thought of living a lifestyle free from financial strain is alluring. And the benefits… My mind drifts to Isabella's home, that dream kitchen and all that space for relaxation and entertainment, not to mention the gorgeous bathrooms and her closet full of designer clothes. I won't allow myself to succumb to envy. Jake and I have a beautiful home and everything we need. But I *do* want the best for our kids.

"Mallory? Are you still there?"

I realize I've been daydreaming for more than a few seconds. "Yes, sorry. It's just that I have a few concerns about Jake working at the casino."

"Oh? Such as?"

"I…um…well, Jake wouldn't want to do anything that might get him in trouble."

"Trouble? What sort of trouble?" Isabella's tone indicates she has no idea what I'm talking about.

I spell it out. "Any sort that is not in accordance with the law."

Isabella hesitates before answering. "Dom is well-connected and well-aware of the law. He operates his business within those laws and is very careful to distance himself from unscrupulous activity. You must know that Dom would never ask Jake to do anything beyond his level of comfort. He looks out for his family and friends."

What about those who cross him?

"Dom can be…intimidating." To put it mildly. "I worry about the stress that could put on Jake's shoulders."

Isabella's laughter tickles my ear, the sound ending with a sigh. "Yes, I suppose he can come across as a bit formidable. Part of the job, I suppose, and part of how he was raised. Dom doesn't let people walk all over him." Her last sentence is set apart from the rest and spoken with a seriousness that requires no elaboration of the fact.

A brief pause in the conversation, and Isabella continues. "I'll let you in on a little secret, since you and I are destined to be good friends. Dom is no pushover. But underneath that tough guy exterior is a cuddly puppy dog." She laughs again, and I imagine her tossing her hair back. "Just don't tell him I told you that. Dom likes to come across as a macho man."

I break off the call, saying I look forward to getting together soon, but right now I have to get back to Jake and my in-laws.

"Of course, Mallory. Family is everything. Talk soon."

I return to my quiet family and stare out the window with them. It's a relief when the boys bound in, giggling about how Grandpa fell down. Steve follows them, brushing snow from his coat and pants.

"I would have gone another few times around the house, but the boys got tired," he says. "I think they need a nap. Maybe I'll join them."

My thoughts go to Baby Jakey and whether his father will allow him to play in the snow with his grandfather. Or anywhere, any time, ever. Sadness flows through me (maybe it's contagious—wafting over from Jake) at the thought that our children won't have a good relationship with their grandpa.

Sensing Jake would rather be anywhere but here, I suggest it's time to go. "Jake and I should be heading out soon. I thought we could do some shopping for the baby while we're in the city. And I'd like to get home before dark."

Jake finally speaks. "Right. Good idea, Mal."

He thanks Gloria for everything, tells John and Deb it was nice seeing them, gives the boys a hug and twirls them in the air, and even nods at Steve. I repeat his sentiments, leaving out hoisting the kids in the air.

Cruising down the street toward the intersection, I ask Jake if something is bothering him.

"Nope. All good, hon. Where do you want to shop?"

"The mall's good."

We drive in silence for ten minutes, snow starting to fall, melting as it hits the salted streets, and traffic zips along. Jake makes an abrupt stop as we cruise by the park and pulls over to the side.

"Why are we stopping?" I ask. "The nightly Christmas light show doesn't start until evening."

He exits the Honda, crosses the sidewalk, strolls over to the snowman structure near the entrance, and pelts it with snowballs. Once he exhausts himself, Jake brushes off his gloves and returns to his seat.

"Everything okay?" I ask as he secures his seatbelt.

"All good. Why?"

"Were you angry with the snowman?"

"Just had some excess energy to burn off. Let's go shop."

I know it's a mistake, but I ask anyway. "What did Gloria want to talk to you about?"

"Grandpa. The photos. His secret."

"She knew?" My mouth flies open. "And she never said anything about it?"

"She knew all right. And more."

"More?"

"You won't believe it." Jake says he'll tell me the whole story later, but there's one thing I should know.

The secrets families keep.

Unbelievable.

Chapter Forty-One

I thought my family was fucked up. So was Mom's. History repeats itself.

I knew something was wrong when I found those photos. But they only show half of the story. Mom said she had wanted to tell me and John, but Grandma told her there was no point. So she kept quiet all these years.

"Tell me, Jake, what do you think is worse?" Mom's words spin round and round in my head. "Staying in a marriage with an abusive drunk you love, or doing what my dad did: living a lie and denying yourself true love because you don't have the guts to leave a marriage? Because I don't know. I just don't know."

Well, I *do* know. Mallory and I won't fall into either of those traps. Living with abuse, living without love, too afraid to do anything about it. I shift the car into park and glance at Mallory. My sweet, beautiful wife.

"Here we are. Where do you want to shop first? Clothes, toys, baby gear, nursery?"

"Are you sure you're up for shopping?"

Nothing is more important than my family. "I'm good. Let's go spend some cash on Jakey."

In the mall, Mallory makes a beeline for the kids' clothing shop. She flips through racks of sleepers while I check out the 'big boy' clothes. Jeans, T-shirts, button-down shirts. I pick out a couple of cool outfits he'll fit into by summer or fall and add a pack of socks and a pair of shoes in corresponding sizes.

"Aww, that's so cute," Mallory coos when I show her. She holds up a bunch of sleepers, a cozy sleep bag, and a pack of onesies. "What about these? And I was thinking maybe a snowsuit, but winter will be almost over by the time he's born. Unless he's early."

As we're discussing Jakey's wardrobe and oohing and ahhing, I spot someone familiar-looking walking by the mall entrance. Setting my stuff on the counter, I tell Mal I'll be back in a minute.

I follow the man down a couple of storefronts, about to call out to him, but I could be wrong. Maybe it's just someone who looks like him. He stops in front of a jewelry store, takes in the window display, and enters the shop, with me on his tail.

A clerk asks if he needs assistance as he examines the diamond rings under the glass.

"May I see this one? I'm looking for something special for my girlfriend. Soon to be my wife, I hope."

Girlfriend? I thought this guy had *a wife.*

And a rush of emotion floods through me as I recall the moment I saw the photos in the barn. Inside the box were a couple of old albums. Wedding pictures of Grandpa and his wife filled the pages. The second album contained more photos—Grandpa and his wife and their new baby. The baby grew into a five-or six-year-old kid. Loads more loose photos sat under the albums. School pics, family holidays, graduation.

Craig asked why Grandpa kept the photos in the barn. I shrugged and closed the albums. I had no response.

Because Grandpa's wife and child are not my grandma and my mom.

The guy ahead of me thanks the jeweler and says he'll have to give it some more thought. When he turns around, recognition sparks in his eyes as he notices me. "Excuse me," he says, lowering his head and trying to circumvent me.

"Dave?"

He shakes his head, keeps moving toward the exit. I call his name again. He quickens his pace.

"Dave? It's Jake." I jog after him, passing the kids' clothing store where I see Mallory piling up another armful of baby essentials on the sales counter.

Has this guy got amnesia, too?

Dave stops abruptly.

"Jake Shelton. You were at my farmhouse when your truck got stuck in the snowstorm," I remind him.

Dave turns around. "Jake. Right. Nice to see you. Sorry. I'm kind of in a hurry here."

"No problem. I just thought I'd say hi."

"Yeah. Hi. Thanks again for your help that night. Appreciate it. Well, gotta run." He walks away.

Back at the kids' store, Mallory is paying for her purchases. "Where did you go?"

I tell her about my strange encounter with Dave. "Not a real social guy. Practically ignored me. You'd think he'd be more grateful after what we did for him."

"Shouldn't you call the police?"

"Because he's unfriendly?"

"No, silly. Because they might want to question him since he was at our house the night before you found Detective Swarovski. In case he saw something?"

"Be right back. I'll meet you out there." I point to the leatherette benches arranged in the mall, just outside the store entrance, before taking off in the direction Dave was heading.

Working my way through shoppers still looking for post-holiday sales, turning my head from side to side, I scan the crowd and the stores. No telling how far he's gotten. When the corridor ends, I know I've lost him. Right, left, or straight ahead to the department store?

On my way back to meet up with Mallory, a mix of scents wafts into my nostrils, pulling me in to purchase some half-price body wash, soaps, and candles for Mallory. Carrying my shopping bag full of fragrances out of the store, I spy Dave in a different jewelry shop across the concourse. This time, I hang back, watching from outside the scent store. I pull out my phone, search for the Brampton Heights Police phone number, and report that I have information in the Detective Swarovski case.

No sooner do I hang up than Dave exits the jewelry store. Deciding I need to keep him here till the police show up to question him, I call out, "Hey, Dave! Any luck finding the right ring for your girlfriend?"

His head swivels around, and his eyes pop.

"It's me, Jake." As though he might have forgotten.

"I know who you are. Look, I appreciate your wife taking me in and you helping me get out of that snowdrift." He removes a couple of twenty-dollar bills from his wallet. "I guess I owe you for your trouble."

I wave the money away. "You don't owe us anything. But if you want to buy coffee and tea for the two of us, you can thank Mallory yourself. I know it would mean a lot to her."

His eyes dart left to right. "Sorry, like I said, I'm in a hurry. Maybe another time."

He takes off again, with me shouting, "I didn't catch your last name."

Short of stalking the man, there's nothing I can do. Maybe there's another way to get his contact information. And beat the police to it.

At the counter of the jewelry store, I inquire about the man who was looking at some items in the case. The clerk is useless.

"I'm sorry, Sir. We can't divulge information about our customers," she says.

"Did he pick out a diamond for my sister? He's planning on popping the question tonight, but he's been having a hard time finding the right ring. I hope you had what he wanted."

Her mouth flies open, then she purses her lips. "Tell your sister to dump his sorry ass. He's looking for a diamond pendant for his wife to celebrate their twentieth anniversary."

My hand flies to my mouth. "What? That two-timing scumbag!"

I thank the woman for saving my sister from a lying, cheating, good-for-nothing womanizer and head back to Mallory, who sits on a bench with four large shopping bags next to her.

"I called the police. But I doubt Dave's sticking around. Something about him isn't adding up."

Worst-case scenario: he's avoiding me because he's got something to do with the detective's murder. At the very least, he's about to become a bigamist.

Just like my grandfather.

Chapter Forty-Two

Waiting for the police. The story of my life.

Jake says they should have been here by now. People pass through the mall concourse, gaze into store windows, and chatter to their friends. Jake swivels his head from left to right and back.

"I found some really cute things." I pull out a sleeper with a barn and farm animals, and Jake smiles, his eyes twinkling.

When I show him the sleeper that says 'My Daddy is the best', the bliss fades, replaced by doubt in his expression.

"I hope I live up to your expectations, Mallory. I know I haven't been the greatest husband. I want to be the best father to our kids. I really do."

"You will be."

He grasps my hand. "I can't promise I'll be perfect. But I *will* do my best."

Gazing into the blue-green sea of his eyes, I believe him. It makes me wonder, though. Did his mother believe in Steve? What was it like when he let her down? What about Gloria's mother? Did her husband do his best?

A police officer approaches the sitting area, and Jake stands, waving to him.

"Mr. Shelton?"

Jake relates the story of how he spotted Dave and why he called the station. The officer takes notes on his pad, stopping now and then to ask questions. When Jake tells him that Dave was shopping in the jewelry stores, the officer thanks him and says he will check them out.

"Where next?" Jake asks once the officer leaves. "Toy shop?"

"Home. I'm tired."

Jake grabs the bags, three in one hand, two in another, and lumbers toward the mall exit with me next to him. As we walk past the food court, I hear my name called. Jilly and her husband, Sam, wave and beckon us to join them for a coffee.

"Wow, looks like you must have found some bargains," Jilly says, indicating the bags Jake lowers beside his chair.

"Baby shopping," I smile.

Jake and Sam carry on their own conversation about Jake's car getting towed, the snowfall, and Sam's snow removal.

"How exciting! Won't be long now, I guess. And I love that dress." She stares at my neck, exposed with the buttons on my coat undone. "I see Santa was good to you."

I look down and realize she means the necklace. "Jake gave me the diamonds," I brag. "A family heirloom."

Sam's eyes shoot toward me, widening at the sight of my 'diamonds.'

"Nice." Jilly shifts in her chair, folds her hands together, and coughs. "Speaking of jewels, did you hear about the jewelry store heist last night? And the…um, murder?"

"We heard it on the morning news."

"Do you think there's any connection to *your* murder? I mean, Detective Swarovski's death?"

"I don't see why there would be." I frown at Jilly's attempt to create a sensational news story out of someone's tragedy. Removing some of the baby items from the bags, I hold them up.

"Did you rob a bank or something?" she jokes. "Sorry, that was in poor taste. So cute! Are babies really that tiny?"

I set aside the sleepers and concentrate on Jake and Sam's conversation, which has also turned to Detective Swarovski. Jake tells Sam about Dave and his call to the police.

"Just in case he may have seen something. That third snowmobiler Mallory saw hasn't been found," Jake says.

"Third snowmobiler?" Sam asks.

"There were definitely three together in our field the night Jake rescued one of them," I confirm. "The second must have been the detective. But there's been no sign of the third snowmobiler."

"Now that you mention it, I saw a snowmobile on the sidewalks in town the night of the storm." Sam leans toward me.

"He was in town on the sidewalks?" I ask.

Sam shrugs. "No one was out walking. Probably figured it was safer than being on the streets with all that snow. Although there wasn't much traffic to contend with. It was pretty clear sailing when I plowed through the main street."

"Could that be the missing snowmobiler?"

Jake rubs his chin. "Maybe we should report that to the police."

Jilly's mouth flies open. "Do you think that was the killer?"

Chapter Forty-Three

The snow gets heavier the closer we get to home. Mallory has been talking about the snowmobiler Sam saw and his possible connection to the other two. One dead, one missing victim with amnesia, and now a third zipping through town not long before I dragged home the dude on a toboggan. Connected? Or just a fluke? And if it *is* the missing piece of this puzzle, how do we find out the identity of snowmobiler number three, who could be a killer?

My concentration drifts like the snow across the road, from the snowmobilers to Mom's revelation. I'll tell Mallory tomorrow; I should let her rest tonight. She has enough on her mind. Besides, I need to get my head around it.

Mom, asking me which relationship is worth saving: the one without true love, where you stay out of obligation, or the toxic one you endure because of love. I didn't have the answer to that. I have plenty more questions, though. About Grandpa. Mom says she doesn't have answers for me. No one has answers. You'd think we were asking about the meaning of life.

Grandpa was a bigamist. That much I now know. The photos I discovered weren't taken before he married Grandma. When I found them, my first thought was that Grandpa had been married once before and divorced. I realize now that Grandpa was older in those pictures than in the wedding photo that stood on the dining room buffet ever since I can remember. I keep replaying Mom's words, my brain tuning out the radio and Mallory's thinking out loud about Dave and the third snowmobiler and whether they are connected to the two men found in our field.

Mom explained how she found out about Grandpa's other family. "Your grandma told me the truth when she was dying. He had married again, three years after exchanging vows with her. A younger woman he met at an estate auction. He had gotten her pregnant. I thought maybe my mother was delirious from the drugs they were pumping into her. Until I checked the barn where she said Dad kept the images of his happy life with another woman, so he could be close to them even when he wasn't physically with them. I wondered whether he kept pictures of us, too, hidden from his second family in his other home.

"Your grandma told me to do whatever I wanted with the photos. She didn't have the heart to throw them out, so she just pretended they weren't there. I did the same thing. I guess I thought they weren't mine to dispose of, and someday the barn would fall down or burn to the ground, taking the evidence with it, and no one would ever know my dad's secret or what your grandma was hiding."

"What do you mean 'what *Grandma* was hiding'? It wasn't her fault. Why would she hide what Grandpa did?"

"When Dad left, she thought he might come back. But, of course, he didn't. She complained that he wasn't there with her, not even when she was on her deathbed."

Mom said she reminded Grandma that he had passed away the previous year, but she kept talking about him as though he were still alive. She recited her own mother's words.

"I hope he's happy with the choice he made," your grandma said as she lay dying. "We didn't know about each other, his mistress and I. When I found the photos just over a year ago, he told me everything. The secret life he led that I knew nothing about. How he fell in love with her. How, even though he didn't love me that way, he still cared about me and didn't want to abandon me and you girls. How he thought he could balance his responsibilities between two families. All those times he told me he was away on farm business, going to auctions, visiting family and friends, taking a much-needed break. How could I have been so blind? All those years of ignoring what was so obvious."

Mom said Grandma told him right there and then that he had to make a decision between the two of them.

"Why didn't she just kick him out?" I asked Mom.

"She said she didn't know how she would live without him. Her whole adult life had been spent with one man, and she wasn't prepared to let him go. It never occurred to her that he would decide to leave *her* so easily. He told her he had spent too much of his life in a loveless marriage, and now that he was seventy, he had the right to be happy. He decided to spend his final years with his other wife. Mom told him if he left, there would be no coming back."

"And then he had a heart attack and died," I said. "Serves him right."

Mom shook her head. "No. Then he left everything behind. His wife, his daughters, his grandsons, his family farm. All for the other woman."

"And then he died," I said again.

"No."

"We had a memorial for him. The year before Grandma died. There's an urn with his ashes in it." I recalled there was no official funeral, no casket, no burial. Just a family remembering the man who died suddenly from a heart attack. Remembering him the way he used to be. Grandma said that's the way Grandpa wanted it.

"Mom said he was dead to her. So she made it final with a service."

Poor Grandma. Her life was spent with a man she didn't really know. A man who stayed out of obligation and because he 'cared about her'. A man who did a disservice to the woman he truly loved. And the three children from two different women who got caught up in his lies.

Now I have to explain to Mallory, and Mom has to explain to John and Deb, that Grandpa is out there somewhere. In a casket in the ground. In somebody else's urn.

Or maybe…

He's alive?

Chapter Forty-Four

Jake has been quiet for most of the trip home. No doubt trying to simmer down after spending the holiday with Steve in the new home he shares with Gloria.

The highway becomes snow-covered, then drifts appear across the road as we approach home, dusk settling in. Such a difference from the city where there is a lot less snow, lights brightening the streets so that true darkness never comes. The darkness that encloses us and the farmhouse every night, its claustrophobia-inducing blanket smothering us. Civilization could cease to exist, and we would never know it.

As Jake signals to turn into our lane, Paul is finishing up the last of the snow-blowing, making a clear path right up to our house. We sit at the end of the lane, the Honda idling, until Paul parks his machine. Jake helps me out of the car and escorts me to the house, waving for Paul to come over.

"Wanna come in for a drink?" Jake asks.

Paul joins us in the family room, and Jake hands him a beer, thanking him for blowing out our lane.

"No problem. Had the day off today anyway. Just Linda and me again. Kids went home last night. Had a nice visit with the grandkids. How was your family time?"

Jake tells him it was great, keeping a straight face, when I know he wants to either laugh or scream. Rather than elaborate on our family visit, Jake changes the conversation to our shopping for baby clothes at the mall. "And you'll never guess who else was there. Dave. The guy you helped out of the snowbank. Pretended like he didn't recognize me at first. Seemed to be in a real hurry to get away."

"Huh. Well, he was kind of an odd fellow, if you ask me. Never even gave much thanks to Mallory or the rest of us for all we did."

"Not the friendliest guy I ever met," Jake agrees. "But he tried to give me a few bucks, which I turned down. What I'd really like is his last name and contact info so the police can question him. In case he might have seen something the night the detective was killed."

Jake tells Paul what happened at the mall. "Dave was gone by the time the police got there. But we ran into Sam and Jilly. Sam says there was a snowmobiler in town that night."

"There's plenty of snowmobilers around."

"Yeah, but Mallory saw three, and the police only found two machines to match two bodies. The third had to be somewhere that night."

"Hmm…" Paul rubs his chin. "You're thinking the third is the killer. He'd have to be long gone by now. But…this Dave guy. Maybe I can help the police find him."

I butt into their conversation. "You can find Dave? How?"

"After we helped dig him out of the snow, I took down his license plate number. I figured you guys might be due some compensation for your time and trouble, going out of your way like that. Dave didn't offer, and he took off like a bat out of hell. I thought it wouldn't hurt to have some way of tracking down the guy in case you or Sam wanted to send him a bill for your services. And besides, there was the issue of the nearly dead guy in your field about the same time Dave showed up. Seemed kind of suspicious, if you ask me. But I'm no cop." He takes a swig of his beer.

Jake picks up his phone. "I'm sure the police will want to contact him. Have you got that license number handy?"

"Jacket pocket." Paul heads to the front closet, brings back a folded sheet of paper, and Jake relays the information to the police station.

"Thanks. They said any leads they can get are useful."

Once Paul leaves, Jake brings in the shopping bags from the car. "Have we got enough space for all this stuff?"

"It's not as much as it looks. And we'll be needing lots more. I was thinking we might consider adding a room or two upstairs now that we've expanded the first floor. So there will be enough room for kids, and we can still keep a guest room. You can start the renos after the baby comes."

If Gloria can have three guest rooms, we should have at least one. I don't think we can expect everyone to sleep on the couches when we have people stay over. Jake glances at me sideways and makes a silly comment about how we should buy Dom's house, and there would be plenty of room for all our family, friends, and acquaintances, even the mailman.

"Seriously, Mal. We've got two bedrooms for the kids. And the den can be a bedroom if we need it."

"I don't see why we can't add a couple more rooms. There's plenty of property to build on. We can expand a little more."

"This is starting to be like that horror book you read. Remember the one—Red Rose or something like that—where the mansion keeps growing? I thought you wanted a cozy home for our family, not some Gothic monstrosity. Jeezus, Mal, this place creeps you out when you're alone at night. Doubling its size isn't going to make it any less scary."

He has a point. But children will bring joy and laughter, keeping the monsters where they belong—off our property and out of my head. This is the first time he's saying no to house renos. When we moved in, Jake told me it was mine to decorate however I wished. Dom and Isabella's home makes our farmhouse look old and worn out. What I wouldn't give to have even one bathroom like theirs. I just can't justify spending that kind of money on our salaries.

"Something's bothering you. I mean, other than Steve. I know you're upset about your grandpa having two families. But you already suspected that. Did Gloria say something else to you?"

Jake holds his head in his hands. "It's a bit of a shocker."

"More of a shock than finding out your grandpa was a bigamist and lived a lie?"

"Yeah. The men in my family aren't exactly great role models. Makes me wonder what chance little Jakey will have of growing up to be a decent man. My old man's a piece of work. His dad was a drunken, depressed old codger who never got over losing his wife to cancer at a young age. And now I find out the grandfather I looked up to as a kid was a scumbag."

"He stood by your grandma, and your mom and aunt, and gave up his own happiness for most of his life. That isn't all bad. He could have walked away completely."

Jake lifts his head, his eyes without spark, their color appearing more of a teal gray than their usual clear blue-green. "He did walk away. It just took him seventy years."

"I'm sorry he died." Maybe if he were still here, his grandpa could explain himself.

"He didn't. At least not when we thought he did. I didn't want to bother you with this tonight on top of everything else, but…Grandpa's memorial was a lie. Grandma's lie."

My mouth flies open. Jake explains what Gloria told him.

"Grandpa could still be alive."

Chapter Forty-Five

But who gives a shit?

I wipe my eyes, obliterating any tears that have had the nerve to seep into the corner. No need to blubber about a man who chose another family. Wherever he is now is of no concern to me.

"Where is he, then?" Mallory voices the thought I have, the same one Mom must have had the past seven years, since her mother confessed on her deathbed.

"Don't know. Don't care."

I grab another beer, turn on the TV, and sink back into the couch. Mallory takes the remote from me and lowers the volume. Looks like I'm in for a 'communication' session.

"I know you *do* care. You told me how much you loved your grandpa."

"Doesn't matter. He was dead to Grandma. He's dead to Mom and me. End of story."

Mallory rises from the couch. "Okay. I guess you don't want to talk about it right now. What do you want for supper? I'll get it started, and I'll leave you with the TV while I read in the living room."

"I'll order in pizza."

She nods.

"I'm not upset. Not with you. It's just a lot to take in," I add. "I'll be fine by tomorrow."

"Okay. But I'm here if you want to talk."

She closes the door in the hallway, leaving me to turn the volume up as high as I want. Having the remote to myself, I flip through the action movie selection. Something with a lot of shooting and blood spilling. No happy families romcom. Pizza ordered, feet up on the table, I settle in for some 'me time'.

The idiots are at it again. The rumbling gets my attention above the blare of the on-screen shooting. Headlights. Ripping around, having a field day in my back yard. The yellow police tape is gone; either these guys don't know bodies have been accumulating back there, or they *do* know, and they're curious. Like spectators at a train crash.

I close the curtains, turn the volume louder, and ignore the trespassers on my property. No point in calling the police.

Or is there?

Would the cops want to know that someone is at the scene of an unsolved murder? I've already called them twice today. Another call might make me the boy who cried wolf. They won't take me seriously when there *is* a problem.

Best to handle this on my own. Scare them away.

I flip the exterior lights on and off, indicating they've been spotted and aren't welcome. They don't get the message. The revving continues, drilling into my brain, my anger rising.

Who the hell do they think they are, using my property like it's their own? What does it take to get some peace and quiet in your own home?

My parka hangs on a hook by the back door, an old pair of boots on the mat. I grab a flashlight from the laundry room and dress to go out and approach the intruders. As I turn the doorknob, I notice the whistle. Still hanging on the hook where I left it the night I rescued Lazarus.

I tromp through the knee-deep snow while they continue to zip around the field. I'm so pissed off about life right now that I hustle with a speed I didn't know I had in me. Through the backyard fence gates, across the field toward the barn, sinking into snow, pressing forward, blowing the whistle. These guys won't quit.

I stop in my tracks, shine the flashlight directly at them, and blow sharp, staccato toots. Whether it's the light or the whistle or a combination of my efforts to catch their eyes, the sleds cease their racket, and the engines shut off. And only now does it occur to me that if these guys are killers, I could be the next body in the cornfield.

One of the guys dismounts. Huge dude. "Hey, what's up?"

"This is private property. That's what's up. Don't want somebody getting hurt. We had an accident here last week. Farm equipment, rocks, stuff lying around. So if you could take your sleds elsewhere, I'd appreciate that."

"Sorry, we didn't know. I didn't see a sign saying it was private."

"The signs are posted. The cops have been called."

"My friend here and I bought a house in town recently. Figured this was public land. Not owned by anybody, so we thought we could take the sleds out for a ride."

"Everything is owned by somebody. In this case, it's *me*."

The other guy dismounts. Equally huge. "And who would *you* be?"

Good thing there's only two of them, or I'd be outnumbered.

"Jake Shelton. Look, I don't want to cause you guys any trouble. You didn't realize it was private land. I get that. There's a conservation area just down the road. Now that you know, if you want to be on your way, I'll tell the cops they're not needed."

"Shelton? Aren't you the guy with the body on your property?"

The other guy chimes in. "Yeah, I heard about you. News travels fast in a small town. And people are saying you were in the newspapers a few months ago. Arrested for murder. You're connected with that casino guy, right?"

"Yeah. Like I said, accidents happen on my turf. Wouldn't want something to happen to you two. You seem like a nice pair. Be a shame if you were to…"

They scramble back onto their sleds, start them up, and wave.

"Hold on," I holler. "Where *exactly* do you guys live?"

Maybe the snowmobiler Sam saw was one of them. In that case, maybe they were a witness. Or one of them is a killer.

They roar off, knocking over another section of fencing on their way, like so many others have done. Hundreds of yards away, our house waits for my return, the lights beckoning. I trudge back home. When I open the back door, the aroma of pizza wafts into my nostrils. Boots off, coat hung on the hook, I head toward the smell. Mallory stands in the kitchen, arms crossed.

"Where were you?"

"Scaring off a couple of snowmobilers. I don't think they'll be back."

"Good. The pizza's here."

"I can smell it. I'm starving."

"I tipped the pizza guy with some change from the entrance table. And I found this."

She hands me a pen. The logo reads 'Tiffany's Jewels'. "Isn't that the jewelry store that was robbed last night? The one where the owner was murdered?"

Chapter Forty-Six

Jake taps the pen in his hand. "Where the hell did this come from?"

"I told you. It was on the entry table."

"Is this the pen Russ found?" Jake rubs his chin, squinting at the logo. "You're right. It's from that jewelry store that was in the news today. And that mall store where Dave was shopping is called 'Gems by Tiffany'. That's one hell of a coincidence."

The ringing of Jake's phone interrupts me before I can say there is no way it's a coincidence. Out in the middle of nowhere near our property? How did a pen from the city jewelers end up here?

"Oh, wow. Seriously? No way. So now what?" He stops to listen. "No, of course. I understand. Sorry that didn't pan out." Jake is quiet again. "I see. Yes, we'll be careful. And yes, we will let you know."

"What didn't pan out?"

"The license plate number. That was Officer Heinz, calling unofficially to warn us. Said he can't share any more info about the case, but Dave's truck is not registered to a Dave or David. It was reported stolen the day he showed up here, snowmobile and all.

"So Dave is a thief? He stole a truck? And he was in our house?"

Jake holds up the pen. "I think we can take a good guess who this belongs to."

The thought that I harbored a truck thief, and possibly a jewel thief, while alone in the house, brings on a wave of sickness, the post-anxiety coursing through me.

Jake reads my thoughts and puts his arm around my shoulder. "It's okay, honey. He's gone. He can't hurt you. And he won't be stupid enough to show his face here again. No wonder he was in a hurry to get away from me at the mall."

My hand protectively on my belly, rubbing the baby, I count the strokes till the waves of panic subside, Jake rubbing my arm in rhythm. "Why didn't you tell Officer Heinz about the pen? Dave must have dropped it. Don't you think that means he was involved in the jewelry theft?"

Jake nods. "Yeah, I do. But let's just keep this bit of evidence to ourselves for now, till the police have more pointing to Dave and away from me. You know what happened the last time they found evidence on our property."

Jake's phone rings again. "I'll be there as soon as I can."

Now what?

"Dom wants to see me in his office. He has info about the case. Says it's best to speak in person. I'll grab a couple of slices now and heat up the rest when I get back."

It would be too much to ask to have an evening with just the two of us in front of the TV, enjoying our pizza and watching a romcom. As if Jake didn't have enough on his plate with Steve back in his life, now there's this whole shocker about his grandpa. It's the perfect chance for an opportunist like Dom to take over as his male role model. Not something I'm going to allow.

"Tell Dom he can wait until tomorrow."

Jake stares at me and opens his mouth to argue.

"Call him back now, or I will. Pick your priority, Jake. Dom or your family?"

Chapter Forty-Seven

Dom lifts his head as I enter his private lair, Nick attached to my arm like we're a couple. I'd suggest we keep the touchy-feely stuff till at least after our first date, but Dom doesn't appear to be in the mood for a joke.

"Jake. You've got some explaining to do." His cold blue eyes lock on mine, and I'm too chicken-shit to blink, so I stare back, waiting for permission to look away.

Nick elaborates, although it's out of character for him. "First off, Dom is not pleased you postponed this meeting from last night to the morning. Dom is a busy man. When he has time to see you, you show up as expected, not whenever it suits you."

"I'm sorry, Dom. But with Mallory expecting—"

Dom rises from his leather seat. "I'm well aware your wife is expecting. Which is why I'm excusing you for the delay. Family comes first. However, don't think you can use that as an excuse to shirk your other responsibilities whenever you feel like it. A man needs to attend to business in order to take care of his family." He nods to Nick and lowers himself back into his seat.

Nick releases his hold on me. "Sit."

Once we're all comfortable, Nick tells me the agenda for this meeting. "Family is what brings us here. It seems you've been holding back some information about your blood relatives. Dom hasn't decided whether that will be a problem or an asset. Maybe you can enlighten us."

What the hell is this about? Grandpa?

"I'm going to need some clues here. Specifically, which blood relatives are we discussing?"

"Specifically," Dom draws out the word, in five syllables, "the cop who's working undercover on the alleged biggest jewelry heist in Brampton Heights."

The blank I'm drawing is no bluff. Yet for a moment, the look that passes between Dom and his brother convinces me Nick is about to hoist me off my chair and reconvene this meeting with some muscleman who will jog my memory.

"Doesn't ring a bell," I answer.

Dom leans forward across his desk. "Detective Marshall of the provincial police. Does *that* ring a bell?"

Marshall? A common last name. Also, Mom's maiden name.

"My mother is Gloria Marshall, but she's a nurse, not a cop."

Nick tilts his head toward me and smirks. "Cut the crap. We're not talking about your mommy."

My brain sifts through all the Marshalls I might remotely know and comes up empty. Grandparents are dead. Mom's older sister moved to England when she got married. No other aunts or uncles or cousins…

"Sorry, Dom. There's only my mom and her sister. She never had kids. The Marshall line continues with me and John, but our last name is Shelton. And as you know, I've taken over the family farm. Now the Shelton farm."

Dom folds his hands together and lets out a deep breath. "I have it on good authority that Detective Marshall is related to you. And I'm concerned that he has been snooping around on your property. What I don't know is what he's looking for. The plants we cultivate? The bodies that seem to keep turning up? Is there something else you're hiding there, Jake, that I'm *not* aware of?"

I haven't got a clue. He must be confused about this Marshall guy. Just a coincidence he's got the same last name as Mom, and he's been on our property, for whatever reason I don't know. I guess *somebody* has to investigate Detective Swarovski's death.

"No, Dom. Nothing's hiding on my property. And, like I said, I don't have any Marshall relatives besides Mom and her sister. Must be another

Marshall family."

Minutes pass before Dom or Nick speak.

"Should you happen to have any contact with your long-lost relative, I want to be informed immediately. In the meantime, I'll see if I can shake more information out of my contacts at our local detachments." Dom pauses. "I also heard you ran into a possible witness, or perhaps a suspect, in the Swarovski investigation. Some truck thief going under the alias of Dave?"

Nick joins in. "Mystery man Dave. Anybody else hanging out on your property we should know about?"

My head shakes, then my eyes pop open. "We *have* had a fair bit of snowmobile activity in the back field. Mallory says there were three of them goofing around the night the detective was killed." I count off on my fingers. "Amnesia guy who took off from the hospital and showed up back at my house to thank me for saving him. Then there's Detective Swarovski. We all know where he is." When I get to my third finger, I shrug. "And somebody else."

"Dave," Nick says.

"No, not Dave. Dave drove a truck, not a snowmobile."

"A stolen truck with a snowmobile in the cargo bed, from what I understand," Dom adds. "And he seems to be avoiding the police for some reason."

"I guess if I stole a truck, I'd be avoiding the police, too."

Dom rubs his chin scruff. "Seems to me, it's clear who the killer is."

I turn to Nick to see if he has any clues to offer.

"It's Dave." He rolls his eyes. "Did you take a course, or does stupidity come naturally to you?"

"I went to college. Business and management." My comment elicits a scoff from Nick.

"No need for insults," Dom defends me. "But this 'Dave' guy needs to be found and identified so we can put a close to this case. And you're the only one who can do that."

My head bobs in agreement. How the hell I'm supposed to find Dave, I have no idea.

"You know what he looks like," Dom continues. "And one of our casino bouncers moonlights as a police sketch artist. I'll give him a call, and we'll see what you come up with."

The rest of my morning is spent describing the elusive Dave.

Chapter Forty-Eight

"Be back as soon as I can," Jake said before leaving me with Nellie and Lucky. Despite the snow that started up during the night, Jake decided to head to Brampton Heights to see Dom first thing in the morning instead of spending his last allotted vacation day with me.

I sit staring out the front window as snow accumulates on the lawn and in the lane. The plow came down our road early, as it usually does, and it's not likely to make another pass today. As if we don't pay enough taxes. People have been complaining to deaf ears about the lack of snow removal in our rural area. The main street in town gets a couple of swipes during heavy snowfalls, but the rest of us struggle to get to work in the winter. Only one more month for me, then I'm off on maternity leave for the year.

A text from Jake tells me not to worry, but things are taking longer than he expected. He's going to search for Dave at Dom's request. My hand supports my forehead as it sinks down toward my lap. Dom has won again, stealing Jake from me. Rather than let myself fume over it, I lie on the sofa and close my eyes. I need my rest so I can confront Jake and get answers when he returns home.

Blanket pulled to my chin, I curl up, joining the cats for a late morning nap. I doze off for a short while, then my phone pings with a notification. A weather alert. Freezing rain is occurring or is likely to occur in the next few hours, followed by high winds and a possible accumulation of up to ten inches of snow by midnight. As if I don't have enough to worry about, now Jake will have to travel home on icy roads. Why is this my life?

I set down my phone, concentrating on warmth and thinking of our honeymoon in Jamaica. Blue-green water, white sand, palm trees swaying in the gentle breeze, and Jake and I strolling hand in hand. The sun in a blue sky with a few puffy clouds, and nothing to think about except the two of us. Before I learned about Jake's gambling, his debts, his little secrets and lies. Before Dom became a household name in *our* household.

Honeymoons are a con. No one's married life is ever a honeymoon for long.

Once I ease myself off the sofa, the cats follow me to the kitchen in search of lunch. Mac and cheese for me with a salad on the side. Comfort food with a dash of health consciousness. Chicken pâté for Nellie and Lucky. Although the scene through the back window shows little sign of a major storm, the pinging of ice droplets on the glass warns of its approach. According to the forecasters, freezing rain is heading up from the south, and with the temperature difference here, it will soon change to snow covering the icy layer. If Jake doesn't make it home before dark, it won't be a pleasant drive.

My meal on a tray, I settle onto the family room sofa, switch on the television, scroll through the choices searching for something to get my mind off my reality. Another text from Jake assures me he is fine and hopes to be home soon. I choose a comedy, hoping it will lighten my mood and cast thoughts of storms, Dom, and bodies in the cornfield out of my mind.

It works for a short while, until the doorbell nearly makes me jump out of my skin. Jilly stands shivering on the front porch, pressing the button again as I approach the door.

"What took you so long?" She breezes past me into the entryway. "I thought maybe you weren't home. Then I'd be stuck out here in the cold waiting till Sam could pick me up."

"Sorry, I wasn't expecting company." I don't mean to be rude, but it's not my fault she's freezing out there. "Why are you here?"

"After seeing you at the mall yesterday, I just wanted to check if there have been any new developments. Sam is out clearing roads before the next blast of snow, and I asked him to drop me off here so we could visit."

More like so she could get the latest gossip on us. Still, I don't mind her keeping me company until Jake gets home.

"That's nice of you. I was just watching TV." I open the closet, and she deposits her coat, then follows me to the family room. "Can I get you something to drink?"

"Coffee, please. Is Jake at work?"

"No, it's the last day of his vacation. He's at the mall. Jake thought maybe Dave would turn up there again." I don't mention that Dom suggested he search for him.

"Oh. That seems unlikely."

"Yes, but the police would like to question Dave. He may be a witness to what happened to Detective Swarovski."

"Or he may be the killer."

We sit in silence for a moment, digesting her words, then I prepare coffee and grab a package of cookies from the cupboard. I don't want to discuss this any further. This week's article didn't paint Jake in as rosy a light as Jilly claimed it would. Although she labeled him a hero and praised him for saving a life, the focus was on the dead detective in our field. I don't need a repeat of that in next week's paper.

"I'm sure the police will find the killer without our help." I turn the volume louder, hoping the movie will grab her attention.

She sips her coffee and bites into a cookie, and takes my cue, her eyes on the screen, accepting that the conversation about Dave is over. Outside, the wind picks up, driving the icy rain against the bay window.

"Let's hope the ice buildup doesn't knock out the power," Jilly says.

"Yes, hope not. At least, we have a working generator."

"That's good." Jilly checks her phone and fidgets on the sofa. "No word from Sam yet."

Does she worry about Sam as much as I worry about Jake?

"What's that?" She points through the snow-encrusted glass.

I peer through the window, straining to see what caught her eye, but there's nothing. The rain, snow mixing with it, a long expanse of white, interspersed with a few trees, and the shed. Beyond that lies the field and the barn, which is barely visible with the misty precipitation and wind that has picked up.

"I don't see anything. Sometimes my imagination gets the best of me out here. That's probably what it is. Especially with what happened last Friday."

"Maybe. I don't know how you manage out here by yourself, all those nights with Jake at work. And everything that's happened this past year."

The unspoken words are clear. I have a husband who has a tendency to go missing and have bodies turn up on his property. What else can you expect, given his association with Dom?

And she would be correct. In some way or another, Dom has been responsible for the bad things that have happened to us. The whole town is familiar with our dirty laundry. I should be thankful they still want to associate with us at all.

"Well, it *is* a bit creepy at night." Maybe that will encourage her to leave before dusk sets in. Hopefully, Jake will be home before then, and Sam will come to take Jilly away before she can dig up any more dirt on Jake to publish in the town's weekly newspaper.

Her phone pings. "Sam is going to be a while. Since he got himself trained and licensed, he's taking over the plow/sander for Corey tonight, who's come down with the flu. I hope you don't mind me staying here till he's done, or Jake gets home to give me a lift. I don't want to walk on the slippery roads and sidewalks. And you shouldn't drive on them, either, in your condition."

The perks of living in a small town. There's always someone to volunteer or lend a hand. Sam is a good Samaritan. And Jilly, for all her nosiness, is kind.

"Of course, you can stay as long as you like. To tell the truth, I could use the company."

We watch the rest of the romcom and polish off half a bag of cookies. As I search for another movie, Jilly bolts off the sofa toward the window once again. And this time, I see what she sees. A flash of color against the misty white landscape. And it's creeping toward us. Slow, steady, with a sense of purpose.

Jilly utters the words I'm thinking. "I'm sure there's someone out there. Coming for us."

Chapter Forty-Nine

Dom gives me three leads to follow. Find Dave. Get the lowdown on Detective Marshall. And figure out what happened to the dude with amnesia.

"I'll send out copies of your sketch to my contacts, but you need to get out there and actively search for Dave. The same goes for the man whose life you saved. They were both on your property the night Swarovski died. You can ID them both. I'm betting if you don't find them first, they'll come back to haunt you. And it may not end well for you."

"I'm not the only one who can ID them." I count off the other witnesses on my fingers. Paul, Sam, Jilly…and Mallory. She spent more time with Dave than anyone."

Dom nods. "And that, Jake my boy, should be an excellent incentive for you to find this guy before he shows up on your property again."

Even if 'Dave' happened to be his real name, that doesn't exactly narrow down his identity. As for Lazarus, even *he* doesn't know who he is. At least Detective Marshall has a name. Dom couldn't get any more information about him.

"I have it on good authority that this Marshall guy is working undercover on the Swarovski case," Dom says. "If you *are* related, as my sources tell me, it would be a good idea to have his support for our little enterprise."

"Enterprise?" I raise my eyebrows.

Nick kicks my shin, and I'm sure he mutters the word 'idiot' under his breath. "The casino. Our related activities."

The weed-growing op, the loan sharking? And who knows what else.

"I can't do all the work for you. As I see it, there are three players in this murder case. Find them." Dom dismisses me with a pat on the back.

As Nick escorts me out, he gives me some direction. "Talk to your mother and find out more about your cop relative. Dom has no use for cops unless they can be of use to him. Check the spots where you've seen Dave and the guy with amnesia. Ask questions. Dom can't involve himself directly."

We stroll through the empty casino, damn near spooky without its patrons. Gaming tables, slots devoid of excitement. All that will change come evening. Lights, sounds, action. To the tune of millions of dollars.

"I'll see what I can do," I say.

"You'd better do more than see. This is your problem. Clean it up. If it becomes *Dom's* problem, he won't be happy."

Nick leaves me at the main doors, and I step through the sliding glass, hitting the button on my key fob as I stride toward my Honda, ice pellets cutting into my face. The ground slides out from under me, sending my butt onto the frozen parking lot. In the moment it takes to hoist myself upright, a plow rumbles onto the premises, spraying sand on the slick pavement. I scan the area to see if anyone else has witnessed my flip and notice Nick standing at the entrance, laughing at my expense.

Inching the rest of the way to my vehicle, I hit the start button, grab the ice scraper from the backseat, and scrub the layer of frozen water from my windshield. With the heated seats on and blower full blast, I consider what Dom said.

Find Dave.

Chapter Fifty

The shape becomes less blurry as it approaches the house. Jilly and I are armed once again, ready with our tools, knives, and Jake's bat. Whoever is out there, they are fixated on getting to us in a hurry, boots lifting and stomping through the crusty snow.

"I don't see any sign of a snowmobile. And he seems to be alone. Could it be Jethro again?" I speculate. "Or the man Jake rescued?"

"This is getting ridiculous," Jilly says. "You're not safe in your own house. And the police haven't been much use. By the time they get here, it'll be too late. I'm calling Sam."

As the person in the back yard nears the house, they stop abruptly.

Jilly speaks into her phone. "Yes, yes, we're okay. But somebody is in the back yard, heading our way." She listens for Sam's reply. "Oh. Well, that's a relief. You scared us half to death."

Jilly pockets her phone and sets down the reciprocating saw she has been holding. "It's Sam. He's in your back yard."

She unlocks the door and waits for her husband to get to the house, while I set down my nail gun and bat and put on a fresh pot of coffee. Sam will need a hot drink after tromping through the ice-encrusted field.

He bursts through the back door, breathing heavily. "Quite the trek," he rasps.

"What on earth were you doing out there?" Jilly takes his parka and hangs it on the hook as he removes his boots. "I thought you were out clearing the roads."

"I was. But as I was coming down the side road next to the field, I noticed somebody wandering around the property. So I got out and followed the guy, but I lost sight of him. I checked around and even took a quick look inside the barn."

I take a mug out of the cupboard. "Should we call the police?"

Sam settles onto the sofa, Jilly joining him. "I wouldn't bother. Whoever was out there is gone now. No point in dragging the police all the way out here for nothing."

I pour coffee into the mug, hand it to Sam, and refill Jilly's cup. "Shouldn't they know someone is snooping around? In case it's connected to the murder case?"

"What if it was the killer?" Jilly's voice reflects her alarm at the possibility. "You could have been in danger."

Sam waves off her concerns. "I doubt it. That whole killer returning to the scene train of thought is just a myth. But I am wondering, Mallory, whether Jake has anything valuable stored in that old barn. He doesn't have it locked. Anybody could take whatever they wanted. Has he noticed anything missing? Or found anything?"

"Mostly stuff his grandpa left behind. I don't *think* it would be of value to anyone. And no, he hasn't mentioned anything is missing." I keep the details to myself. No need to have Jilly report in the weekly paper that Jake's grandpa hid all sorts of secrets in the barn.

"That's good. Break-ins aren't too common around here, but you and Jake have had some problems."

Jilly nods. "Trouble seems to come looking for you. I hope things quiet down before the baby arrives in February."

So do I.

Chapter Fifty-One

"Thanks for having me over." Jilly grabs her coat from the closet. "And be careful. Especially with Jake not home. You never know who is going to show up here. If there's somebody snooping around the property…"

"Keep the doors locked and don't let anyone in. Call if you need anything tonight, and I'll be right back," Sam adds, having returned from retrieving his truck off the side road.

I saunter to the dining room, check the weather conditions, and watch them pull out of the driveway, grateful for their friendship. One of the good things about small-town country living is the neighbors. You can always depend on the locals when you need them. No matter how nosy they may be. Now, if only Jake would get home. Apart from a short text saying he had a few more things to do, I haven't heard from him for a couple of hours. And the weather isn't improving any. With darkness settling in, I switch on the outdoor Christmas lights. Jake will appreciate a beacon when he comes home. Snow has been falling steadily, covering the icy layer formed by the brief period of freezing rain. Plows and sanders will be out in the city. Jake is safe there. Until he passes the city limits and enters an alternate universe in the country. No lights to illuminate the road, hardly a plow or sander in sight.

Double-checking the back and patio door locks and closing the curtains, I do my tour of the lower level, thinking about supper. Should I go ahead without Jake? Thank goodness for convenience food. I'll pop some frozen breaded chicken cutlets into the oven, boil a packaged rice dish, and open a can of peas. Jake can heat up his food when he gets here. Nellie and Lucky run into the kitchen as soon as they hear me bustling around the stove. I turn on the television to keep me company as I wait for my meal. The six o'clock news headline is the current weather situation.

"Significant snowfall is expected throughout the evening, with high winds reducing visibility. Blowing snow following this afternoon's flash freeze will make roads treacherous. Police are advising against unnecessary travel."

I text Jake and ask if he has checked his weather app. He answers immediately.

A bit slick here, don't worry. I'm at Mom's. Will call when I'm ready to leave.

A bit slick? It's just like Jake to make light of the weather. You'd think that last Friday would have reminded him of how bad things can get out here. But no, it's just 'a bit slick, and I shouldn't worry'. The weatherman claims I *should* worry and is advising people to stay home, especially in outlying areas.

Refusing to focus on the weather and the fact that Jake will have to drive home in it, I immerse myself in a sitcom, bringing my meal to the sofa once it's cooked. Following supper, I call the cats to snuggle, and I choose a movie to pass the time. Forgoing anything horrific, a cozy murder mystery seems tame enough. Even though I know the murder isn't real, it makes me think of Detective Swarovski. Maybe not the best choice for tonight. I switch to something romantic, but it only makes me upset that Jake isn't with me, so I flip to a Christmas movie I've seen before to drown out the wind, and I pick up the novel on the coffee table. A psychological thriller about a wife with a controlling husband. Again, maybe not the best choice, but I need to occupy my mind with something.

"Hello. Is anyone there?" A voice, louder than the rest, on the television takes me out of my book.

My eyes on the screen, the voice calls out again, but the words don't come from the mouths of the characters. I push myself to a sitting position. Where is the voice coming from if not the TV? Is it my phone? My iPad? Did I click on something? An audiobook? A social app? An ad?

"Hello? Hello?" The voice rings through the house as I turn down the volume on the television.

Someone is in the house.

My bat lies on the floor next to the kitchen table, several steps away. As quickly as my pregnant belly will allow, I scramble toward it and pick it up. Down the hall, a shape approaches, the floorboards creaking. My phone sits on the coffee table, forgotten in my haste to grab the bat. Before I can reach it, the dark figure enters the kitchen, and an involuntary scream escapes me. The intruder raises his hands in the air, indicating he's unarmed. Recognition sets in as my eyes settle on his face and the set of his jaw.

The man whose life Jake saved.

"It's okay. I'm not going to hurt you. I did knock, but I guess you didn't hear. And the door was unlocked, so I let myself in. Sorry if I startled you." He stands where he is, hands raised, no attempt to move closer.

My bat ready to strike, I step toward the table to pick up my phone. "I'm calling the police."

"There's no need for that. I'm here to see Jake. To thank him properly."

"He's sleeping."

"Kind of early, isn't it?"

The stranger scans the room as if searching for something. "This is nice. A new addition?"

Why does it concern him?

"My grandfather grew up on a farm. I love these old brick houses. You've done a great job on remodeling, opening up the space to a living area. I'm city born and raised, but my heart's in the country. I'd love to have a place like this someday."

"I'll let Jake know you were here. If you leave your name and number, he'll get back to you." I step further away and wave toward the front of the house. "You can show yourself out."

"Thanks, Mrs. Shelton. I'd prefer to speak to Jake in person. I'll come back another time."

He turns, glides through the hall, and out onto the porch, without another word.

The rumble of his truck starting up snaps me out of the shock of my brief encounter with the unnamed man Jake rescued last week. I've only seen this guy twice before, but something about him is familiar. If I could just figure out what it is.

I set the bat in the corner, turn on the exterior lights, and latch the door, pulling on it to check that it is locked this time. I must have been distracted when Jilly and Sam left, and I looked out to see what the weather was doing.

My phone pings in my hand, startling me.

I'm heading out now.

I don't need the stress of waiting for Jake to make it home on icy roads when it's not necessary. There's no need to tell him Lazarus was here and cause him to rush home and get into an accident. I call him to say he should stay put at his mom's till morning, and drive home in the daylight.

"No way, Mal. I'm not leaving you alone."

"I'm not alone. Paul is next door. Sam said to call if I need anything. Everything's locked up tight, and Nellie and Lucky will keep me company. I'm going to bed soon, and I'll sleep a lot better knowing you're not out on the roads." Even though I want him here, and part of me hopes he will refuse to listen, I assure him I will be fine.

Jake continues to insist that the roads won't be *that* bad, but Gloria takes the phone from him. "Mallory, are you sure you're okay on your own for the night? Our street is a sheet of ice, and now it's snowing."

"I'm fine. Don't let Jake leave. It will be more stressful for me and the baby if he drives in this weather. Especially after what happened last week."

In the background, Jake and Steve argue about whether he should stay or not. Steve is on Gloria's side, telling Jake not to be stupid.

"Ask Paul if he and Linda can keep you company," Jake says, back on the phone. "Call Sam and Jilly if there's a problem with the baby. They'll take care of you and get you to the hospital. And if there are any more snowmobilers, call the police."

"I will. But I'm sure everything will be fine."

"Honey? Are you sure?"

"Love you. See you in the morning." I purse my lips and smack a kiss at him, which he returns.

Parting the living room curtains, I gaze at the scene out front. The woods across the road are barely visible, obscured by the slanted snowfall. Drifts form on the white lawn, like waves under a surfboard, heading toward the house.

Headlights brighten the road, snow sweeping across. A vehicle slows in front of the house. I hold my breath, waiting for it to move on. It backs up, inching toward the lane.

Don't stop. Keep going.

The driver turns down our lane, headlights closing in on me, shining through the window, shutting down as the roar of the engine ceases.

A man exits the small vehicle, steps onto the walkway, and continues toward the porch steps. When his head turns toward the window, his face clear now, he gets a glimpse of me spying through the curtains. I grab Jake's bat.

And run. To the kitchen for the carving knife.

Chapter Fifty-Two

I'm stuck at Mom's place with Steve. I tell her about my unsuccessful fishing trip to the mall and the hospital before landing in to visit her. "Leave that to the police. I don't want you putting yourself in danger over this. It's not your fault that Detective Swarovski died on your property," Mom says.

Steve adds, "You sure this has nothing to do with Dom? This is what you get for associating with his kind. You've been in trouble since the day you walked into his casino."

I draw in a deep breath and restrain myself. He's not worth it. Killing Steve will send Mom to the psychiatric ward and me to jail. Instead, I ask Mom if I can speak with her in private. Steve says whatever I have to say to my mother, I can say to him. We're family.

Family? What a joke.

My family is at the farm. Which is where I should be. But Mom and Mal decided I should stay put, and I don't need two hysterical women thinking I'm dead in a ditch somewhere. Besides, I don't want to leave till I get some answers from Mom.

Who is Detective Marshall?

Seeing that Steve has no intention of leaving the room, I blurt out the question.

Mom blanches. "I…don't know. But I suppose…it could be my half-brother. I never did meet him. I was never told anything about him. I just saw the photos of him as a child."

Steve doesn't appear surprised by Mom's revelation, which tells me she's confided her family history to him. As if it's any of his business.

"I've been told he's on the police force. A detective."

Mom's mouth flies open. "Oh. Wow."

"If he's my uncle, I'd like to meet him."

"I...I...can't help you. I honestly don't know where he would be."

Steve butts in. "Couldn't you ask the police? Seems pretty straightforward."

I hate to admit it, but Steve has a point. "So I should call a bunch of police stations and ask for Detective Marshall?"

Steve shrugs. "Good place to start."

The rest of the evening is spent looking up phone numbers for police detachments within a two-hour radius. Over and over, I'm told there is no Detective Marshall working at the station. When I finally get a positive response, I'm told he's unavailable, and another detective can assist me.

"No, thank you. It's a personal matter." I hang up.

It turns out my half-uncle, also known as Grandpa's son by another woman, has been working close to home, less than an hour away. In the biggest city in Canada. Downtown Toronto.

Chapter Fifty-Three

Dave.

Here he is on my doorstep. Ringing the bell. Knocking on the door. In the middle of a storm. Just like last Friday. Deja vu.

Only then, I thought he was Jake, and I let him in the house. Now, I know he's a thief and could be a killer. And Jake is not on his way home.

It will take too long for the police to get here, especially with the road conditions. I call Paul and Sam, barricade myself in the laundry room with the cats, and wait for the cavalry to arrive.

Lights off, hoping not to attract attention, should Dave break in, I gaze out the snow-encrusted window. A faint light seeps into the room. Wind howls a ghostly refrain, shaking the pane. It offers no escape, too narrow for me and the baby to squeeze through. Nowhere to run, even if I could, with an endless field of white. A dark sky, white crystals slanting down, builds another layer to trudge through.

No escape. Trapped like a cat in a cage, with my cats curled up on the counter, their glowing eyes questioning what I'm doing in the dark, my breath quick and shallow.

I pray they will keep quiet. I try to slow my breathing.

The doorbell has stopped chiming. No more banging on the door. Maybe Dave gave up and left. Maybe he's looking for another way in. Maybe Paul has arrived and is talking to him.

He's banging on the back door now, closer, only steps away from the laundry room. My hand clamped over my mouth, I inhale through my nose, deep breaths. The knife is pointed out, ready to stab the intruder; the bat in my right hand is ready for a swing. The chiming resumes. Front door? Back door? Both? And now a new pounding. The patio doors? How can Dave be everywhere?

In spite of using the breathing techniques Dr. Falcon suggested, I'm ready to pass out. Lightheaded, disoriented, waves of panic flowing through me. Frightened to death.

More ringing. Or pinging.

My phone lights up.

"I'm at your front door," Paul says. "Let me in. Sam is at the side door."

I drop the knife on the counter, the bat on the floor, and bolt out of the laundry room toward the front of the house, unlock the door, and collapse into Paul's arms.

"It's okay, Mallory. We're here."

He hollers for Sam, who joins us, and they lead me to the living room sofa. The back door pounding continues, and the bell rings as well. Sam and Paul leave me to confront Dave. Through the front window, I glimpse Dave's vehicle sitting in the driveway, snow dusting the windows.

And someone is getting out of it.

I need to warn Sam and Paul that there are two of them. Rising from the sofa, I tread through the hall to the kitchen and into the mudroom.

And come to a dead stop.

Sam and Paul's backs are to me. Facing them is the man Jake rescued. His eyes flit to me and back to the two men. "Stay back, Mallory."

His jaw set, his hand steady, gun pointed at my would-be rescuers, he tells me again. "Get out of the way, Mallory."

To the men, he says, "On your knees, hands behind your backs."

I scream with an intensity I never dreamed possible, my hands covering my belly. "Please, please, don't. My baby…" I whimper.

Sam and Paul drop to their knees. The man doesn't move, his weapon braced to shoot. Behind me, I feel a rush of wind as the front door opens. The pounding of footsteps resounds through the hall and stops. I turn around.

Dave stands there, eyes wide. "What the hell?"

Chapter Fifty-Four

I punch my pillow out of frustration. I've wasted a day I could have spent with Mallory trying to find Dave, who may or may not have anything to do with Detective Swarovski's murder, and come up with nothing. And Lazarus, who likely did kill the detective, is still out on the loose, and I'm no closer to figuring out his identity. My uncle can be tracked down where he works, but what am I supposed to do? Walk in and say, "Hi, Unc. You don't know me, but your dad was my grandpa. Why don't you drop by for a visit, and we'll catch up on the last several decades? I'd like to introduce you to my friend, Dom."

When Dom finds out I've made no progress in finding the detective's killer, it won't help our tenuous relationship. Any bad press for me, by association, reflects poorly on his business and personal integrity, according to him. If I can at least get my uncle on friendly terms with Dom, it might appease him somewhat. The only cops Dom likes are the ones that can be swayed by his money and power. Not that they're crooked or anything, just amenable to Dom's way of doing business, which may or may not always be strictly according to the law.

And who knows? Maybe this Detective Marshall will solve the Swarovski case. Kill two birds with one stone.

Stuffed away with packing boxes in 'my room' in Steve's effin' house with him lying next to Mom, brings my temper to a boil. A few more thwacks into my pillow, and I lie staring at the ceiling, trying to calm down. Not much chance of getting any sleep tonight. I consider checking in on Mallory, but I don't want to disturb her if she's sleeping. If she's asleep, she isn't worrying. If she's awake and worrying, she'll text me.

I'll be out of here the minute daylight cracks through the sky, and the plows have the roads cleared and sanded. Tomorrow, I'll call the police station again and set up a meeting with my uncle. He'll probably be glad to learn he's got a couple of nephews, although John doesn't need to know about it until I test the waters. If he turns out to be as deadbeat as Grandpa, there's no point.

Even though it's past midnight, brightness pours through the curtains, courtesy of the city streetlights. You'd think it was the middle of the day. Slick roads haven't stopped people from motoring past. Car doors slam, horns honk, headlights flicker, dogs bark, laughter, and voices carry through my window. Sirens shriek out in emergency mode. Airplanes roar overhead. Throwing back the covers, I venture a peek through the curtains and jump back, hoping no one's seen me in my underwear. Hordes of people walk along the sidewalk not far from where I stand. Groups chat by their cars. Families are visiting. Somebody's having a party. On front porches, people hug and scurry off to their vehicles. Others are just arriving. It's a fucking carnival out there. Can't wait to get home and get some peace and quiet.

Mom and Steve retired early, leaving me in the family room to twiddle my thumbs. I decided I'd better get some shut-eye, too, and rise early to get home to Mallory. As soon as I hit the sack, I realized sleep wouldn't be coming any time soon.

I pull on my pants and T-shirt and slip out of the bedroom. Mom's room is just off the family room. If I turn on the closed captioning, maybe I can watch TV without waking her. Hopefully, the light from the screen will filter into her room enough to irritate Steve.

As I step along the hall, a slicing and scraping noise stops me, and I listen in the near dark. Someone is in the living room. Why haven't they turned on the lights? I tiptoe toward the sound. When I turn the corner, a glow bounces around the boxes piled in the room. As my eyes adjust, I realize the glimmer comes from a flashlight. A shadowy figure slits open a box and roots through.

"Hey! What are you doing?"

The bulky balaclava-wearing shape turns toward me as I shout, then bolts up, knocks me aside like an empty beer can, and races through the front door. By the time I regain my balance, slip on my boots, and run after him, he's off the property. Frigid air hits my chest; my teeth chatter. He's out here somewhere. Mixing in with the crowd on the street?

I turn to the left and the right. There he is, skirting the lawns, snow crunching as he jogs along. I shout again, then run after him, my feet sliding on the sidewalk. It occurs to me too late that the lawns might be less slippery. My butt hits the snow-covered ice, and an expletive resounds through the street. People turn to gawk, then return to what they were doing before my fall. No one checks to see if I'm okay.

Exterior lights illuminate Mom's porch. Steve wanders out in his robe and slippers, spots me on my ass, shakes his head, and goes back inside, but not before yelling at the top of his lungs. "Get in here! Now!"

Once again, people stop to stare before going about their business. I twist onto my side, get on my knees, push myself up. Ice burns into my hands as the tread on my boots attempts to grip the ground. Frozen to the bone, I stomp across the lawn on an icy layer of snow.

Steve waits for me, the door partly ajar. "What the hell are you doing out there?"

I breathe into my hands and rub them together. Steve shuts the door, removes his robe, and hands it to me. "Here you go. Now, do you mind telling me what you were doing, freezing your ass off out there?"

I'm too cold to turn down his offer of the robe. "Thanks, Dad."

It's as close to a father/son moment as we're ever going to get. He flips on the living room lamp, and his mouth flies open, seeing the boxes ripped open and stuff strewn about. I explain that there was an intruder in the house, and I chased him out.

Steve doesn't thank me. "What the hell did you bring down upon us?"

"Me? It's not my fault somebody broke in." I scan the mess. "Do you think anything is missing? I didn't see him carrying anything."

Steve surveys the room, moves things around, taking inventory. "Hard to tell. Not much of value here, just knick-knacks, that sort of stuff...how the hell did they get in?"

"Beats me." I check the door, and seeing no signs of forced entry, do the same with the other two exits and the windows. Nothing else seems to have been disturbed. I report back to Steve, who is still checking out the boxes. "Doesn't look like anyone broke in."

Steve glares at me as though it *must* be my fault. "So someone just walked in? Did you happen to leave the door unlocked?"

I scratch my head. "No? No. I wasn't even outside after you locked up and went to bed. Not until I chased the guy down the street."

"Where's your key?"

Besides Mom and Steve, John and I have a key to their house to use in case of an emergency, just as Mom has a key to our homes.

"In my pocket." I open the entry closet and dig through the coat pockets till I find my car key and house key. No key to Mom's house.

"You lost your key," Steve bellows. "We'll have to get new locks for all the doors."

Mom walks in to find me turning my coat pockets inside out and Steve cursing. "What on earth is going on?"

"I'm looking for my key to the house. I must have dropped it somewhere."

"Just take the spare one and get a copy made." Mom pulls a key from the entry table drawer and hands it to me. "Why do you need it in the middle of the night?"

I explain what happened, and Mom rushes into the living room.

"I didn't see him run off with anything. Dad says there's nothing valuable, so I guess the guy wasted his time."

Mom's mouth flies open. "Nothing of value? Everything here has sentimental value. Photos, gifts, keepsakes, souvenirs…"

"I meant not of monetary value to a thief," Steve qualifies.

"Well, it's a good thing I labeled all the boxes with their contents. I'll know if anything is missing."

As Mom checks the list on one of the boxes, replacing items that belong, the spare key in my hand jogs my memory. I didn't bring Mom's key with me. It's still hanging by the front door at home. I tell Steve he can't blame me after all.

"So you're saying someone just walked right in? Through the locked metal door?" Steve glares at me.

"No, I'm saying you must have forgotten to lock the door."

"Do I look like I'm senile? I lock the doors every night."

As tempting as it is to make a snide comment about his mental capacity, I resist and help Mom take inventory and repack her precious possessions. Steve, seeing I won't be goaded into continuing the argument about who allowed our home to be invaded, joins in.

A couple of hours later, Mom's belongings are boxed back the way they were before being violated, and nothing has been found missing.

"It's a good thing I got up when I did and stopped the guy before he could grab anything," I say.

Whatever Steve was about to say, mouth open, glaring at me, he reconsiders when Mom thanks me for being alert. "Right. Good job, Son," he says.

"Let's get some sleep. You can head home after breakfast," Mom says.

I don't plan on waiting till then. I'll be out of here before they wake up.

Mallory and the baby need me.

Chapter Fifty-Five

"What are you doing? Drop your gun. They're Jake and Mallory's friends. They were here the night I was stranded, and Jake saved your life," Dave says.

Lazarus keeps his gun trained on Paul and Sam and addresses me. "These are your friends? I thought someone was breaking in, and you needed assistance."

"They were. I did."

His eyes flit from me to Sam and Paul to Dave. "What's going on here, Mallory? Are you safe?"

He seems as confused as I am. Except another emotion overpowers my confusion. Much like the last time a man with a gun held me captive in my home, fear disconnects me from reality. This can't be happening.

"No. Dave was trying to break in. And you…you're with him." My voice trembles as I accuse him.

The man whose life Jake saved puts his gun back in its holster, motioning for Sam and Paul that it's okay for them to get up from their kneeling position. "I think there's been a misunderstanding. Dave and I aren't here to hurt you. Maybe we can sit down and talk. When are you expecting Jake?"

"Anytime now." I won't let him know that Jake isn't coming home until tomorrow. A man with a gun can't be trusted. That much I know.

"We'll wait, if that's okay."

Paul speaks up after being silent since the man pointed a gun at him. "Maybe you should come back another time."

"I remember you now. From the last time I was here. You suggested then that I should call before coming back. My memory has been playing tricks since the head injury, but things are coming back to me."

"What do you want?" My voice is still shaky.

Sam must read my mind. "Mallory would like you to leave."

The man makes himself at home on my family room sofa and addresses me. "I'd rather stay. At least until Jake gets home. I thought I spotted someone lurking around your property when I was here earlier; that's why I entered your house—to check that you were okay. Then, I parked my truck down the road and kept watch on foot. I saw Dave pull into your lane and slipped into his car. He thought it would be less intimidating if he talked to you on his own rather than have the two of us approach you."

"So you and Dave know each other?" Paul asks.

The man doesn't answer. Paul has caught him on that. A connection between him and Dave that Dave neglected to mention Friday night.

"When you didn't answer the door, Dave gave up and returned to the car. Then these two guys," Lazarus motions to Paul and Sam, "pulled up behind Dave's car and ran to your door. I thought you were in danger, so I trudged around to the back of the house and drew my gun when they opened the door."

As far as I'm concerned, none of this explains why he's here, why Dave is here, and their connection to each other. Making out Paul and Sam are the threats? Pretending he was guarding the house to protect me?

"I want you to leave," I repeat, emphasizing each word, my voice steady this time.

Sam rises, grabs the bat leaning against the wall, and Paul backs him up, saying, "You heard the lady. She wants you out of her house."

Expecting him to pull his gun out again, I bluff, "The police will be here anytime now. I called 911."

The man runs a hand through his hair. Why does he seem familiar? He nods and rises. "Shit. There's no need for police again. Call them off. If you're sure everything is okay, we'll come back another time to talk to Jake."

"Call first," Paul says.

As Dave and Lazarus leave, escorted by Sam and Paul, I know I haven't seen the end of them. There's more to this than wanting to thank Jake and to protect me from some unknown predator outside my house. I'm sure the only threats here are Dave and this man who Jake rescued.

Sam and Paul return after moving their vehicles to allow Dave out of the lane. Paul puts his arm around me and says he'll call Linda and tell her he's staying with me till morning.

"You shouldn't leave Linda alone if those men are still out there." Sam volunteers to stay instead, saying Jilly will be fine in town, where plenty of neighbors are close by.

The front door is closed against the storm, but the wind has blown a scuff of snow onto the hardwood in the brief moments that the men slipped in and out of the house. Sam removes his boots and leaves them on the mat at the front entry to dry. "It's nasty outside. Slick. A layer of ice under the snow, a layer on top, and more snow coming down."

"I'm not sure how far Dave will get in that small 2WD drive vehicle of his. I wonder what happened to the truck," Paul says. "If he stole it, he traded down. He'll be in a ditch before long."

"What if they come back?" My voice trembles. I know I can't expect the police to drive here and be stationed at my house all night in case someone *might* come to the door, but I don't want to be alone.

"I won't let anyone in. Don't worry. I'll be right here," Sam assures me, the bat hanging from his hand.

"And I'll be right back if you need me. Call." Paul nods to Sam before heading out to his vehicle.

"Any weapons around here?" Sam asks once we're alone.

"Downstairs."

I watch Sam climb down to fetch the toolbelt, nail gun, and reciprocating saw from the tool bench where I left them. He glances at Jake's office space next to it. "Nice layout Jake has down here."

I assemble the tools on the kitchen counter, Sam's eyes on me. "That oughta do it," he says, sinking into the sofa and grabbing the remote. "Go on upstairs and get some sleep. I'll keep watch."

Bat and knife in hand, I thank him and head toward the stairs. I won't bother Jake with this; he'll insist on driving home. And it's not necessary. Sam is here.

Chapter Fifty-Six

The smell of bacon half-rouses me from a nightmare where I'm wielding a hammer and box cutter at Dave. Where did that image come from?

A plow scrapes its way along outside my window, so close I could swear it will crash through the brick any second. It takes a minute to orient myself, to realize I'm not at home, and Mallory isn't with me. I grab my phone to check for texts. Nothing.

A glance out the window tells me the worst is over. The snow and freezing rain have stopped. The wind has died down, and the sun peeks through clouds in an orange and yellow glow. We've weathered another Ontario storm. Then I remember. And with the memory, my butt aches from hitting the icy sidewalk last night. Someone broke into Mom's house looking to rip her off, but I stopped them before they could take off with something valuable. How the hell they got in is a mystery.

A call comes through for me, but it's not Mallory. Dom skips the formality of wishing me a good morning. "Jake. How's it going with locating the persons of interest?"

"Uh, not so good, Dom. No sign of Dave or amnesia guy. But I do have an idea of how to reach my cop relative who I've never met before. I'll be in touch with him soon, get buddy-buddy, and report back to you."

Dom sighs, a deep, loud sound that lets me know he's not pleased. "I don't want to involve myself directly, but this case needs to be resolved. I may send Nick out to the farmhouse to have a chat about the situation and discuss next steps. My regards to Mallory." He hangs up.

I need to haul my ass back home before Nick shows up to 'discuss next steps'. Wolfing down my breakfast, my brain trying to figure out what to do next about the two suspects in the murder case, both to appease Dom and to keep myself out of jail, I disregard the conversation between Mom and Steve until Mom mentions my name.

"He asked for Jake Shelton specifically, but I didn't want to wake you, so I said you'd return his call. Maybe after you finish breakfast, you can check in with the station."

I swipe my napkin over my mouth and turn to Mom. "Huh?"

"Pay attention." Steve nudges me with his elbow.

Mom tries again, handing me her phone. "Someone called for you early this morning. He didn't give his name, but I wonder if it could have been my half-brother."

I scramble to make the call, knowing initiating contact with this cop might buy me some time with Dom and possibly assist in finding Dave and Lazarus. I'm told again that Detective Marshall is unavailable to take my call and asked whether I would like to leave a message.

"Just tell him Jake Shelton called."

"When you talk to him," Mom bites her lower lip, "can you tell him I'd like to meet him?"

"Sure." We'll be one big happy family. The cop son of her bigamist Dad, her sorry excuse of an abusive husband, and her son, whose property is a dumping ground for murder victims. "But right now, I need to get home to my pregnant wife."

I push back my chair, thank Mom for the bed and breakfast, peck her on the cheek, and narrow my eyes at Steve, who has extended his hand, saying, "It's been good to have you home with us this week, Son. We hope to see more of you and your lovely family come to visit."

I grit my teeth, and my hand springs forward to meet his, knowing Mom is holding her breath. If he thinks he's going to make me look bad in her eyes, he can forget it. I'll be the bigger man. "Good to be home. I'll see you soon."

"Group tonight," Mom reminds me as I head out the door. "I'll bring leftover Christmas cookies from the freezer."

The city streets have been cleared, salted, and sanded. It's clear sailing down the main highway half the way home, then the terrain changes from white salted road to partly snow-covered with increasingly higher banks. Every so often, gusts arise, sweeping a new layer of white slickness under my wheels. By the time I near our corner, it's snowing. Home, sweet home.

When I turn into our lane, the dread courses through me. A black pickup sits next to Mallory's Toyota. I should never have left Mallory on her own. If Dave hurt her…if he hurt the baby…

I *will* kill him.

No man is above murder when it comes to protecting his family.

Chapter Fifty-Seven

"What the hell are you doing here with my wife?" Jake's voice bounces up the stairwell.

I crawl out of bed, half-asleep, and stumble down the hall to the top of the stairs. "Jake? What's going on?"

Sam stands at the bottom of the steps, face-to-face with Jake. "I stayed over on the family room couch. You had some unwanted visitors last night. Paul and I chased them off, but we didn't think Mallory should be left on her own."

"Mallory? Are you okay?" Jake bounds up the stairs. "I'm so sorry I left you alone. When I drove into the lane, I saw the pickup and thought Dave had come back to hurt you. Then Sam met me at the door, and for a second I thought…never mind what I thought."

He runs his hands down my arms, brings his chin to rest on my head, then draws me close, kissing my forehead. Sam shouts up the stairwell that he's heading home to Jilly, and the front door clicks closed after him. Jake takes me by the hand and leads me to bed.

"I'm fine, but it was a scary night." I recount the evening's events, with Dave and Lazarus dropping by, and how Sam and Paul came over to protect me, but the man with memory loss was confused and thought they were going to harm me. When I mention the gun, Jake rises and paces the room, running his hand through his hair.

"I should have been here instead of traipsing around the city," he says. "You must have been scared to death. If anything had happened to you…"

"It didn't. And to tell the truth, I'm not sure Dave and the man you rescued are a danger to us. They wanted to thank you in person for what you did. Although, I don't know why that man had a gun. It wasn't a hunting rifle. It was a handgun. Is that even legal? Oh, and I almost forgot. He was here earlier in the day, looking for you. And Jilly was here visiting in the afternoon, and Sam said he saw someone in the field when he was driving by clearing the side road."

"You had one heck of a busy day. Thank God we've got good friends who looked out for you. But I should have stayed home." Jake kisses the top of my head, holding me close.

"I *was* exhausted after the stress of having all those people in the house, but I'm fine. I had a good, long sleep once everyone left, and Sam kept guard. We *do* have good friends and neighbors. What about you? Did you have a good visit with your mom and Steve?"

"I had an eventful day myself." Jake tells me about his trip to the mall and the hospital. Shaking his head, he says, "But all the time I was searching for these guys we helped out, they were looking for me, right here. I'm not leaving you alone in the house again, not till they're caught."

We cuddle in bed, Jake assuring me I'm safe now. "By the way," he says, "I seem to have a long-lost uncle who's a detective in Toronto. I've been trying to get in contact with him at the police station."

"Your grandpa's son? The child in the photos?"

"Looks like it." Jake caresses my hair. "Something else happened. We had a break-in last night, but nothing was taken. I chased down the guy, but didn't get a good look at him."

With the high crime rate in the city, it shouldn't come as a surprise. We always assume it will never happen to someone we know, but the odds put everyone at risk. Each year, there are a couple thousand break-and-enters and robberies in the area.

"Jake, you shouldn't have gone after him. What if he had a gun?"

We lie in each other's arms, silent for a time. I wonder whether Jake is thinking the same thing I am: There is no safe place. Not in the city. Not here in the middle of nowhere. Jake snores in my ear, and I extricate myself from him. I'll let him rest after last night's encounter with the would-be robber. I put on my new robe and head downstairs for breakfast, Nellie and Lucky appearing out of nowhere when I open the refrigerator.

"Hi, sweeties. Are you hungry?"

The usual chicken pâté for them, and a fried egg and cheese slice on a bagel for me, then we sit on the window seat and gaze out at the winter wonderland. A gentle snowfall, coming straight down, brings peace to the open landscape. I sip my second cup of tea, no snowmobilers disturbing the quiet. This is the way it's supposed to be. No strangers coming to the door, no trespassers on the property, no bodies in the cornfield.

In two days, we'll be back to work, back to our regular routine. If the police don't solve the detective's murder, I'm not sure I can sit here alone while Jake is at the warehouse. Don't killers always return to the scene of the crime?

A nice, uneventful weekend will be nice. Just Jake and I hanging around the house, watching TV, relaxing.

My phone brings me out of my daydream. "I'll bring treats tonight," Vicky says. "We're new to the group, and I felt bad showing up out of the blue and not bringing something last week."

I'd forgotten about Group. "Jake said Rod and Sid told him they're not coming."

"Oh. Are you cancelling?"

It's a tempting thought. The weather is okay, but not great. "Maybe we should. Hold on, I just got a text from Beth."

Hope we're still on for tonight. I'm so mad at Jason I just might leave him. Is your guest room available?

She must be joking. She and Jason have everything they could want, with all that new money and the baby coming.

"Beth and Jason are having some major issues, from the sounds of it. I'll see you tonight." I complete my call with Vicky before returning Beth's text.

Hope everything is okay. You're welcome to stay here.

Not the first time Beth has sought shelter at the farmhouse. Last fall, when Jason went missing, she was at her wits' end. She's as likely to leave her husband as I am to leave mine. But if she needs a break, I'm her only friend.

"Honey?" Jake saunters into the kitchen, a perplexed look on his face. "Did you happen to move the key to Mom's house from the holder?"

"No. Why?"

"It's missing." He rubs his chin. "That's odd."

"You must have misplaced it."

Jake prepares the coffee. "Yeah, I guess. Keep an eye out for it, will you? Steve blamed me for dropping it somewhere. He wants to change the locks after last night. By the way, Mom said she'll bring treats for tonight. I think it was Rod and Janice's turn, but since they're not coming…."

"I don't think Group is going to fix that marriage anyway. What Janice needs is a new husband. That's the only cure for her marriage."

Jake chortles. "Yeah. But you've got to give Rod some credit for giving Group a try. He must care for Janice if he's willing to air all his shit just to please her."

"Hmmm." I'd bet that the last thing Janice wants is for everyone to know what a major creep her husband is. Group is likely her last resort, a final plea for help. If only she could meet someone new. Someone who appreciates her. It's amazing what some women will put up with.

"It'll be a small group tonight."

"Something's up with Beth and Jason. Did he say anything to you?"

Jake pours his coffee into a mug and joins me on the window seat. "Nope. Why? Trouble in their millionaire paradise?"

I shrug. Everyone has troubles. Not everyone admits it. I've been guilty enough of burying my head in the sand when it comes to Jake. The nights at the casino and out drinking, borrowing money to finance his gambling addiction, lying about it, involving himself with Dom…not to mention his jealousy, his anger management issues…

"Mal?"

"What?"

"I love you. I know I'm not worthy of you." He must have been reading my mind.

"I love you, too. And no, you don't deserve me."

His brow furrows, his mouth turned down in a little boy pout.

I can't help but smile. "But you've got me. And you're going to spend the rest of your life making yourself worthy."

Am I another Janice? Another Gloria? Blind to my husband's faults?

A rumble outside diverts our attention from the difficulty of marriage. Jake rises to check it out and shouts from the front entry that it's Paul blowing out the lane. "I'm going out to clear the walkway and shovel a path around the house."

The front door slams shut behind him. I turn on the television and settle onto the sofa. The midmorning city news reports the usual gang-related shootings and drug busts. Crime doesn't stop during the holidays. An update on the latest jewelry store robberies includes video of a storefront in the Brampton Heights mall, where Jake and I shopped for baby clothes a couple of days ago. I turn up the volume.

"It is believed that thieves entered the mall after hours through the skylight and smashed through the jewelry store doors. Security cameras were temporarily disabled, and guards chloroformed. Police are calling this another targeted heist, the third in the area in recent months."

No, the city is not a safe place to live. A scraping sound snaps my head around. Through the patio doors, I observe Jake's hooded form shoveling snow off the wooden steps. He waves before continuing to clear a path between the house and garage and moving along toward the back door. Paul's snow blower continues to rumble out front.

I grab my phone and search for jewelry store robberies in the Brampton Heights area. There is more information online and on social media groups than what the local news reported. Much of it is speculation or comes from unconfirmed sources. Fake news. You can't believe everything you read. I sift through news reports, videos, and posts, piecing together common threads.

Smash and grab. Hammers used. Cars plowing into jewelry stores. Masked men. Brazen armed robberies. Injured store employees. Some suspects were caught, others escaped.

According to reputable news sources, there has been a drastic spike in jewelry store thefts this past year, with thieves becoming more professional. I search for jewelry heists in the greater southwestern Ontario area.

Disarmed cameras and alarms. Entry through skylights. No sign of forced entry. Suspects got away. One headline catches my eye: **Are Jewelry Store Heists Across Ontario Connected?** I keep scrolling and find more interesting articles: **Is Organized Crime Behind the Recent Spike in Jewelry Store Robberies?** and **Jewelry Thefts Fund Other Criminal Activities**.

What's taking Jake so long? He'll be interested in hearing about the mall robbery last night. Thank God nothing happened while he was there.

News articles provide limited information. But related social media posts and videos, as ripe as they can be with conspiracy theories, offer more details. People speculate about a global crime syndicate involved in money laundering, insurance scams, and jewelry smuggling to and from India, Italy, and the Middle East.

Italy? My thoughts immediately shift to Dom and Isabella, who hail from Sicily.

Chapter Fifty-Eight

I shovel my way back toward the driveway, widening the path between the house and garage. Paul exits the cab of his snow blower and stomps through the snow toward me.

"Thanks for clearing the lane again," I shout.

"No problem. We had one crazy night here," he says.

"Mal told me about the visitors. I appreciate you coming over and looking out for her. What the hell do you think they wanted?"

"I don't know. Sniffing around your place, looking for something. Said they wanted to talk to you personally. These guys keep turning up like a couple of bad pennies. And they seem to know each other. I got to tell you, that's the first time I've had a gun pointed at me." Paul wipes his brow. "That was a bit beyond what I expected when I exercised my neighborly duty. Nearly made me wet my pants."

"A gun will do that."

"What's the deal here, Jake? You got something these guys want?" Paul sets his hands on his hips.

"Me? What could I possibly have that they want? Besides, I don't know these guys. They just showed up out of the blue." Or out of the snowstorm.

One of Paul's hands waves toward the back field. "What if they thought there was something valuable here? Like out in the barn? That jewelry you found?"

"The costume jewelry? Why the hell would they risk coming out in a blizzard to take Grandpa's stash of fake diamonds and gold?"

"Have you been following the news lately? Jewelry store robberies—

there's a ton of them recently in the area. Not here specifically, of course, but *in the city*." Paul spits out 'in the city' as though it's a disgusting place.

"I may have heard something."

"And you don't think it's strange that you found jewelry in your barn last week? Or that these guys keep snooping around? And coincidentally, a dead detective was found in your field?"

I shrug. "Coincidences happen all the time."

"Maybe. But I find it a bit suspicious that nothing criminal (apart from a few speeding tickets through town and that Peeping Tom incident a while back) ever happened around Idlewood until you moved in. So I'm inclined to wonder whether the recent events on your property aren't coincidental. Especially considering your friendship with that somewhat dubious character at the casino."

"Are you blaming me for all this?"

Paul's eyebrows shoot up. "Not *you*, and I've got your back, don't get me wrong, but something's rotten in the state of Denmark, if you know what I mean."

"Huh?" What's Denmark got to do with any of this?

Paul shakes his head and removes a glove to rub his chin. "Something's off here. I haven't figured it out yet, but I've been thinking…especially since that gun was pulled on me last night. Take care of Mallory. Don't let her out of your sight until this murder thing is resolved. I'll be around, keeping watch. Let me know if you need anything."

With a wave, Paul heads to his snow blower and backs out of the lane. Putting the shovel back into action, I work my way toward the front walkway, my mind running through the 'coincidences' that have taken place in the last week, trying to link them together.

Jewelry thefts. Grandpa's stash. Grandpa's secret life. Detective shot dead. Nearly dead amnesia guy thrown off his snowmobile. Dave's stolen truck stuck in a ditch. Dave in the jewelry stores. Mom's house broken into. A key missing.

I embed the shovel into a snowbank and rush into the house. My safe is *safe* in the basement. Isn't it? With its dual lock—key and combination—no one would be able to break in. Except Mal, who has managed to sneak into it before. It's unlikely she'd go to the basement, though. In any case, the key is hidden in such an obvious place she'd never think of it being there, and I've changed the combination from our anniversary to the baby's due date. She'd never guess it.

I root through the keys in the entry hall holder and remove the riding lawn mower key ring, the safe key still linked with it. Storming through the entryway without removing my boots, I head toward the basement. Mallory turns to face me as I open the door off the kitchen. Certain she's going to comment on the snow I've dragged in, my hand goes down to my laces. But she takes no notice. "Jake?"

"Hon? What's up?"

"Where's Dom from?"

"The casino. Brampton Heights. Remember, we were just at his place a few days ago." Memory loss must be a pregnancy thing.

"I mean, originally. His family. Where he was born."

"Sicily."

"That's what I thought. Is Sicily in Italy?"

"I don't think so; I think it's overseas somewhere. One of those exotic countries."

"I don't mean Little Italy in Toronto. I mean the one in Europe. Didn't you say his cousin is a pilot and flies home frequently?"

"Are you looking for a free flight? Planning a family vacation?"

Mallory draws in a deep breath and exhales in a rush. "No, silly. Did you know there was a jewelry store robbery last night in the mall where we saw Dave the day before?"

I stand staring at my wife, trying to assimilate this latest bit of information into the rest of this crazy scenario. Dave is a thief. Did Dave know about Grandpa's stash and think it was genuine? Did he come here to look for it? What is he willing to do for it? Is Dave a killer?

Mallory narrows her eyes. "Stolen jewelry sometimes comes from, or ends up, in Italy, from what I've read. And if Dom is from Italy, do you think—"

"I think you read too much. Why don't you take a nap before the gang shows up for Group? I'm going downstairs to check on something."

"Your boots." She motions to my feet. "And mop up the mess you left behind."

I do exactly as I'm told, even though I need to get to the basement ASAP.

A pregnant wife with an overactive imagination, along with her anxiety—not a good combination. Need to keep her happy. Boots on the back mat, mop out of the laundry room, a few swipes along the hardwood, then I scoot down the wooden steps. The workbench on the right looks off. Tools missing, moved around. Someone's been down here messing around with my stuff. Stealing shit? My eyes zip to my desk.

A gold chain lies on the carpet in front of my safe.

Chapter Fifty-Nine

Jake bursts into the kitchen and flops onto the sofa next to me.

"Everything okay down there?" I ask.

"Did you happen to need some tools lately? They seem to be missing."

"I used them as weapons when we had company. I guess they worked." I open the cupboard under the sink where I stuffed the tools in case I might need them again. Jake's mouth pops open, forming an 'O'. I grin at my husband, making it clear I don't need a man to shoo away unwanted visitors. The truth is far from that. "What were you looking for down there?"

"Just checking the safe. With you and Paul going on about these jewelry thefts, I wanted to be sure Grandpa's stuff was still there."

"Is it?"

"Yeah, I guess. I didn't get an exact count of the pieces. One was on the floor. I must have dropped it when I stashed the jewelry there in case somebody stupid enough to think it's real decides to rob us. Like this Dave guy. Or Lazarus. The joke would be on them when they took it in to be appraised."

"Soup okay for lunch?"

"Tomato? And grilled cheese? If it's not too much trouble." Jake's face takes on a darker cast, and I know what he's thinking. We've had more than our share of troubles over the last six months.

"Sounds good to me. It'll just be a few minutes." The mention of cheese and tomato has brought on a craving for smooth and gooey food.

Jake grabs the remote and flips to a romantic movie, upping the volume so I can stir and flip while I listen and watch. The smell of comfort fills the air as the pot boils and the frying pan sizzles. I balance two cups of soup and a plate of sandwiches on a tray and transport them to the coffee table so we can enjoy our meal while watching TV.

Our stomachs full, Jake pulls me close. At least we'll have a few hours of peace and quiet, just the two of us. Nellie and Lucky, upright on the window seat, watch the eerily quiet vast whiteness outside. The footprints left behind last night have been covered by the snowfall and wind. A few flakes continue to stir up, not enough to obscure the view straight out to the red barn.

Twenty minutes into the movie, Jake's snores interfere with the actors' dialogue, prompting me to turn on the closed captioning and let him rest. My lids close, and I allow myself a few moments of peace, the rise and fall of Jake's chest soothing, the comfort food making me sleepy.

When my eyes open, dusk has settled, darkening the room. Jake's steady breathing continues, nothing interfering with the tranquility of our home. Nellie and Lucky lie curled up on the bench cushions under the bay window. This is the way it should always be, just the two of us and our little family. Soon, our guests will arrive for the evening's meeting, and that's okay, too. I'm proud of our old home. It's a place for family and friends to gather.

Out of the corner of my eye, a movement flashes, and my head snaps to the window. Gray, white, a vast expanse of nothing out of the ordinary. My mind is playing tricks. I imagine an intruder lurks just out of my line of sight. Nellie and Lucky haven't moved from their sleeping position. Jake snores on. No sound intrudes from the outside world.

I slide away from Jake, ease myself off the sofa, and step toward the back door. My hand reaches the knob, unlocks it, and I gaze from left to right, then straight ahead. Snow. Darkness settles in around the endless expanse of white fields. Flipping on the exterior lights, I scan the back yard again.

Footprints. They weren't here earlier.

Shivering, I listen for any crunching of snow, watch for any sign of whoever made the tracks. A hand touches my shoulder. My squeal cuts through the cold.

"What are you doing?" Jake pulls me away from the door and shuts it against the frigid air.

"I thought I saw something. And there are footprints."

Jake opens the door again to see for himself. "Those weren't there when I was out shoveling. Turn on the front lights. Make sure everything's locked up after me and call for help if someone strange shows up. I'm going out to have a look around the house. I'll be back before Group starts. Set out those tools you used as weapons."

From underneath the sink, I remove the box cutter, hammer, screwdriver, nail gun, and saw.

"I guess that'll do the trick. Don't be afraid to use them if you need to." He takes the box cutter for himself and grabs the bat that Sam kept in the corner of the kitchen last night, dons his coat, hat, gloves, and boots, retrieves a flashlight from the closet, and disappears out the door, pulling on the knob to check the lock has engaged.

With the front exterior lights on, I pace from the living room to the dining room, gazing out the windows. Jake rounds the corner of the house, tramping through the snow, waves to me, and continues past the porch toward the garage. Moments later, his shape passes the patio doors, then the back bay window as I track his progress around the house. From there, he marches straight out the back yard, toward the shed.

The cats have awakened and stand guard at the window. Jake fades into the darkness, a faint beam of light visible as he heads out to the field and the barn in the distance. On the television, the local six o'clock news begins with a report that the weather has improved, and all roads in the area are center-bare with fair visibility. The severe conditions of last night have settled into a normal winter weather state.

The rumble of a vehicle catches my ears. Gloria and Steve must have decided to come early to help set up for Group. When I approach the entry hall, the car door slams. Footsteps clomp up the porch steps, shaking off snow. The bell chimes. I pull open the door to allow my in-laws into the warmth of the house.

Lazarus stands outside my door. Behind him lurks Dave. The ringing of my phone startles me. Something clanks in the house. It sounds like it's coming from the basement.

Chapter Sixty

"What in the flippin' hell do you think you're doing on my property?" As I followed the fresh footsteps around the house, I noticed they continued past the garage, into the back yard, and out to the field. Halfway to the barn, my flashlight beam landed on the large shape in a snowmobile suit crackling through the crisp snow. It came to a halt when my voice rang through the frosty air.

Now, his hooded face comes into view as he turns to face me. I can't believe this man has the nerve to show up in my cornfield again. The light blinding him, my bat raised, I demand answers. "You? What do you want? Why are you skulking around, scaring my wife?"

He tilts to the side. "Can you point that thing away from my face? It hurts my eyes."

"How about you tell me what the hell you're doing?" I bellow, stepping closer, swinging the bat.

"Shhh…keep it down, Jake. You tryin' to alert the whole fuckin' town?" Muscle Man, who used to harvest the weed in my field, holds up his hands, gloved palms out. "I'm here under Dom's orders."

"Dom? I thought he fired your ass." Not to mention, there is no weed to tend in the winter.

"He re-hired me. To hang out in case the killer comes back to the scene of the crime. And to protect Mallory. Not that she needs it. She seems pretty handy with power tools."

"I don't think so. Dom wouldn't hire you back. He doesn't put up with the kind of shit you pulled." Sounds like BS to me. I tell him to turn around and drop to his knees, his hands behind his head. "Down. Now. Don't make me clobber you. I hit more home runs as a kid than you blasted joints. And this box cutter is digging a hole in my pocket, itching to come out."

He complies under my threat, crunching down through the surface of the snow as he slumps. "Take it easy, Jake. Call Dom yourself."

"Lie down flat on your stomach, face in the snow, hands where they are."

"Are you fucking kidding?"

"Do you want your kneecaps broken?"

I risk taking my eyes off him for a couple of seconds and call Dom's cell.

He answers on the second ring. "Have you located any of the parties of interest?"

"I'm working on it. I did, however, find *something* interesting on my property. Jethro. Claims he's working for you, keeping an eye out on the property."

"That would be correct." His mellow voice provides no clue as to why he re-employed a man who crossed him.

"I'm about to cripple him. Unless you can explain why he's stalking Mallory."

"I would strongly suggest you refrain from injuring him." Dom's voice is even, but I detect a hint of a sigh. "I should have informed you he's back on the payroll."

"Care to enlighten me further before I maim him?"

"He came to me at an opportune time, unable to find employment elsewhere due to a lack of positive references. I needed someone to help you resolve your problem. Jethro knows you, your property, and the types of situations you find yourself in."

While I believe Dom made it impossible for Jethro to get hired anywhere, even flipping burgers, I doubt he would trust him again. "Are you forgetting he double-crossed you?"

"The beauty of it is, Jake, my boy, he's not likely to do so again."

The possible consequences of crossing Dom twice flash through my mind. "I see."

"I believe I made myself clear to our friend, Jethro. The slightest hint of disloyalty will make a prison term seem like a vacation in paradise compared to option B. Let me know if there are any issues when you review his work performance, and he'll be terminated. But not before the proper severances, of course. Have a good evening and give my regards to the little woman."

I clamp my open mouth shut when Dom hangs up. Time to assess Jethro's ability to do his job. I kick his leg. "You can get up now."

He pulls his upper body up, braces himself against the ground, which gives way under his weight, and struggles to a standing position, turning to face me. "Satisfied?"

I wipe the smirk off his face. "For now. You might want to keep in mind that if you work for Dom, you work for me." I let that sink in. "So have you seen anyone around the property while you've been skulking around?"

Jethro shrugs. "Just the usual suspects. Your folks, friends, neighbors popping by. The cops doing a drive through town now and then. And there's those two guys you helped out the night of the big storm. One our age, the other older. I've had my eye on them, but your friends scared them off last night."

"Are you armed?"

"Gun. In my pocket."

I set my bat between my legs and take the liberty of fishing out his weapon. "Let's go."

"Where?"

"To the house. And you'd better pray nothing has happened to Mallory while I've been chasing you. Or you'll be begging me to hand you over to Dom for a disciplinary hearing on your work performance."

I wave the gun in the direction of the house. "You first."

We march home, and I use my key to enter through the back door. In the family room, Mallory sits on the recliner facing Dave and Lazarus. Her eyes are locked on them, the reciprocating saw aimed toward them, a hammer in her left hand.

I wave my gun at the two men, Muscle Man backing me up. "Entertaining guests, honey?"

Mallory's eyes widen. *"Jake?* Why do you have a gun?"

"I met our friend, Jethro, when I was out for a walk around the property. He carries a gun for protection. Do we need protection, hon? Or have you got things covered?"

"Um, I think everything is okay. He…" Mallory gestures to Lazarus with the hammer, "wants to talk to you."

"Okay. Talk." I turn my attention to him.

"In private would be better." The guy's right hand flies to his back pocket. "Just let me—"

"Don't move." I direct the gun at him.

The doorbell rings. I motion for Jethro to answer the door.

Between the stomping of boots to shed snow, voices drift through the hall.

"Jethro! What are *you* doing here?" Beth asks.

"Just visiting, cuz."

"Jake? Mallory? Everything okay?" Vicky calls out.

"Come on in," I shout down the hall, inviting my friends to join the party, the gun tucked into the back waistband of my jeans, after I've checked the safety so I don't shoot myself in the ass.

"Oh. You have company. Are you joining us for Group?" Vicky sets a box of baked goods on the counter and nods toward the men on the couch. I assume she thinks they're a couple with marriage issues.

"They're just leaving. So is Jethro."

"More renovating?" Craig raises his eyebrows, noticing the tools in Mallory's hands.

"Where's your car?" Jason asks Jethro. "I didn't see it in the driveway."

"I left it down the road," Jethro answers.

"If you gentlemen will excuse us, we have a meeting." I motion for Jethro, Dave, and Lazarus to follow me to the front door. Time to get these clowns out of here. This circus is over as far as I'm concerned. They grab their outerwear, but the doorbell rings before the four of us get to the hallway. "That'll be Mom and Steve."

"No," says Mallory. "Your mom called to tell us they wouldn't be coming. Steve didn't feel good about leaving the house after the break-in last night."

"Break-in?" Vicky's voice rises. "Was anything taken?"

"No, I caught the guy in the act before he could find anything of value, and he ran off." I continue showing the intruders to the exit. Before we get there, the front door swings open, and Janice bursts into the entry, bawling her eyes out. What is she doing here? Rod told me they weren't coming tonight.

"I'm getting a divorce." She removes her coat and throws it to Jethro as though he were a butler or something.

Her announcement is followed by Rod rushing in. "Sweetheart. Honey. Darling. Let me explain. It's not what you think."

"Not what I think? You…you cheated on me. And I'm going to make sure everyone knows about it. I'll take you for every penny you've ever earned."

Suddenly a smooth-talker, Dave intervenes, jabbing Rod in the shoulder. "What is it with men like you who think they can get away with treating women like that? Either cheating *on* their wife or cheating *with* somebody else's wife. How could you disrespect a beautiful woman like this? And use another woman to do it?"

Rod advances toward Dave. "Mind your own 'effin business. And keep your eyes off my wife."

"It was with another man." Janice thrusts herself between Rod and Dave, beats her hands against her husband's chest, then slaps him so hard he stumbles backward. "Someone he met at the bar. I heard them on the phone. Talking about a secret meeting place. And…and he bought him jewelry. *I* never got jewelry from you."

"That's not what happened. I was seeing a guy I met in the bar, and you overheard me talking about our partnership, but—"

"I smelled aftershave on your shirt. And you don't use any. You always smell like sweat."

"I was just earning some extra money."

"Having sex with men in bars?"

Talk about secrets, Rod.

"What? No. Making deliveries for this guy."

Lazarus butts into the conversation, "Hey, I remember *you*." He pulls out a wallet from his pocket and flashes an ID card, then cuffs Rod. "You are under arrest for trafficking stolen goods. You have the right to retain a lawyer. You have the right to remain silent. Do you understand?"

I sure as hell don't understand. Janice and I stare open-mouthed at this guy making ridiculous claims about Rod. We both know he hasn't got the brains or moxie to pull off something like that. The exclamations from the family room indicate everyone has heard the exchange in the hallway.

Mallory waddles over to where the action is, followed by Vicky.

"Can I see your ID?" Vicky asks Lazarus. After ascertaining he's a legit cop, she tells Rod not to say a word. She will make sure he gets the best representation.

Mallory peeks over Vicky's shoulder and gets a look at the ID, her hand flying up to her mouth. "Oh, wow. Jake? Is this guy your uncle?"

"Cousin," the cop clarifies. "I've been trying to find a chance to speak in private about it. I recently found out about you. We have lots to talk about."

"Cousin?" I stare, open-mouthed.

"Half-cousin. My dad's your half-uncle."

"Pleased to officially meet you, nephew." Dave extends his hand. "Sorry for the subterfuge. There were reasons."

My knees buckle, and Dave's arms reach to hold me up.

What the hell is happening here?

Mallory pulls out her phone. "You and Steve need to get here now. Your brother and nephew are at the house. And I think Jake may be in shock."

I was wrong. The circus is just beginning.

Chapter Sixty-One

"Jakey hasn't got a chance." Jake sits on our bed, trying to recover from the revelations that knocked him off his feet. "Two more scumbags in the family who give men a bad name. Lying about who they are. Showing up here, scouting out the house. They'll probably lay claim to the farm property. Find developers and turn it into a subdivision or something stupid. Jakey's birthright is gone, all because Grandpa couldn't keep it in his pants."

My hand caresses Jake's back, and I struggle for words to assure him everything will work out. "We don't have all the facts yet. Let's wait and see what they have to say."

"Dave is Grandpa's son. He'll have rights to the property."

"Maybe we can buy him out."

Jake's hand rubs the stubble on his chin, the darkness matching the circles under his eyes. I could swear he's aged in the last week. "Do you think we could? We might have to spend all our savings. And I mean, all of it. Your parents' money, too."

The thought of throwing away my inheritance, along with Jake's, to stay in the house we've taken for granted was ours to keep, is too much. Maybe it's time to make the move to the city that I've been pondering. But I can't stand seeing Jake like this. "If that's what you want, it's what we'll do."

Downstairs, our guests await our return. I'm sure they understand that Group is cancelled for the night. Janice accepted my invitation to stay in the den. If there's anyone who has more to sort through than Jake, it's the woman whose cheating, criminal husband has been arrested. My reflection in the dresser mirror mocks me. Am I so different from Janice? Twenty years down the road, will Jake remain faithful? As for criminal activity, I don't allow myself to question his innocence.

I rise from the bed, take a closer look at myself in the mirror, and run my fingers through limp golden locks. "We'll be okay. As long as we have each other, it doesn't matter if we live here or elsewhere. I'll support you, whatever you decide. We'll deal with it together. Right now, we'd better head back down. Poor Janice."

"Yeah, that was one hell of a shocker."

On the dresser, my hairbrush sits next to my jewelry box. An impulse propels me to open the doors on the wooden chest. Cherished pieces from my parents and from Jake hang on hooks as usual.

"Jake?" My voice quivers. I turn to Jake, my mouth wide.

"What's wrong? Honey, is it the baby?" He jumps off the bed, arms encircling me, blue-green eyes boring into mine.

"My necklace. It's not here. Did you put it somewhere else?"

"What? No. I didn't touch it."

Jake fingers each piece of jewelry as though the 'diamonds' might be hidden amongst the chains and bracelets. The zirconia bracelet is in its spot. He pulls open the drawers, searches through the earrings and brooches. "Where are the earrings?"

Everything is where it should be, except for the two pieces from Grandpa's stash. I run my hands over the surface and under the doily while Jake reaches underneath the dresser and peers in behind.

Jake's face scrunches up. "Why the hell would someone take that and not the rest?"

"What if…I know it's a stretch, but what if they aren't fake? Maybe that's why Rod was arrested."

"Come on, Mal. Do you have any idea how much a string of rocks that size is worth? Probably tens of thousands. And the earrings to match? I don't know, we could be looking at a hundred grand. No way Grandpa had that kind of cash. And why the hell would he leave it in the barn if that stuff was worth anything?"

We stare at each other as though we'll find answers in each other's eyes. Is Jake thinking the same thing I am? Could Rod have stolen my diamonds?

Jake's face contorts as he voices another possibility. "Unless…Grandpa was a jewel thief?"

A tentative knock on the door distracts us temporarily. I pull open the door to find Dave standing there, ill at ease.

"I…uh…thought maybe I should explain. If it's any consolation, I didn't know about this until a couple of weeks ago when Ryan told me about the case he was working on. The previous owner of one of the properties used to temporarily stash stolen jewelry was Alex Marshall, my dad. We confronted Dad, and he told us the truth. All the time we thought he was a traveling salesman, he had another family. He said it really wore him down, running between the farm and city, trying to sustain his double life. When my mom was diagnosed with cancer, he quit his job and stayed by her side. She lasted over three years with all the surgery and treatments. He took care of her, and kept her out of hospice, right to the end."

A moment of silence follows, then Jake asks the question that I'm itching to ask. "What's this about our barn being a hideaway for jewelry?"

"Ryan said it was one of many locations. All he knows is he and others are supposed to work together to drop off and pick up the goods from various spots at specified times. The inventory rotates from one place to another, making it impossible for the authorities to track. And anyone who gets caught doesn't have enough information for the police to find the jewelry or who's behind it all. Ryan was directed to keep his ears open and try to work his way up in the organization. Police suspect the product is circling around in a money laundering scheme—sold cheap to jewelry store owners, who are then robbed, eventually sent overseas to be altered and sold again. Insurance companies are being hit hard with payouts."

"And what was your role in this?"

"Nothing. My son's the cop. Damn good one, too. But he suffered a nasty bash to the head when he hit Dad's farm implement out in the field. To make matters worse, when I visited him at the hospital, I was told he had been drugged before he was brought in—given something that causes memory loss. When he took off from the hospital, it was starting to come back to him. He remembered he was undercover, but couldn't put the pieces together, so he thought he'd be safer staying with me until he figured it out."

"None of that explains why you were here Friday night when he was injured, and the detective was killed." Jake pulls his gun from his back pocket and trains it on Dave.

"Whoa! Put that thing away. I didn't hurt anybody. I was hanging around your place for two reasons: I wanted to see Dad's farmhouse and maybe meet you or your mom. And I thought I could help out Ryan if I noticed any strange goings-on here."

"What were you doing in the jewelry stores?" Jake asks, not lowering his gun. My brain jolts as I think of Jake and 'his gun'. I doubt he'd pull the trigger, but he exudes an intimidating aura just the same. Reminds me of Dom.

"I was playing amateur sleuth, seeing if anything jumped out at me. It didn't. Except for you stalking me. And I thought I should keep our relationship secret till Ryan sorted things out."

Jake puts the gun back in his pocket, sits down, and rubs his forehead.

"And Rod?" I ask. "What's his role in this?"

"No idea," Dave yawns. "Maybe Ryan can give you some answers in the morning.

Chapter Sixty-Two

Paste a smile on my face and pretend everything is normal. Just another night at Jake and Mallory's place. Nothing out of the ordinary. A couple of new members to add to my family tree, a friend who got led out in handcuffs, a stash of jewelry that has caught someone's attention, and a gun sticking out of my back waistband.

In the family room, Jethro stands by the bay window, looking out, as if he expects more action. Dave sits precariously on the arm of the rocker beside Janice, patting her back. Jason, Beth, Vicky, and Craig turn their heads toward us as we join them on the sectional.

My best bud, Craig, remains silent, but his raised eyebrows and slight shake of the head, followed by an eye roll, convey his thoughts.

Since it's my house, for the time being, I speak first. "As you may have surmised, tonight's group session is cancelled due to all hell breaking loose in my house. So if everyone could beat it, I'd appreciate it."

Mallory nudges me with an elbow to the gut. "What Jake means is that he's a little overwhelmed by the sudden revelation about his family. We could use some private time. Beth, the offer of the guest room stands if you need a break. And Janice, you're welcome to stay, of course. You shouldn't be alone at a time like this."

The woman's sobs escalate, rivalling a stray cat's yowl, causing Dave to startle and fall off the armrest. Jason helps him up, saying no thanks to the offer for Beth to stay over; he and his wife will work out their family issues at home.

Then he addresses Beth. "Our problems pale in comparison to this. If it'll keep the peace, I'll meet you halfway." He turns to his cousin-in-law. "Jethro, if you need more help financially, I can spare some additional cash till you get yourself back on your feet."

Jethro nods his thanks, and Beth says, "That wasn't so hard, was it?"

"I'll go warm up the Hummer so we can get out of your hair. The four of us came in one vehicle," Jason explains. A blast of cold air rushes in as he opens the front door, then it slams shut. Jason returns to the family room, shaking his head. "Sorry, Janice. I'll have to ask you to move your car so I can back out. You're blocking me."

I didn't think she could blubber any louder, but Janice proves me wrong. "I don't…" she wails, "Rod…has the key."

I bolt toward the front door and peer out onto the driveway. My Honda. Mal's Toyota beside it. The Hummer behind the Toyota. And then Rod's Escape, in which he's unlikely to make an escape tonight. Dave's vehicle is gone, which I assume was Rod's ride to the police station. I slump back onto the family room sofa, next to Jason. "You're right. It's blocked in."

"Guess we're stuck here for the night," Craig says, offering up my house as though it were a hotel.

Mallory picks up the ball. "Beth and Jason, you can stay in the guest room. Vicky and Craig, the pull-out couch in the den. Janice, the new sofa's fairly comfortable. I hope that's okay. Dave and Jethro…" She turns to me. "This is exactly why we need another addition."

"Don't worry about me. I'm good on the floor," Dave says, perched back on the armrest. "Although, there is a nice B&B in town. Ryan and I stayed there last night after Mallory kicked us out. Bit of a walk, especially in this snow."

"I'll be staying up, patrolling the property. I'm on duty. Gainfully employed again, thanks to Dom." Jethro directs his comment to his cousin-in-law, Dom's new partner in the Kingston casino project.

Jason nods his approval. "Good. Glad to hear you ironed things out in that regard. It means I won't need to dole out quite as many handouts your way. Speaking of which, what about your car? Did you get that piece of crap fixed? Will it get us to the city?"

"I'll go fetch it."

Minutes pass, seeming to be hours, as we sit and stare, chins in our hands, waiting for something to happen. Ryan to bring Rod back, saying the arrest was all a misunderstanding. Rod to explain his infidelity to his wife. Janice to quit howling like a sick dog. Dave to head home with his son, the cop. Jethro to get his piece of crap car up the driveway so our friends can leave this god-awful circus.

An engine cuts through Janice's whimpers, Dave having subdued her with an arm around her shoulder, whispering that everything will be okay, and she can do so much better.

A car door slams, then the front door whooshes open, boots clomping straight into the family room. Snow melts from Steve's leather footwear onto our new hardwood. "What in blazes is going on now, Jake?"

The lead clown has shown up for his performance, having missed the first half of the show. I've got a feeling there's a lot more to come.

Chapter Sixty-Three

Jake's about to blow. And I don't think there's much I can do to mitigate the effects of the explosion. Fortunately, Gloria enters the room, pushes her husband aside, and maneuvers herself between Steve and Jake. Her eyes flit around the room and land on Dave; she studies his face.

"You look…a bit like Dad. Is it true? You're my brother?"

Dave slides off the armrest and extends his hand. "I'm glad to finally meet you. Sorry it's under these circumstances. I just recently found out I have a couple of sisters."

They stand awkwardly, appraising each other, with no one making a sound, not even Janice. I want to help Gloria. I don't know how.

Jethro provides a distraction from the uncomfortable scene of dysfunction in our home, barging in and tossing his keys to Jason. "Here you go. She's running good. But that kind of leaves me stuck here without a vehicle."

Jason hands over the keys to his Hummer. "Bring it home when the lane is clear, and you're done work. And there better not be a scratch on it when it pulls into my driveway."

Our friends rise from the sofa, scurrying for the front door where they fumble for their coats as though they can't get away soon enough.

Vicky hugs me, whispering, "I hope this all works out. What a shock."

Craig catches my eye, tilts his head, a barely perceptible nod. "Mallory."

"It's okay. We'll be fine. It is what it is."

Please don't remind me that Vicky got the better deal in the husband department.

Beth and Jason wish us the best of luck.

Jethro leaves as well, saying not to be alarmed if we see him wandering around outside.

And now there are six.

Jake stands where I left him, less ready to blow his top now that Gloria and Dave are sitting side-by-side on the sofa. Steve has taken a neutral position on a dinette chair.

Janice remains on the rocker. "Maybe someone could give me a ride to that B&B? I don't want to be a bother."

Playing the role of hostess, I place on a plate one of the pastries from the box Vicky left behind, grab a juice bottle from the refrigerator, and tell Janice to make herself comfortable with the television in the living room. "I'm sure they'll release Rod by morning, and everything will work out. It's a mistake. Just like when Jake was arrested."

Been there, done this. Better not have to do it again.

I close the hallway door after Janice and take Jake by the hand, leading him to the sectional where Dave and Gloria sit, and I settle onto the other end. Dave's mouth twitches, and he purses his lips, but no words come out. Gloria folds and unfolds her hands. Steve observes them, cool for now, but I have no doubt his fists will fly if Dave says or does the wrong thing.

I decide there is no better alternative than to have Dave speak and hopefully clarify his role in this family. "So, Dave. Maybe you could start by explaining…um…things."

Dave stands, motions for Steve to take his place on the sofa and settles into the glider rocker. "It's a convoluted story. Where to start? It started when Ryan got assigned to this case, taking down an international organized crime ring."

"Oh!" Gloria's hand flies to her mouth.

"Not single-handedly, of course. He's part of a province-wide team investigating jewelry store robberies and heists. The authorities believe the entire operation links to a crime syndicate in Sicily…"

"In Sicily?" Jake sits forward. "Is there a connection to anyone here?"

"A theory. No proof. Ryan says these kinds of crime organizations are almost impossible to take down. But the provincial police and local authorities are working on putting an end to the network of criminals involved with jewelry thefts here in Ontario, starting with the lower rung."

Gloria's face is ghost-white, remembering the man who she thought had died years ago, but left to be with another family she didn't know about. "Mom said Dad died. We had a memorial. I never got to see the body."

"Well, I guess you've got that to look forward to at some point down the road. Right now, he's looking pretty good for an old goat of seventy-eight."

"Are you telling us that son of a bitch is still alive?" Steve butts in.

Gloria covers her face with her hands, sobbing. "Mom's been gone for seven years, Dad for eight. I think she died of a broken heart. Even if they called it a heart attack. She didn't get over him leaving her."

"What do the jewelry thefts have to do with you coming forward now?" Steve demands.

Dave explains how our barn was used as a stash house, and how the title search led to Ryan's discovery about his grandfather's other life.

A sound between an inhalation and a hiccough erupts from Gloria, and I'm certain that she's going to break down. Steve has the sense to keep quiet. Jake's eyes dart from one of us to the other.

But Dave has more. "Dad lives with me now. He'd like to reunite with you and Jake."

"So he thinks he can waltz right back here and take over our home?" Jake rises and advances toward Dave.

Dave holds up a hand. "You don't need to worry about losing your property. Dad said he gave up his claim to it when he abandoned his wife and daughters. He had a lawyer draw up paperwork to that effect. The marriage between him and my mom was never legal, even though Mom believed it was."

"I don't know…if I want to see him," Gloria chokes out the words.

"I get it. *I* don't know if I want to see him now that I know the truth. But I'm kind of stuck looking after him in his old age. And he took good care of Mom when she got sick. You don't have to make a decision until you're ready. I'm going to give that B&B a call, see if they can put me up for the night. I'll leave you and your family to digest what I've told you."

Dave pulls out his cell and books a room.

"Can I get a lift into town?" he asks Jake.

Steve says he'll take him since his car is blocking Jake's Honda. As Dave and Steve walk past the living room, Dave calls out to Janice. "I've got a room at the B&B. Wanna join me? I can book another room for you."

Janice is by his side in a hurry. "That sounds like a good idea. I've made enough of a fool and nuisance of myself here." Still sniffling, she turns to thank me for being so understanding of her situation in light of all my problems.

My problems?

We've all certainly gotten to know each other well since our house became a 'fix your marriage' venue. Once it's just the three of us on the sofa, I say, "I hope this 'date' of Dave and Janice's works out to be the first of many."

Gloria agrees. "I think Janice is due for some respectful treatment. Dave seems really smitten with her. Love at first sight."

Jake squints. "She's not going to be my aunt, is she?"

Chapter Sixty-Four

"All the men in my family are doomed. Miserable excuses for fathers. I'm scared, Mal. That I won't do right by you. Scared for Jakey. That he won't have a good role model and will end up like the rest of us."

"You and Jakey aren't doomed to repeat the mistakes of your father and grandfathers. It's your choice to make. Look at John. He's a good family man. And Ryan is a respected member of the police force. And Dave is…well, he's Dave. He seems decent. You're a good person, too, Jake, deep down. You have a good heart. As long as you keep working at it, the good will win out. I believe in you."

Mal and I are snuggled under the covers, her head resting on my chest. I stroke her head; the soft, silky blond hair is calming to my touch. Nellie and Lucky lie curled up at our feet. With the door left open a crack, Steve's snores travel down the hall. At least he's sleeping, not having intimate relations with my mom. The thought puts me off having any fun time with my wife.

Dave's crazy story has us all exhausted. Grandpa's secret life has been exposed. He wants to see Mom and me. I know what Mom's answer will be. I'm not so forgiving. Sure, he did look after his so-called second wife when she was dying. Missed his real wife's demise in the process. But when he 'married' wife number two in the first place, what was his excuse for that? It's like he's two friggin' different people.

Which reminds me of Dom. Who the hell is *he*? I've known him for years, and I don't really know him at all. Dave's talk about a crime ring and a syndicate from Sicily knocked me sideways. To think that I, even for one minute, thought about working for this guy. With a cousin who is a pilot and frequently flies to Italy, where the 'family' lives, Dom's wealth, his dubious methods of getting what he wants from people, and his goal of running the local government, I'd be stupid not to wonder whether he's involved in something shady.

And I'm not stupid.

I'm cutting all ties with Dom. I roll off the bed, head for the bathroom, and call my 'friend'. Big brother? Benefactor? Fairy Godfather? The Big Boss?

"Jake. What's up?"

"I just wanted to let you know that I've made a final decision. And it is *final*. I won't be working for you in any capacity."

A big sigh blows into my ear. "Jake. I understand your reservations. It's a big decision. And from what Jethro reported, you've had a rough night. Not the best time to make a life-altering choice. Why don't you sleep on it? Give it a few more days. There's no rush. But I have announced my intent to run as Mayor. With my strong platform for positive change, I expect a win. I was really hoping I could depend on you. It goes without saying I will be disappointed if things don't go my way."

How to respond? Dare I air my suspicions?

"There's been some talk, Dom."

"There always is. What specific talk?"

Do I dare?

"Well, Dom. It's like this. I've found my long-lost cop cousin."

"Glad to hear you've been reunited with family."

"Yeah. So this jewelry crime ring he's working on busting seems to have ties to Sicily, or so they think. It crossed my mind that your family is from Sicily."

"There are a lot of families residing in Sicily."

"Wealthy ones?"

"All kinds."

"Your family is wealthy, from what I understand."

"You understand correctly. Also, powerful. But I'm making my own way here. I've cut most of my business ties with my family."

Might as well go all in and take my chances. "I'm not accusing you of anything, Dom, just to be clear. But if what my cousin says is true, you should watch your back."

Another heavy sigh. "Jake, Jake, Jake." His words crisp, each one enunciated, flow into my ear. "Do I strike you as a man of low intelligence?"

"No, no, Dom, of course not. I'm just looking out for your best interests."

"I appreciate that. But I always watch my back. I'm watching yours, too. Those rocks around your wife's neck? I'd lose possession of those if I were you. Unless you've got a legit receipt and a money trail. Especially now that you have a cousin in law enforcement. Family is family. But you can't always trust your blood relations, believe me. Sleep on it, and we'll talk tomorrow."

Too much spinning in my head for sleep to come. Dom has neither confirmed nor denied any culpability. And I just don't know.

But holy shit! I'm rooting for him.

Chapter Sixty-Five

The snorts and snores resound in synchronization, Jake beside me, Steve down the hall. We called it an early night after all the stress of the evening. Despite my exhaustion, I can't get back to sleep. I rise and pull back the curtain to a view of snow on the front lawn, snow on the trees across the road, and banks along the sides. All is clear, all is quiet.

Tiptoeing to the door and continuing to the stairs, I listen. The nightlight guides my way as I grip the handrail, the sidelights from the front entry shedding a glow up the stairs. So much got worked out tonight, and it's been a lot to take in for everyone. If only Ryan could find out who is responsible for Detective Swarovski's death, this ordeal would be over, and we could start to heal from our family traumas. And there are plenty of them.

I close the hallway door so as not to disturb anyone's sleep while I watch TV in the family room. In the kitchen, I flip the light switch and put the kettle on for tea. Outside, the back yard is still, no shadows creeping around the house, no snowmobiles ripping around the field. With one of Vicky's pastries and my cup of tea, I pull the throw over myself and curl up on the sectional with the television on, closed captioning, volume low. Another one of those romance movies lights up the big screen. Maybe I'll just float off to sleep right here, dreaming of a perfect relationship with the perfect guy in a perfect small town.

Footsteps intrude on my blissful daydream. My head whips in the direction of the basement door. It creaks open, a massive shape coming through.

"Jethro! What were you doing down there?" As I approach the door, my squeaky voice echoes down the steps. "How did you get in the house?"

"Anybody who knows you can get into your place. You keep the keys by the front door. It's not that hard to get a copy at Wilken's Hardware."

A clatter snaps my head past him, and to the left, to the doorway of the unfinished cavernous part of the basement we don't use. "What was that?"

Jethro takes a step back. "There's a rat in your cistern. I'm taking care of it. Just waiting to hear back from Dom to see how he wants it exterminated."

A scream catches in my throat as a shadow slips through the door of the cavern. When I point, Jethro whips around, pulling a gun out of his back pocket, loses his balance, and tumbles down the wooden stairs. It happens so quickly, I stand frozen. The shadow approaches Jethro's body on the newly carpeted basement floor, and Sam's face comes into view. I breathe a sigh of relief. A moan escapes Jethro, who lies on his side.

"Quick! Help me tie him up before he wakes," Sam says. "I saw this guy hanging around your property while I was out plowing, so I followed him to see what he was up to. I caught him stealing your jewelry, and he forced me into the cistern at gunpoint. I'm lucky I was able to hoist myself out."

Jethro's gun is now safely tucked in the waistband of Sam's pants. Holding the railing, I inch down the stairs, my eyes on Jethro in case he makes any sudden moves. Sam holds Jethro down and instructs me to grab a coil of rope from the pegboard, along with snippers. A wrench lies on the workbench, the snippers tossed next to it.

"Thank God you're okay, Sam." My eyes land on the sparkles in front of Jake's open safe, a bag lying on the floor, jewels spilling out as Sam binds Jethro's hands and feet.

Sam rises from his kneeling position, setting the rope and snippers on the bench. "Watch him while I back my truck into the driveway, and I'll get Jake to help haul him to the police station."

As Sam bends over Jethro and turns him onto his stomach, Jethro grabs at Sam's shirt pocket, and a necklace spills out. *My* diamond necklace.

"Sam? Why do you have my necklace?"

"He was going to frame me. Then take off and leave me to blame."

In the cistern?

A chill courses through me. Something isn't right.

Jethro squirms on his stomach and rasps. "Run, Mallory."

I make it up a couple steps, my heart pounding in my chest, ever mindful of the baby. "Help! Jake!"

"Stop. Get back here." Sam scurries after me and pulls shut the basement door. He grabs my arm, dragging me toward the floor as I keep a grip on the handrail.

"You're hurting me." I don't resist, fearing I might fall. "What's going on, Sam?"

Jethro struggles against his ropes, flipping himself onto his back. "Let her go."

Sam deposits me on the swivel desk chair next to the tool bench and backhands Jethro across the jaw, knocking him out again. As he runs his hand through his hair, pacing the floor, my hand slides toward the wrench. Sam stops, noticing me stretch toward it, and pulls out Jethro's revolver.

"Don't even think about it. I'm sorry, Mallory. I never thought it would come to this. I don't know what to do. I mean, I can't *shoot* you. But I can't let you go, either. So…I don't know."

I struggle to breathe. A wave of nausea rushes through me, and darkness threatens to overtake me. But the baby needs me. My only hope is to convince Sam that there is an alternative to using the gun. "Please. I'm pregnant. I know you don't want to hurt me and the baby. Maybe you could just leave. I won't say anything. I promise."

Sam shakes his head and resumes his pacing. "I don't see how that can work. This is bigger than just a bit of stolen jewelry."

"What do you mean?" If I can keep him talking, maybe I'll figure out a way out of this.

He lowers the gun. "Things got out of control."

"I'm sure none of this is your fault."

"I got in over my head, Mallory. I never meant for anyone to get hurt. But it's become a nightmare. And I can't face Jilly. What am I supposed to tell her?" Sam pulls a hand over his face, and my eyes move from his expression to the gun next to his hip. I don't dare move until he sets it down.

I watch him struggle with his inner self, the good and the bad, unsure of which side is going to win this current war. I've seen Jake battle his own demons, and I know that sometimes it's simply too much to handle. Just like the fights in the school yard, just like the tragic domestic situations reported on the news, just like workplace violence. Frustration and pressure lead to desperate actions.

"Tell *me*, Sam. What happened?"

He looks away, and I consider whether to grab the wrench and lunge at him. Overpowering Sam is a fantasy, nothing more. I have the baby to think of, not just myself. "Sam? You're a good man. I'm sure there are mitigating circumstances. Don't do anything to make things worse."

He talks to the wall as I consider my options. Sit and wait for someone to help. Hope for Jethro to wake up. Strike out. Fight back if he attacks first. "I was recruited when I went out on an emergency call where a guy got hurt during a robbery. Claimed he was a store customer. But in the ambulance, a stash of jewelry spilled out from his backpack. He begged me not to turn him in, saying he'd split the money he earned with me. I should have left it at that. But I didn't. I wanted more. And it just spiraled out of control."

Like addiction. Like abuse. Like anxiety. Like grief.

I keep my eyes on Sam as my hand inches toward the wrench. "We could just pretend none of this happened and go on as normal."

Sam snickers, turns to me, and notices that I'm reaching for the tool on the bench. The hand holding the gun jolts up, shaking as he waves it in the air. "Do. Not. Even. Normal? Yeah, we'll all go on as normal. This therapy session is over. Let's go. Into the cistern."

"No. My baby…" I whimper, appealing to the Sam I know, the good Samaritan.

"I'm not asking again. Maybe I should tie you up and gag you before throwing you into the cistern. That'll buy me some time so I can figure this out." He approaches the pegboard above the workbench, his back to Jethro.

Jethro's eyes open. He mouths to me, "The snippers. Over here."

As Sam reaches for the duct tape, I grab the snippers off the bench, but I'm too slow, and Sam slides them out of my reach. "Please, please, Sam…don't hurt my baby."

"Quiet. Or I'll *make* you shut up." Sam unrolls the tape and clips off a chunk, tossing the snippers back onto the tool bench.

"What would Jilly say if she could see you now? She's always so proud of you."

It stops him long enough for me to take action as he sticks the duct tape to the bench and covers his face with his hand, shaking his head.

I wrap one hand around the wrench and swivel to face him. The wrench comes down hard enough on his ankle to elicit a shout as his leg buckles. "Fuck!"

"The snippers," Jethro mouths again, seeing Sam with his head bowed. "Cut me loose."

I lunge for the cutters and toss them toward Jethro, who rolls over and grabs them. Sam has recovered his balance; he points the gun at Jethro. "Not happening."

A gun trumps scissors.

Jethro doesn't seem to realize that. With his bound hands, he points the snippers at Sam. "Drop the gun."

Sam laughs. "Are you serious?"

I ease myself off the chair, reach for the battery-operated drill on the pegboard. Jethro sits up. "Yeah, I'm serious. Are you?"

My grip on the drill steady as can be given the circumstances, I advance toward Sam's back as Jethro pulls himself to his feet, still groggy. "It's over. Give it up. Before you do something you'll regret. There's a woman and baby involved. Man up."

We don't get the opportunity to witness Sam's next move. From the corner of my eye, I see a shape at the top of the stairs; it slowly descends, one step at a time, mindful of possible creaks in the old wood.

"Turn around, you cowardly piece of shit." Steve's voice bellows through the basement. "No one fucks with my family."

The bat connects with the inside of Sam's knees as he turns to face him, and Steve hits a home run, knocking him to the ground.

Jethro maneuvers the snippers to the ropes on his hands while I grope for the gun that sprang out of Sam's hand as he went down. But I'm too slow in my condition. Sam grabs the gun and pulls himself to a kneeling position as Steve swings again.

The crack of the bat on the floor coincides with the shot. There's no time for me to process what happened. Footsteps pound on the stairs, matching the pounding in my chest.

"Police! Don't move." Ryan stands in the middle of the stairs, his gun pointed down.

Jake shoves past him, racing down the stairs, disregarding the danger, and scoops me into his arms. "Oh, thank God, thank God. Honey. Thank God. Are you okay? The baby. Is the baby okay?"

Ryan collects the gun Sam has dropped again. "Hands behind your back."

I melt into Jake, and he cups my face, telling me I'm safe as Ryan cuffs Sam, then Jethro, and reads them their rights.

It's over. I'm okay. The baby is okay. Jake is here with us.

Ryan's voice is all I hear through the buzzing in my head and whooshing in my ears. Only two words make sense. "Ambulance. STAT."

Who needs an ambulance? I look down at myself, expecting blood to spurt through my nightgown. Am I losing the baby? My hands fly to my belly, my eyes downcast, searching for blood. Jake's hands join mine. Jakey kicks against my palm.

"I need some help here, Jake," Ryan shouts.

I lift my head. Sam and Jethro sit propped against the stairs, hands behind their backs, chained to the railing, looking like they've been in a barroom brawl. Maybe *they* need to go to the hospital?

"Dad?" Jake slips away from me, crawling on the carpet. "Dad!"

Blood seeps from Steve, pooling around Jake's knees.

In a blur, the action in front of me moves in slow motion, a video on playback, each scene elongated. Ryan, leaning over Steve, ripping off his own shirt to staunch the blood flow. Jake, sitting on his heels, rocking back and forth as Ryan shouts for him to get an emergency kit. Gloria, scurrying down the stairs, keening an unnatural song of death. Sam shouting, "He's going to bleed out before the ambulance comes. Uncuff me. I can save him."

Ryan swears in response as he applies pressure with one hand and throws me the key to the handcuffs, shouting back at Sam. "You'd better make sure he survives."

To Jake, he screams, "First aid kit, Jake!"

Jake jolts from the floor, up the stairs.

It's in my hands now. Wait for the ambulance? Let Sam go and trust he won't run off?

No time to think. It's time to act.

As soon as I uncuff Sam, he hobbles over to Steve to assist Ryan in applying pressure. "Take off your belt so I can make a tourniquet," he directs Ryan.

When Jake returns from the back bathroom to hand over the first aid kit, Sam is securing the tourniquet with a screwdriver. He takes over from Ryan, packing the wound with gauze, checking Steve's airway and his pulse. Jake sits back, watching them work on his father, his arm around Gloria, whose shrieking has settled into wracking sobs. Jethro asks me if I'm okay, saying Dom won't be happy if I'm hurt.

Dom? Dom won't be happy?

Chapter Sixty-Six

It's over. Or as over as it's going to get.

Steve lies unconscious in the hospital bed, tubes and machines hooked up to him. Beeping, colorful, wavy lines and numbers on the monitor, nurses flitting in and out, staring at the screen and checking Steve to make sure he's still among the living. Lights, sound, action.

Mom sits quietly on a chair next to Steve, nearly comatose herself, a hand on his arm. Mallory sits next to her, one hand on Gloria's arm, another on her belly, a chain linking our unborn child to his grandfather, who nearly died, as though the baby can transfer his vitality. On the other side of the cot, I'm on my knees, head in my hands, fighting the sobs, embarrassed to be seen pining over my old man. No one speaks. My thoughts are so tumultuous I wouldn't understand the words if anyone did have something to say.

Earlier, when they wheeled Steve off to surgery, I broke down and confessed my love to my biological father. The man I hate, the man who ruined our lives, the man who thought he could worm his way back into our hearts. The man whom I didn't realize I still love.

"Dad, Dad, hang in there. Dad, please don't die on me. I'm so sorry. I forgive you. Dad, I love you." I didn't know if he could hear me, but he squeezed my hand as they loaded him onto the stretcher to wheel him off to the operating room.

How fucking sick am I? Blubbering over this man I despise.

Now, the surgery's over. And we wait.

I rise from my knees, as though I've finished praying (and I swear to God

I haven't been).

Who the hell am I kidding?

I gesture for Mal to join me in the waiting room, so that John and Deb can have a turn watching over Dad in the ICU. We amble through the double doors, hand in hand, out to the waiting area where my brother, John, and his wife sit staring through the windows of Grandview Medical Center as the snow falls on a blustery afternoon, waiting for their first glimpse of Dad since the gunshot wound to his thigh. We take their place on the vinyl chairs. I know John has plenty of questions about what happened. Deb casts her eyes my way, but her look is sympathetic, not accusatory.

A figure appears from around the hall. Tall, imposing, strolling in as though he owns the place. But his face betrays his emotions. Dom approaches, greets Mallory, and takes her hand. "I'm so relieved that you and the baby are okay."

He then sets his hand on my shoulder and gives it a squeeze. "Jake. I'm sorry about your father. How is he doing?"

"Hanging in there. Got through surgery. We're waiting for him to wake up. Waiting to hear from the doctor." I'm surprised I can string together a few coherent words.

Dom sits beside me and waits with us, Mallory on my other side. An hour, according to the clock on the wall, passes. It may as well be a year. I'm caught in a vacuum. Sucked in like a piece of lint. Worrying about Dad. About Mom. About Mallory. About the baby. Tick, tick, tick.

John bursts into the waiting room, his face unreadable. "The doctor's coming. Wants to talk to the family."

Deb escorts Gloria from the ICU to join us, and we wait in silence. Within minutes, a middle-aged male doctor appears. I can't tell if it's good news or bad.

What could be a slight upturn of his mouth graces his face. "I'm Dr. Sorini, the surgeon who operated on Mr. Shelton. So, the bad news is your husband," he nods toward Gloria, "lost a lot of blood, and he'll be needing rehab to regain use of his leg. The good news is he's tough, and I expect he'll recuperate quickly. He should wake up soon, and we can better assess his condition then. At that point, I can answer any questions you have about his recovery."

Dr. Sorini turns to Dom. "And how are you, my friend? And the family?"

"We are all well. Thank you for taking care of Mr. Shelton."

"Of course, Dom." The doctor heads back to the ICU.

Dom's 'friends' seem to extend well beyond the casino and hotel complex.

Chapter Sixty-Seven

A fog lifts from around us as we all hover at Steve's bed in the private room where they have moved him, and his eyes open. He tries to speak, but it comes out as a squawk. Gloria holds up a glass of water with a straw, and he takes a few sips. His first words are directed at Jake. "Son. Is everything okay? Mallory? The baby?"

Jake's voice catches. "All good, Dad. Thank you for saving Mallory."

Steve lies back on his pillow. "What's a father for? Although, I think Mallory can handle herself. You've got a brave woman, Jake. Hold on to her."

"I intend to."

This is the moment for Jake to accept Steve's attempts at redemption. It's now or never. But he needs a nudge.

"I don't think Jethro and I were a match for Sam and his gun. Thank you for saving us. I don't know what would have happened if you hadn't shown up." I speak the truth; I really don't know. Sam could have gone either way. My eyes beseech Jake to make his peace.

He takes a deep breath, clasping his hands under his chin. A slight nod, and his eyes meet Steve's. "I really mean it, Dad. I appreciate what you did. You kept my family safe. Even if you couldn't do the same for your own."

He needs another nudge. I elbow him in the gut, as much as it pains me.

"Oof." He holds his stomach. "Anyway…you know what I mean. I'm really, really grateful. It means a lot to me."

Jake sets his hand on Steve's shoulder, and Steve nods, saying, "I'm trying to do better. It will never be enough, and I can't take away the pain I caused the people I love, but I swear I'll do my best."

I'm not so naive as to think this love relationship between father and son will continue once this is behind us, but there has been a definite shift in Jake's attitude toward Steve.

"It's been a long night and day," Gloria says. "Why don't you all head home and get some rest? I'll stay here with your dad. The nurse said they can set up a cot for the night."

Our steps to the hospital exit are much lighter than last night's entry through the emergency doors. When Jake rushed ahead, checking that I was behind him, he stopped to inquire about Steve at reception, his face ashen.

Now, he is calmer. I squeeze Jake's hand.

At Gloria and Steve's house, the four of us collapse on the sofa. Deb checks in with her neighbor, who is looking after the boys. Then John starts to fire off the questions he's been holding back.

Jake holds up a hand. "I wouldn't know where to begin. But our cousin, Ryan, may have some answers. I asked him to meet us here."

The bell rings in response to Jake. Ryan enters, and Jake introduces him to John and Deb. "Cousin Ryan, courtesy of Grandpa's secret life."

Despite our exhaustion, we listen to Ryan explain how he found out we are related. What catches John's attention is Ryan's words that Grandpa is alive and well. He wants to see him.

Jake's twisted sarcasm has returned now that Steve is on the road to recovery. "Great! We'll have a big family reunion and live happily ever after. Too bad Grandma can't join us, seeing as she died from a broken heart."

I change the topic to Sam. It was *he* who shot Steve, the gun discharging when he stumbled, trying to avoid Steve's attempt to bat him back to the ground. "What happened at the station? Did you arrest Sam? What about Jethro?"

Ryan provides all the details. "Jethro was released after being questioned. Domenic Pappalardo confirmed that he was working for him, guarding the farm, and that you were aware of that."

Jake nods. "Yeah. And Sam?"

"Sam is awaiting a bail hearing. He confessed to being involved in the jewelry thefts. He's likely to be charged with attempted manslaughter in Steve's shooting, but the fact that he saved Steve's life will be in his favor. Moreover, he's offered to give testimony against the people who hired him. Unfortunately, they're only low-level operators; we're not likely to find the real criminals, the ones at the top of the pecking order."

"So your investigation is over?"

"It's never over, but we'll shut down one small operation, and we've got more leads. I was working undercover, transferring stolen goods to a safe, temporary hiding spot till the heat died down, and trying to flush out who was in charge of the operation. Things went sour when Sam, Detective Swarovski, and I met up in your back field to deposit more swag. As we scouted out another good hiding spot, Sam got greedy and wanted to pocket some of the goods."

We all draw in a breath at the same time, but Jake is the first to ask, "Detective Swarovski? He was undercover, too? And Sam killed him?"

"Yes, no, and yes. Detective Swarovski *was* undercover, but he was suspected of being on the take. I was brought in to keep an eye on him as well as to break into the organization."

"On the take?" Jake's voice rises an octave.

"He was turned down for a promotion he expected. Shortly after he falsely arrested you for murder this past fall. He was bitter about that." Ryan shoots Jake a look. "Not all cops are on the straight and narrow, especially after years of seeing criminals get away with so much. Still, he didn't deserve to die, guilty or not. And the jury is out on that. The official stance is he was working undercover and was killed in the line of duty."

"So you don't know?"

"A lot of cash was discovered in his bank accounts. No trail of where it came from."

"Who killed him?" I ask.

"Swarovski and I tried to convince Sam that the higher-ups would find out if some of the goods were missing, and we'd all be in trouble. Sam and Swarovski got into a fight, and when Sam pushed him, Swarovski cracked his head on the feeding trough in the stable. Sam panicked and told me to help him drag the body out to the field, but I took off and was going to call for help. My snowmobile hit something as I tried to get away, and well…you know the rest. I didn't remember much after my head injury, not to mention the roofies, which Sam must have slipped me on the way to the hospital."

"But you saw Sam in our house," I exclaim. "If you saw him kill the detective, why didn't you arrest him then?"

"I didn't know it was him. Although his voice was familiar when I met him at your place. He wore a balaclava under his helmet that night. Obviously didn't want people to know who he was."

"I guess none of us knew who he was," Jake says. "Sam was our friend; he lived in our neighborhood and kept the roads safe in the winter. He was the good guy. A paramedic, saved lives. I can't believe he would do this."

"Jethro caught him red-handed, loading the jewelry from your safe into a backpack. That, combined with the treads on his snowmobile, some still visible near the shelter of the stable where Swarovski died, should be enough to put him away. With my testimony, he'll face charges for involuntary manslaughter in Detective Swarovski's death and Steve's shooting, along with attempted theft and possession of stolen property. Several pieces from the recent heist were found hidden in his home."

"How did Sam break into my safe?"

I have his answer. Jake is no expert at keeping things hidden, hard as he tries. "You keep the key on the ring with your riding lawn mower key, hanging at the front entrance. He must have discovered it when he stayed with me the night you were at Gloria and Steve's place. And Jilly knows the baby is due at the end of February. Sam must have finally figured out that was the combination and tried possible numbers."

Poor Jilly. There will be a big news article to print, but I think this will end her journalistic aspirations. I wonder whether she saw any signs that her husband had criminal tendencies. A woman would have to be blind not to know that about her husband, wouldn't she?

Chapter Sixty-Eight

I t's going to be okay," I say once we're alone. "Steve's going to make it."

"Yeah," Jake nods. "Not that he deserves to."

Back to square one. I remind him that his father almost died, and he was beside himself, in tears, worried that he was going to lose him.

"That was for Mom's benefit. You know how I really feel."

"I do know, but I'm not sure you do. I understand that you hate the old Steve. So do I. I think he hates himself more than the rest of us combined. But I think your mom is right. Everyone deserves a second chance. I don't know what you went through growing up, but I can see Steve wants to be a good husband and father, and he's great with the boys. I trust him to be a grandpa to Jakey."

"I won't *ever* leave him alone with my son. Or daughter." Jake's eyes take on the steely cast that tells me to leave things be.

"No. I agree. But supervised visits? He did save Jakey."

Jake swallows. "Yeah."

I set my hand on Jake's. "Honey, I think you need to let go. You owe yourself that much. Forgiveness is the best gift you can give yourself. If not for Steve, do it for you. For us. All of us. You are going to be a great dad. *You* don't need to repeat your father's mistakes. Don't let our future and our children suffer because of the past.

"You're right, hon," Jake says, "I need to forgive. I just don't know if I can. But I'll try."

"Okay."

It's the best Steve is going to get. Steve is trying hard. Jake is willing to try harder to accept him. Gloria will be relieved. As an about-to-be mom myself, I understand the importance of family. We all make mistakes, we forgive, we love. Sometimes the mistakes are horrific. And love doesn't conquer all. But hate conquers nothing.

It's going to take Jake a long time to process what has happened. "I know you've had a lot thrown at you the last few days," I say, recognizing the emotional toll this has taken on him, "with the news of your grandpa and the family you didn't know about. And to find out Rod and Sam betrayed your friendship and used our property for profit."

Jake shakes his head. "Yeah, hard to believe my friends were involved in this whole mess. I still can't get my head around it. I mean, I kind of get it with Rod. He was after some quick money, not bright enough to consider the consequences of getting caught. Maybe he can plead stupidity and get a lighter sentence. But Sam? He was supposed to be the good guy. I still can't believe he would do this. He caused Swarovski's death because he was greedy for more money. He nearly killed Steve. And he almost..." Jake's voice cracks, the words sticking in his throat, then his expression hardens. "I can't forgive what he did to you and Jakey."

"No." Some things are harder to forgive than others. "But I don't think he meant to kill anyone. The detective and Steve—it was an accident. And I don't think he wanted to hurt me, but the way he was waving that gun around scared me."

"What kind of man threatens a pregnant woman? I don't get it. I thought I knew Sam."

"He did save Steve in the end. And he confessed his sins."

"Because he was cornered. He was trying to save his own skin. If he felt any remorse for Swarovski's death, he would have turned himself in, instead of trying to find the missing jewelry."

"Everyone has their flaws." The words slip out of my mouth, and I don't know where they came from. Subconscious thoughts? Jake is by no means perfect himself. Nor are some of his family members. Or some of the people he associates with. But who am I to judge?

"Humph. Some flaws are greater than others."

"Speaking of forgiveness," I say, "Janice called me to apologize for her husband. She's decided to file for divorce. She said this was the final straw that broke her back, and she's cutting all ties with Rod."

"He'll be tied up in prison time for a while anyway." Jake furrows his brow, and I can tell he's pondering something. "If *I* spent time in jail for trafficking stolen goods, would you stand by me?"

"Yes," my answer comes without hesitation. "But you would never do that."

Then I think about the illegal marijuana that was growing in our fields. And the hold Dom has on Jake. What else would he be willing to do for him?

He rubs his chin. "No. But I've made some mistakes...which I won't make again."

"It's only human to make mistakes. It's how we learn." This is what I tell the kids at school.

We all err. The only mistake is if we refuse to admit that we were wrong.

Chapter Sixty-Nine

Steve has regained his color. He sits propped up on his family room sofa, surrounded by his family. Gloria, Jake and me, John, Deb, and his new in-laws—Dave and Ryan.

"Ryan has some information about the break-in at our house," Jake says. He turns to Ryan to allow him to explain.

"It was Rod. He confessed to being involved in the transportation and concealment of stolen goods. I remembered when I saw him at your house—he was one of the guys in our group. He said he just wanted to make a few bucks. Didn't realize it was against the law."

And Beth thought Jethro wasn't the brightest?

Ryan continues. "He's been charged and will be serving time. Might be able to make a deal, though, to cut down his sentence. He's willing to talk, along with Sam. Turns out he was in a partnership with Sam. They thought nobody would miss a few pieces if they took them. Rod was the fourth snowmobiler on your property that night. He just didn't make it to the meeting spot in time the night we made our deposits. But he did arrive in time to see Sam load his sled on his truck and take off like a bat out of hell, placing him at the murder scene."

"It was Sam's truck that zipped past me that night as I was getting close to home," Jake says. "I thought he was just plowing the roads. But he was making his escape."

Ryan nods. "And there were plenty more deposits in your barn. Several. You only found one. The police seized the rest during the search for evidence in Detective Swarovski's death. Sam visited me at the hospital, thinking I'd made off with the jewelry. When Sam saw Mallory wearing those diamonds, he figured you might have found a stash and helped yourself. But Rod and Sam couldn't find where you'd hidden it, so Rod thought you might have planted it in Gloria's house, mixed in with all the moving boxes. Then Sam noticed the safe in your basement, found the key, lucked out on the combination with Mallory's delivery date, and struck gold. Among other metals and gems. Thanks to Jethro, he didn't get away with it."

"Wow. Poor Jilly. Poor Janice." I shake my head. "Finding out your husband is a criminal."

"I'll take care of Janice," Dave says. "She's due for some good loving."

"You're right about that, brother." Gloria reminds us that someone is missing from our family reunion.

"I'd like to see Grandpa, too," John says when she mentions him.

"Me three," Jake adds. "Glad to see you're doing better, Dad. We need to head out, but we'll stop back in tomorrow."

"We'll be in touch about a family get-together," Dave assures us, "once you've recuperated, brother-in-law."

Jake hugs Gloria, and to my astonishment, he pats Steve on the arm. "Get well quick."

Dave and Ryan leave with us, and we walk together to our vehicles parked on the street.

Something is still bothering me. "What about your truck? The police said you stole it."

Dave blows out a big puff of air, his breath coming out in a fog. "That was a mistake. I just found out my ex-wife has a new boyfriend. One with a fancy truck and snowmobile. I figured if he could take my wife, I could take his truck."

"Mom's not your wife anymore," Ryan reminds him.

"Like I said, a lapse of judgment. And I didn't outright take it. I made a trade—left him my old car. I plowed his truck into a snowbank, so I'd have an excuse to get into your house that night and get to know Dad's other family."

Knowing Dave isn't above breaking the law makes me wonder if Jake is right—all the men in his family are doomed to fail. I turn to Ryan, Jake's cousin, who operates on the right side of the law.

Ryan rubs his jaw, now clean-shaven. "I convinced Mom's boyfriend not to press charges by negotiating a deal where he got to keep Mom and get his truck back, and I wouldn't turn him in for finding the marijuana I planted in his glove compartment, in exchange for telling the police it was a domestic misunderstanding."

Jake nods. "Negotiation is the way to go. Better than involving the cops in family business."

Ryan laughs. "You got me there, cuz. But I've got a job to do that's more important than a stolen truck and a domestic dispute. I'm going to keep on trying to find out who's behind these jewelry store thefts and shut them down."

"Speaking of which, who killed that jewelry store owner, Leo, what's his name?"

"All we know, from our sources, is that it was a contracted hit. Leo was involved in the money laundering/insurance scam, like we suspect some of the other jewelry store owners are, and he wanted out. So they took him out."

Chapter Seventy

Work can wait for now. Mal and I asked for an extension of our holidays in light of the circumstances. We have a lot to digest before getting back to the grind, although it looks like life will go on as normal. Except for Rod and Sam and their wives.

As if sensing I've been strung out, Lucky hops onto my lap and rubs against my arm, purring. I pet his smooth, silky black fur, telling him he's my good boy.

The sun shines in a cloudless sky as we look upon our back yard, diamonds twinkling on the white canvas. In the distance, the barn stands as a reminder of the ordeal we went through. We've weathered another storm, literally and figuratively.

Mal and I sit at the kitchen table, enjoying a second cup with our cheese omelet and hash browns.

Mallory surprises me with a request. "I called Jilly and asked if I could come over after breakfast. She said she could use a friend. Want to come with me?"

I open my mouth to ask why the hell I would do that, then stop myself when I notice the expression on her face. Pity? Concern? Disbelief?

"Sure, hon, but don't you think it's going to be a bit uncomfortable for everyone?"

Mal stirs her tea, staring into the amber liquid. "She's going to need a lot of support to get through this. I'm not sure she's going to get it. People tend to be judgmental. I don't know how her friends and neighbors will react to this. They may blame her for not seeing what was going on under her nose.

Maybe they'll think she was involved, too."

"Yeah." I get the feeling she's talking about us as much as about Sam and Jilly. I've hidden things from my wife, too, and dragged her into the messes I created. "This *is* the biggest scandal to ever hit Idlewood. And you know how people in Idlewood love to gossip."

Mal raises her eyebrows but doesn't say anything more on the topic. I'm sure she's thinking about the scandals I've been involved in and the resulting gossip.

After breakfast, we dress and head to the car, Mal saying she's not sure what to say to Jilly. I nod, indicating I'm not likely to be of much help. The road to town is clear, thanks to county plows, and snow has been hauled away from the main street and sidewalk, the residual mess of the so-called storm of the decade leaving little evidence of the recent extreme weather.

Sam and Jilly's older story-and-a-half white-sided home is one street over from the 'downtown' core, the black pick-up parked next to Jilly's Nissan in the short driveway. Leaving the Honda on the street, Mallory and I walk up to the stoop and ring the bell. When no one answers, Mal checks out the front window and finds the curtains drawn.

"Guess she's not home," I say, turning to head back to our car.

"She should be expecting us. I called her an hour ago." Mallory pounds on the door. "Her car's here. I'm worried."

"Maybe she went for a walk." I scan the ground looking for footprints and find none other than our own.

Mal keeps up with the pounding and ringing, stopping only to call Jilly on her cell. No answer. I join her efforts, pounding on the front window.

"You don't think she would do anything…she wouldn't hurt herself, would she?" Mal asks, concern etched in her face.

A thought occurs to me. Spare key. Everybody locks themselves out of the house. There's nothing on the stoop but a mat. Nothing under it. No garage. The vehicles are locked. I scan the area. Snow. Maybe not everyone has spare keys all over the place.

"I'm going to the back," I say. You keep trying."

Knee-deep snow impedes my progress, but once I get to the back yard,

I'm rewarded with the sight of a small deck off the back door. Where there's a door, there's a mat. Maybe. The snow has blown right up against the door, a shovel next to it. I uncover the mat and the spare key. Not bothering to knock, I enter Sam and Jilly's home, my phone ready to call 911. It may already be too late.

Chapter Seventy-One

Jake unlocks the front door from the inside, and I rush in, expecting the worst, recalling the time not too long ago when I thought Jake was gone for good. The bottle of pills had been too tempting; the only thing that saved me was the child growing in my body. I had called for help before succumbing to total despair. Am I Jilly's call for help? Have I come too late?

With all the curtains shut tightly against the sun, Jilly sits in the dim living room staring ahead into the nothingness her life has become. I know the feeling well. There's no point in telling Jilly everything will be okay. But I can be there for her.

"How many did you take?" I motion to the coffee table, a few pills spilled out of the bottle.

Jilly doesn't speak, continuing to stare. Jake's eyes meet mine, and he mouths, "Should I call for help?"

"Jilly? Are you okay?" I wrap an arm around her shoulder. "Do you need us to call 911?"

The irony of the situation sinks in. A medical emergency call from Idlewood would normally be answered by Sam and Jilly, our local paramedics. Jilly's body heaves in response to my question, sobs sputtering from deep within her chest.

"I…I didn't know…how many…to take…to make it stop…"

Jake makes the call.

* * *

Several hours later, we sit by Jilly's side in emergency at our local hospital. Having been examined by the doctor, she is waiting to be released, her physical health not in immediate danger. But sometimes suffering goes deeper than the physical body. I should know. The emergency doctor also knows. She arranged for the on-site psychologist at Grandview Medical to come for a quick assessment of Jilly's mental health.

Equipped with a contact for a social media support group for wives with incarcerated husbands and a prioritized appointment for counseling next week, Jilly is on her own, sent home to pick up the pieces of her shattered life.

"You should stay with us for a few days," I say as I sit in the back seat of the Honda with Jilly on our way back to Idlewood. Jake's eyes flit to the rearview mirror, then he voices his agreement.

"Okay," Jilly's voice is small, and she shrinks into her seat as if she would like to escape. "Thank you."

After stopping at her place so she can pack a bag and checking that her house is secured, we head home to the farmhouse. Jake leaves us alone in the living room, closing the hallway door, as if sensing that Jilly will be more comfortable without his presence.

"I guess the joke's on me. I'll be the laughing stock of the town," she says once we are alone.

I take her hand in mine. "Why would you think that? You've done nothing wrong. People will understand. You're a victim in this. Sam's actions were his own."

"All this time, I couldn't understand why you stood by Jake after what happened this summer. The rumors, the police, his association with Dom. And here I am, living with a criminal worse than what I imagined Jake might be."

Jilly's words sting, but it's not a time to defend myself or my husband. I make no comment, deciding to listen instead.

"They let me see him, finally," she continues. "He cried throughout our whole visit. Said how sorry he was, and he wished he could take it all back. He never expected anyone to get hurt. All he wanted was some extra money so he could give me the kind of life I deserved. He saw an opportunity and took it, but it all spiraled out of control."

I nod and want to say that there are better ways to make money than criminal activity. A better job. Wiser investing. But I bite my tongue.

"He told me not to wait for him, that I should find someone new and go on with my life, have a family and a nice home. But I can't...how am I supposed to go on? I don't want anyone else. Just Sam. And he's gone." Her tears spill onto my hand, and I let them dry onto my skin. We're blood sisters, connected by the tears we've shed thanks to our husbands.

"He's not gone. Just away for a while." At least he's not dead. "He made a mistake. A good lawyer, maybe Dom knows one, can help. If he repents and behaves, he might get a lighter sentence. And I'm sure you'll be allowed conjugal visits."

Does Sam deserve any of that? I don't know. But if the shoe were on the other foot, which it easily could have been and might be at some point in the future, I would want my friends to support me.

Jilly lifts her head and makes eye contact. "I don't know if I can forgive him. I want my old Sam back."

"He's still in there somewhere," I say. "The part of him that's sorry is him."

Jilly considers this for a moment. "You're right. But no one else is going to understand that. He's not a Good Samaritan anymore. He's a...Bad Sam. I'll be the topic in the headlines instead of the reporter, the stupid wife who lived with a criminal and didn't know it."

"You can make your own headlines. Write an article from your point of view."

Jilly shakes her head. "I don't...even if I could, no one would take me seriously. I'm going to sell the house, move far from here, change back to my maiden name."

Why should she be the one to go on the run? Give up her life? Because of her husband's actions? "No, you've done nothing wrong. Stand your ground. This is Sam's doing, not yours. And maybe writing about it will help you to deal with it."

"Write what? That I didn't know my husband? That he's responsible for someone dying? That he almost killed someone else?" Head in her hands, Jilly leans over, defeated. So unlike her usual confident, chatty self.

"I'll help you write an article for Idlewood Chatter. A human interest story. We won't gloss over what Sam did, but we'll focus on how he regrets it. How one small mistake led to more, and he found himself in too deep to get out. People will relate to that."

"Will they, though? Most people aren't criminals."

"Sam is more than a criminal. We can remind people of all the good he did for the community as a paramedic and clearing the roads. His volunteer work. Sam was everyone's friend. He got Ryan to the hospital in time. He saved Steve's life."

As I find myself defending Sam, I wonder at what point did I blur the thin line between legal and criminal, good and bad?

Chapter Seventy-Two

Dom has been on my mind throughout all this. I can't for the life of me decide whether he's the villain in some global scheme to take over the world, or an anti-hero in some ancient Sicilian/Greek tragedy. As if in response to my thoughts, Jake's cell goes off. I grab it and check the caller ID. Dom. I could ignore it. I should ignore it. Tell Jake it's spam.

I hand over the phone. Jake puts it on speaker.

Dom's powerful voice comes through loud and clear. "Glad to hear things worked out well for you. Everything has been dealt with in an appropriate manner. Nice job."

"Yeah. All good in the end."

"Exactly. That's all that matters. The end justifies the means. Which brings me to the other reason I'm calling. I wanted to let you know my nomination for mayor of Brampton Heights has been endorsed and filed, and I'm ready to go to the polls and serve the citizens of our fine city."

"Good luck."

"I don't need luck. You know that. What I do need, or rather what I *want*, is your support, Jake. And that entails the job position that puts you second-in-command, save for Nick. I need an answer. And it better be the right one. Are you in or out?"

I know my husband has aspirations. There is more to life than going through the motions in a job that is not your passion. Jake's passion is the casino, not the warehouse. The casino could also be his downfall. It's his fatal flaw. I've read enough Greek tragedies to know how that can end.

But family comes first. Jake has acknowledged that, and he supports my need to have a big family in a large, cozy home. Every good husband stands by his wife and her dreams.

Jake bows his head. "I hate to disappoint you, Dom. Nothing personal. I need to do what's right for my own family. So, I'm afraid I'm ou—"

And every good wife stands by her husband and his dreams.

I finish Jake's sentence. "He's in. We're in. We're *all* in. Thank you for the opportunity, Dom, and for everything you have done for us. But of course, I want your word that there will be no illegalities involved and that Jake can leave the position on good terms should we decide it isn't a good fit for our family."

"Of course. You have my word. And thank *you*, Mallory, for being supportive of your husband. Jake has a great future ahead of him."

"Thank your wife, as well, Dom." With the final word, I hang up.

I smile at my man and pat my belly as he stares at me in amazement. Dom and I both know how he built his empire. Not without the help of a certain 'little woman'. I won't ever again allow anyone to look down their nose at me, dismissing me as weak. Jake and I are equal partners in life.

Isabella's words have stuck with me.

A woman should stand side by side with her man. That's the only way he can succeed.

And the only way he can keep from going down with his ship.

* * *

After breakfast the next day, we head out to Brampton Heights. "I need to go to the casino to firm up my acceptance of Dom's offer," Jake says.

We're welcomed at the casino doors and ushered in like royalty. Word must already be out that Jake is in charge, if not on par with Dom or Nick, a close second. Jake struts onto the gaming floor, his eyes lit up to match the slot machines. As we pass the pit, I stop. "Do you want to play the cards one more time?"

Jake takes a deep breath in through his nose and swallows. His mouth turns up and his eyes meet mine. "No. I'm done with being a player. I nearly lost everything to the games. Never again. How about you and I play at home? Strip poker. A better payout for me."

"You think you'll beat me?"

"It doesn't matter who beats whom. We both win."

We stroll hand in hand, Jake surveying his new empire, nodding and waving to people he knows. Clients, dealers, croupiers, attendants, servers, the bartender. Jake is in his element.

Dom rises to greet us when we enter his office. He takes my hand and brings it to his lips. "Mallory, always a pleasure."

Shaking Jake's hand and welcoming him to his new position, Dom pats him on the back, then draws him in for a hug. "Glad you stopped in to make things official. I've taken the liberty of having the paperwork drawn up."

Nick, who has been standing by the window, joins Dom in shaking Jake's hand. He hands Jake some documents. "Take them home. Get your attorney to go over them with you. I think you'll find it more than acceptable. And Mallory, the terms you requested are laid out in black and white. Welcome to the family."

Jake's eyes widen as he zeros in on the salary offered. "This looks very generous, Dom."

"Make sure you earn it," Nick advises. "As outlined in your contract, you'll be in charge of overseeing casino operations and ensuring regulations are adhered to. Keeping the cop presence down and avoiding unnecessary visits from government officials. It's not as easy as it looks, keeping the customers and employees happy while ensuring the money flows to the casino, and everything appears above board. We're looking to improve profits."

"Of course. Profits." Jake nods.

"Let me show you to your office." Dom holds the door for me, then leads the way out, pointing to the door across from him. "Nick is here, as you know. Your office is next to his. Formerly Adam's office. Don't worry; there's no trace of him left. It's decorated in a style to match Nick's workspace and mine, but if it doesn't meet your expectations, it can be redone to suit your tastes. And of course, you can add your own finishing touches."

Jake's jaw drops as he scans the room. Massive mahogany desk with a state-of-the-art computer system, leather chairs, bookcases, recliner, big screen TV, fully stocked bar. All the amenities Dom himself enjoys. "Well…Dom, it isn't quite what I'm used to."

Dom raises his eyebrows. "Is that so?"

Jake chuckles. "This makes my warehouse workspace look like a Budget Rent-an-Office. Thanks, Dom. Nick. And speaking of Adam, if you don't mind, I'd like to recommend someone to take on part of his former duties, if it's okay with you, Dom. And Nick."

"That depends. Who have you got in mind?"

"Jethro. You need muscle, he's your man. He's not the sharpest tool in the shed, but he'll keep your clientele in line should they require straightening out. I know he crossed us both before, and you don't put up with that shit. But maybe you could give him a break? Give him a full-time job? He did try to look out for Mallory."

"Mallory looks out for herself," Dom reminds me in case I don't already know. "I'm not an unreasonable man. I'll leave it up to you. Your call. But if he screws up again, I don't offer third chances. To anybody." He pats me on the back. "Except family. I'm looking forward to you joining us. Once your two-week's notice at the warehouse comes to an end, Nick will start your training. In the meantime, stay out of trouble. No more bodies in the cornfield. Being associated with that kind of stuff can give you a bad name, and it's tough to regain people's respect. Trust me on that."

As Jake and I do a final walk-through of the casino floor before going home to our paradise, I ask one more time if he wants to play for old time's sake. But he has mastered his addiction.

"No. The old time is done. It's time for new times. Better times." His arms wrap around me, and his lips brush mine. "Starting with a trip to the jewelry store for a replacement of your necklace and earrings, and the gold pieces I gave to Mom and Deb. Followed by more renovations and additions to the house for all those kids we're going to have. Three, maybe four."

Everything I've ever wanted is within my grasp. A family. A beautiful home. Me staying home with the children while they're young. No worries about how to pay the bills. I smile at my handsome husband, his blue-green eyes twinkling. And I know he is no longer a slave to his abusive past and the addiction that ruled him. No more than I am controlled by my guilt and grief at losing my parents, and the anxiety that ruled my world. We don't have to be prisoners of the past. We aren't puppets dangled by fate unless we allow ourselves to be. It's time to move forward with the royal flush we've earned.

New adventures await. We're ready for them.

I cup my hands around Jake's face. "Till death do us part. We're in this life together. It's going to be perfect."

Ackowledgments

As always, thanks to my husband, Brian, for standing by me (literally and figuratively) at every book event and for his suggestions and edits to my manuscript. Also, thanks for sharing your last name with me, which fits well with the mystery/thriller genre, and for allowing the use of your family farmhouse as the inspiration for Jake and Mallory's homestead.

Thank you to my family for their support of my author adventures. A special thanks to my son, Bryant, for providing the necessary equipment so I can attend outdoor markets and book fairs, and to my daughter, Brittany, my son-in-law, Eric, my grandchildren, Rowan and Violet, and my brother, Joseph, for coming to my book events.

To my critique partner, Norah Blakedon, thanks for sharing your thoughts and advice about my manuscript. To my friend and co-worker, Deb Robinson, thank you for being a fan and advocate of my books.

And, of course, thanks to my agent, Cindy Bullard of Birch Literary, for taking me on as a client and providing me with the opportunity to become a published author.

My appreciation to Shawn Reilly Simmons for her editing expertise and wonderful cover. You continually amaze me with your abilities. Thanks to Deb Well for all you do and to the rest of the staff at Level Best Books for getting this book out to the readers.

To my friends, neighbors, and community, thank you for asking about my books and telling me you enjoy reading them. Thanks to my local bookstores and libraries for hosting author events and carrying my books. And to my readers, please know that each and every one of you is much appreciated. If you enjoy this book, I hope you will consider leaving a review on Amazon, Goodreads, or elsewhere. Thank you!

About the Author

Ivanka Fear is a Slovenian-born Canadian author. She lives in Ontario with her family and feline companions. Ivanka earned her B.A. and B.Ed. in English and French at Western University. After retiring from teaching, she wrote poetry and short stories for various literary journals. Ivanka is the author of the Blue Water Mystery series and the Jake and Mallory Thriller series. She is a member of International Thriller Writers, Sisters in Crime, Crime Writers of Canada, and Vocamus Writers Community. When not reading and writing, Ivanka enjoys watching mystery series and romance movies, gardening, going for walks, and watching the waves roll in at the lake.

AUTHOR WEBSITE:

https://www.ivankafear.com

SOCIAL MEDIA HANDLES:

Facebook: https://www.facebook.com/ivankafearauthor

Instagram: https://www.instagram.com/ivankawrites

X: https://x.com/FearIvanka

Also by Ivanka Fear

The Dead Lie, A Blue Water Mystery

Where is My Husband?, A Jake and Mallory Thriller

Lost Like Me, A Blue Water Mystery

What Lies in the Cornfield?, A Jake and Mallory Thriller

Cold Query, A Blue Water Mystery